Lety's Gift

Coralie Hughes Jensen

Ward Hill, MA

Lety's Gift

By

Coralie Hughes Jensen

ISBN 0-9787318-0-8

Photo: Franky De Meyer, Brussels, Belgium

Cover art and book design: Pam Marin-Kingsley,
www.far-angel.com

Published in 2006
by
Lightning Rider Press
Ward Hill, MA

Thunder is good, thunder is impressive;
but it is lightning that does the work.
- Mark Twain

www.lightningrider.com

To Bruce, Megan, Michael, Hannah, and Charlie.
A haven in the real world where
I can rest from my dreams.

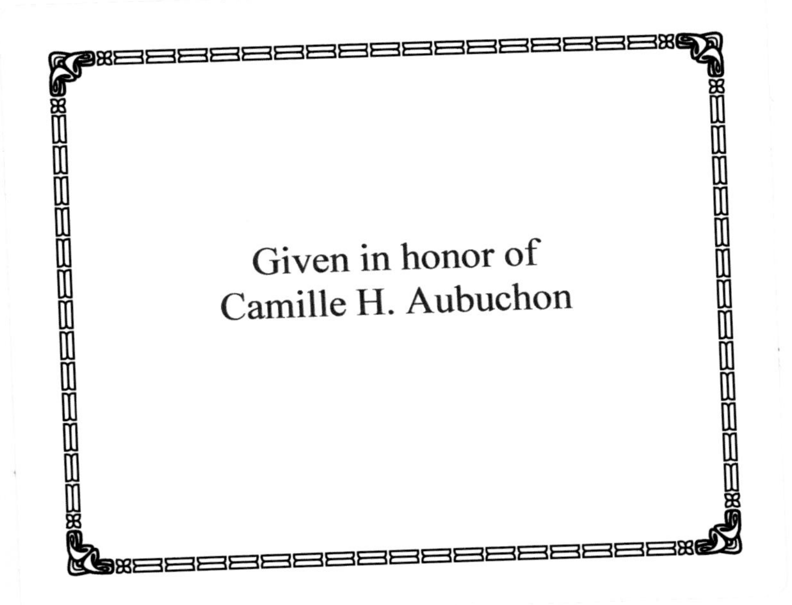

Acknowledgements

Thank you to the Phoenix Writers' and Artists' Group and the Haverhill, Massachusetts Library staff for giving me the support and opportunity to write this book. To artist Pamela Marin-Kingsley for a beautiful book cover. Also to The Reverend Alexander Daley who encouraged us to take supplies to the Western Diocese of Newfoundland so we could meet people and interview priests. To The Reverend Cannon Frank Cluett and his wife, Mathilda, who helped me polish the Newfoundland dialect, and The Reverend Daphne Parsons who inspired me with her life in Newfoundland and who had the determination to follow her dream to return to Queen's College and become a priest. A special thank you to my husband, Bruce, who always works very hard to make it possible for me to continue to write.

Book 1

A winter storm descends on an ill-fated ship,
Winds howling triumph before the first strike;
Sea washing over the secured decks
Until the ship submits—
The lofty mast cracks, the greedy water hisses,
And the sea devours the hapless sailors.
Just as quickly, the winds die; gentle breezes
swamp the void.
The vessel rights itself,
The flutter of shredded sails
proclaiming its surrender.
Sated, the storm picks its teeth with the timber
that floats on its still-rumbling surface.

Chapter 1

In a Pebbly Cranny

The thunder crackled, echoing through the clouds. Electricity bounded from cell to cell. The howl of the wind rattled the windowpane, and when it stopped, hail drummed the glass erratically. Granny Ivy looked out from her rocking chair and then returned to her knitting, paying little attention to the low groans from the bed just a few meters away.

"That's it, Lety, blows yer air out slowly. It'll pass," she said, not once taking her eyes off her half-finished sweater.

Light flashed across the dimly lit ceiling, and the two women froze, waiting for the assault. They were rewarded by a crash not far from their doorstep that mimicked a giant wave.

"I can't take it," Ivy finally said, rising from her chair. "It's gettin' chilly in here. I'm stokin' the fire to see if I can get more heat from it. Hell if I wants to go out fer more wood in this weather. Can I get another blanket fer you, Lety?

Lety released a moan, low and gravelly, like it came from the deep pit of her huge belly.

"Now don't be goin' on, girl. You gots yerself into this muddle. I knows yer mother warned you not to. All them sailors got one, and had you used yer brains and taken a look at one of 'em, you would have throwed *IT* back at 'em. 'Stead, you let 'em jig you like you was a fish, and they maked you sick. I knows Ester told you 'bout what those sailors always have in mind—can't wait to come on shore and take *IT* out. Why Ester didn't give you the polly pitchum or saffron or somethin' else that makes you well again, I don't know."

Lety screamed. Ivy stood there and waited until the contraction ended. Then she walked over to wipe Lety's face.

"There, there, Lety darlin'. I knows you thinks you loved him but he's gone now. What was his name again? Jasper? Jason? Jackoff? *Damn!* If his ship ain't gone down, he's in another port by now not even 'memberin' yer name and tryin' to use *IT* on some other fool girl."

Lety grabbed Ivy's hand, vivid crimson assaulting the young woman's fat cheeks.

"Don't push yet, Lety! I'll stop talkin' 'bout him if you promises to breathe. There I stopped," she said, zipping her lips.

And so the evening went on. Water crashed over the rocks and barely retreated before surging forward again. Ice rained in from the sea, pelting the side of the house.

Some time before morning, a nearby building burst into an angry fire. Ivy stood at the window reporting the progress of the flames to Lety who wriggled uncomfortably on the bed.

"Ooh! I can't believe there can be such a fire in this storm. I wonders what Fergus was storin' in his fishin' hut, Lety, that would make the flames so tall. I'll bet it's not fuel fer his boat he gots in there. More like he's storin' his moonshine can. Damn fool! Won't last long, I'm sure. Nothin' can last long in this weather. It'd surprise me if that fire is lastin' longer than a quarter-hour. I just hopes Fergus didn't lunch on his store and dwall off in his shed."

Lety wailed so loud she rivaled the howl of the winds.

Ivy stooped over the end of the bed and peered under the blanket. "Nearly there, Lety. But I don't want you pushin' just yet. Gives me a minute to heat up some tea so I'll have the strength."

But Lety started to push anyway. An hour later, Lety was still pushing. Ivy kneeled by the woman's head and pressed down on her swollen belly.

"Bore up! You gots to push harder, girl. That baby ain't gonna jump out of you. You gots to *make* him come out!"

Lety puffed out a long sigh.

"Where do you think yer goin', Lety? You still haven't got that baby out. I knows you ain't no noody nawdy and won't go nowhere so that I'm the only one here fer the next 'traction," Ivy counseled, sitting back and beginning to worry for the first time that night.

Ivy got off the bed and began to tug at Lety's arm. "Come on, girl," she said, her voice shaking. "You gots to get out of this bed and do some of the work." Once she had Lety on her feet, she continued to yell. "Now coopy down! I'll hold you so you don't fall. You gots the pain now?"

Lety began to scream.

"Don't scream! That blows the pressure out in the air. You gots to get that pressure buildin' up inside. Now *PUSH*!"

Lety awoke on the pumbly rocks. The sea was smooth, and the sun's rays pulsed down, warming her arms. She had just begun to show, but no one had noticed, at least she didn't think so. Ester would have if she hadn't moved to Tooley to be with her new man. But Lety didn't care what the others thought. Jeremy would be back soon, and they would get married.

"Good mornin', Lety," the gruff voice said.

"Mornin', Fergus."

"What you doin' out here?"

"Waitin'."

"Waitin' fer what?"

"Waitin' and thinkin'."

"You just can't sit round here doin' nuthin'. Why don't you and I take the boat out and see what we can catch? Yer goin' to need somethin' to eat. Aunt Ester said we should all take care of ye. But you ain't helpin' yerself."

"I'm takin' care of myself, Fergus, but I could use some extra fish."

"I don't have extra. Yer goin' to have to get up and come fishin' with me if you wants any dinner."

Lety rose and brushed herself off. She followed Fergus to his shed and helped untie his skiff. Then she looked out over the bay.

"Who you waitin' fer?" Fergus asked, climbing in and starting the engine.

"Nobody in particular," Lety responded, sitting on the thwart and examining the poles by her side.

The wind blew up as they rounded the end of the bay. Lety felt the breezes loop through her hair. She screwed up her eyes, searching for a boat on the horizon.

"Who's that?" she asked, pointing at a schooner in the distance.

"Looks like Strong out of Wolf Point. Wonder what he's out fer."

"Oh," she grunted.

The waves rolled under them.

"Who you be lookin' fer, Lety? You looks awful dishy. Maybe we should set the lines down here so we can head back, and you can get somethin' in yer belly."

Lety didn't want to think about it here. She wanted to wait until she got back to her house where she could dream about it in bed. She wanted to ponder what it would be like to have Jeremy beside her on that bed, not out among the rocks where she felt the stones and shells poke her in the back. Sure she tried to concentrate on him. She kind of liked his fishy smell and his bristly whiskers. But his muscled form pushed her farther into the gritty crevice and did not let her get comfortable. Jeremy told her how pretty she was. He told her that her soft foxy hair made her special and did not make fun of her shape like the other boys did.

Lety was big. She was a whole head taller than her mother and brawny too. Everyone who saw her could not believe "how she'd growed so big when her dad and Ester be so skinny." She liked food. There was no doubt about that. She was hungry and relished her dinner. But there was not that much food to be had in the Hawkins household so no one knew where her extra portions were coming from.

Even Jeremy was several centimeters shorter than she was. But he did not let on. He seemed to love her bulky figure scrawling along the shore. He bought her some candy and picked her flowers—everything a lover was supposed to do. So it was not so strange that he would take her down the beach and into the rocks and want to kiss her. And it was not so strange that he would want to grope under her sweater. After all, Lety never dreamed in a million years that anyone would want to love her so much. But he did. And when he got her going too, she was in heaven, not knowing what to do next, but enjoying it even though she could not move out from between the rocks.

She was surprised by the reaction when she returned to the house, her hair mussed and clothes rumpled. Aunt Stella was planted in front of the stove, cooking a meal for her.

"Where've you been?" she asked after one look at the big girl.

"Me and Jeremy was out lookin' for turtles," she lied.

"Who's Jeremy?" the woman asked, her eyes scrunched up into slits. "Don't tell me you've been out with one of them sailors."

"No. I mean yes. But he's lookin' to settle here. He told me he loves it here."

Aunt Stella banged the pot down on the table. "Yer in trouble, girl! No man off one of them boats is lookin' to settle here. They just tells you that so they can get you with *IT*! You didn't let him put *IT* in you, did you?"

Lety's eyes went blank. She was not sure. Not only was she not sure what *IT* was but did not remember what he was doing down there while she kept adjusting herself so the shells and pebbles would not poke her so much. All she knew was that she was enjoying herself for the first time in her life—so much so that she screamed when she could not take any more bliss—

and that Jeremy was so tired from trying to make her happy that he fell asleep right there on her bulging bosom.

"Yer a darn fool if you did, Lety. No boy is goin' to come round if you have a baby hangin' from yer tit," she said, spooning stew into a bowl. She looked up at Lety's face and reached out to touch it. "It's just that yer so big, Lety. Big enough to scare all the guys away cuz you make 'em look so scrawny. They scutters off when they sees you comin'. You needs someone to come here and take care of you full time. Yer growed like a woman but you gots the mind of a girl."

In the wee hours, gray light shown through the window. Even though the winds had died down, the restless bay bridled. A layer of ice slowly melted over Fergus' ruined shed.

Ivy continued to shout at the lump that now lay prone on the bed. "The baby's here, Lety! You just needs one more big push, and it'll be over. Oh, look, girl. I can see the head. It's got hair. Yer hair, Lety!"

Lety let out a tired *scroop*.

"That's the 'traction. Push hard. Here it come. What's this, Lety? *OH MY GOD!* She's got the caul! Now let me see. I takes it off over her ears. If I takes it off perfect, she'll have the *gift*."

Lety hauled her exhausted body onto her elbows to watch.

"There we go," Ivy said, wiping the tears from her eyes. "She's beautiful, Lety. She'll have flamin' hair, just like you. And she's special. The caul confirms it. Yer daughter will have the *gift*!"

"Lemme see her, Granny. I wants to hold her."

Sophie pushed away from the podium, taking a microphone with her. "Are there any other questions?"

"What made you want to go into the priesthood?" someone in the audience asked.

"I would like to say I was convinced that I wanted to be a priest since I was very young. In those days, women weren't allowed to go into the priesthood, however. I'm not sure I admired a particular priest. What I saw of the ministers I knew disgusted me. But I was curious about what it would be like to speak my mind and have people listen. I was told that God had given me a gift, but at the time, couldn't identify what my gift was."

Sophie drove through the rain to the house on Burton Road.

"Do you want some hot chocolate, Sophie?" asked Ben. "You look tired. Maybe you need a martini."

"No thank you," she said. "But I am beat. I think I'll go upstairs and lie down before dinner."

"Rachel left us a casserole. She went to the movies with her friend. I can heat it up any time."

Sophie smiled and slowly climbed up the stairs. "I feel like I've been on my feet for hours."

"You *have* been on your feet for hours. You should've had a chair on stage with you."

She opened the door to her room. Heading directly to the suitcase and pushing aside her clothes, she reached inside and removed a packet. Sitting on the edge of the bed, she took a letter out of the first envelope and began to read it, tears filling her eyes. Sophie had read it before—many times before. The edges were tattered and the paper brown and splotched. And she had it memorized; her lips continued to move after her eyes wandered away from the letter. She held the crinkled paper to her breast as she lowered her head onto the pillow and slipped into a dream.

Sophie clambered up the long road that circled the mountain. The road narrowed into a path that turned into a dark expanse of trees. The heavy boughs twisted lower to block her way, but she climbed over them and continued. When the path came to an end, a huge gate loomed in front of her. The gate was locked. She scaled the branch beside her—first one tortuous limb and then another until she was higher than the walls on either side of the gate. Looking down into a large courtyard, she first heard the peel of bells from a steeple that equaled her altitude. In between the chimes, she listened to the chants as a long column of men emerged from the church two by two. She could not see him. They all looked alike, their blond scalps shorn and their heads bowed. Sophie jumped to the top of the wall and hung her feet over. When she was secure, she called out his name. But no one in either column was drawn away from the ongoing mantra of prayers. The men walked around the courtyard and began to disappear into another building. Her heart ached as the line evaporated.

When she sat up to scream his name again, she was in a bed.

"Are you all right, Sophie? That casserole is just about warm if you want to freshen up and come downstairs."

"Thank you, Ben. I'll be ready in a moment."

She sipped her wine and took another bite.

"This is great, Ben. You sure can cook."

"That's what I tell Rachel, but she keeps retorting that I ought to at least try to do it some time."

"Where's Jessie?"

"Out with friends. She's out more than in nowadays. She's looking for an apartment so she can live on her own."

"That's good. I know you miss her, but at least she *can* get out," Sophie said, finishing another bite.

"You were right to warn Rachel, you know. She watched Jessie like a hawk and knew when to get help," Ben said. "How did my class do today?"

"I told them the story of my priesthood and how I managed to move up through the ranks, but in the end, they were more interested in my talking about my childhood and early days as a priest."

"I didn't tell them what to ask," Ben said. "They're sharp."

"Are any of them graduating in May?"

"Some are."

"Are they planning to go on to Queens?"

"A few. But I'm not sure if their goal is ordination. Some only want to get their masters."

"You've got to work them harder, Ben. You've got to convince them that the priesthood is rewarding."

"Aren't you going to ask me?"

"Ask you what?"

"About *him*, Sophie. You always ask me if I've seen him."

She put her napkin to her lips, wondering if she should ask. Finally she did. "Is he coming Saturday?"

"I don't know. Yes, I talked to him, but he didn't answer. I left the program with him. I'm sure he read it."

"What did he say? Is he happy?"

"Yes, very serene. Not like he used to be. *Mr. Charisma*, isn't that what we used to call him? I can't believe he's happy where he is, but he insists."

"Did he ask—?"

"I told you we talked about the celebration tomorrow. He was very curious. Yes. But he knew it was coming. We always talk about you—and Cyril, of course."

"You haven't answered my question, Ben."

"I'm not sure he asked directly. I always forget what prompts me to talk about you two. The conversation just turns that way, and he listens and smiles and nods his head."

Sophie picked up her glass and took a swallow. "So. Tell me what you told him about Cyril."

"Cyril's definitely coming. Wouldn't miss it for the world. He's bringing his friend—Kieran, I think his name is. I'm really going to have to write these things down in the future. I'm getting old. That's why I'm opening this other bottle. But before I cry about my age, let's use it to toast your success again."

"Cyril and Kieran are coming all the way from Toronto? That's quite a trip. How can he get away from work? What is it he does now? Something to do with technical gizmos for production companies?"

"You're worth it, Sophie. You make us all proud."

"Not that it hasn't been done before, Ben."

"You must be in shock. You've reached the top, Sophie. We all started with you but you're the only one who made it. You can't minimize that."

But the woman's mind had already wandered back to that afternoon.

Sophie saw another hand go up. "Okay. This is the last question or I'll be here all night. I'm sure the staff wants to close up."

"What happened to Fergus? Did they find him after the fire?"

"Everyone had to take cover from that storm. Aunt Stella told me later that Fergus had no place to go since he either lived in his dinghy or in that tiny red fishing shed."

"You gots to 'member, girl, that we was all hunkered down, tryin' to keep warm. Fergus was doin' the same."

"How did you find him, Stella?"

"In bits and pieces. You must 'member that his old moonshine can had to be workin' full time. We always warned him that he shouldn't be lightin' up his pipe round that 'stillin' machine, but old Fergus wasn't one to give up any of his vices. The splosion throwed body parts all over the pier. Anyway, we picks up the pieces and puts 'em in a box. We would have buried him that day, but the ground was still froze hard as iron; so we sends for Father Mercer who comes from Pinehorn and we all says prayers over his box," she said, taking out a pipe of her own and sucking on the tobacco without lighting it. "Lety was 'specially sad cuz they was close, bein' neighbors and all. But Lety had a baby on her hip and had trouble keepin' her mind on the prayers every time you lets out a gurgle or a coo—you not knowin' Fergus at all cuz you was too busy bein' born when he blowed himself up."

"Tell us what happened next," the young man said. "We know you were born illegitimately in a small village in the north. But it must have been hard for your mother to raise you."

"That was just the beginning. I barely got to know Lety at all before life forced me to move on. It was never easy, but it was about to get harder."

Chapter 2

The Crow

"I don't really remember my mother. I mean, I know her from a picture, the only one I could rescue from my grandmother's mantel. But Aunt Stella tried to bring the memories back years later when I returned to Tooley."

"Of course, you 'members her, girl. Didn't Ester ever talk to you 'bout her? You gots to hear the stories over and over 'til they lives in yer heart—a part of yer memory."

The old woman leaned back in her rocker, listening to the waves break over the rocks. There was no threat. It was summer, and the sea birds managed to make more noise than the rising tide.

"You knows Lety was no more than a child herself, don't you? A big child, but one nonetheless," she began. "She loved her new baby. She'd suckle you out on the rocks while she waited for her lover to come home. Do you 'member any of the stories she told you about him? Most likely not. She hardly knowed him herself. That nuzzle-tripe cozied on up to her with foolish words that he'd got out of a book somewheres or from the more sperienced sailors. He bamboozled her, making her think she was 'sireable. Then he gots her afore she had time to run."

Stella gave Sophie a side glance, realizing the young woman might not want to think of her mother as foolish, or ugly, for that matter. She took out her pipe and tapped it on the arm of her rocking chair. When she had stuffed it again, she lit it and slowly let the smoke curl upwards before it was carried off by the winds.

"Anyway, we'd all help her with the things she didn't know 'bout havin' a baby round. When her milk wasn't 'nough, we showed her how to cut up bread and greens and teached her how to cook eggs. You was growin' just fine. Afore you knows it, you was gettin' up and walkin' on yer own. You even talked some, but mostly grunted cuz Lety weren't no talker and teached you only what she knowed."

"Why didn't she keep me?"

"She'd have kept you forever if she could of, girl. Not even a government 'ficial could've pried you loose from her strong arms. She was healthy as a horse, and when her nostrils flared, there was fire comin' out of 'em. No one was gonna take you away. You was her life."

Stella and Sophie rocked for several minutes while the old woman puffed on her pipe. Both had to ingest what had passed. Sophie fingered the picture of Lety she kept in her pocket.

"You has her hair, you know. Ester must have told you that much, didn't she? Lety had wild red hair that gots tangled so badly in the wind that we had to cut out pieces so we could get the brush through it. I sees you keeps yers under control, though a bit short for my likin'. Girls today don't seem to want to look like girls. I thinks the boys must get awful 'fused when they comes wooin'. How can they tell you from the boys?"

Sophie smiled.

"That's what I like. You gots yer mother's smile, though yer teeth are a bit straighter and you most likely still have all of 'em," Stella said, pausing to look the younger woman over. "And yer smaller than Lety, though nearly just as tall. Must be a picky eater. You looks like a matchstick that's on fire. A baby's gonna have to do lots of searchin' to get a meal there, girl."

"What happened?"

"We all knowed what was gonna 'cur 'bout two weeks afore it did. There was a sign, and Ivy sees it, knowin' right then she'd seen somethin' as sure as a wind hound predictin' a storm." The old woman screwed up her eyes to make the picture in her mind clearer. The color drained from her cheeks. "It was a bright day, no threat of weather. The sky was a light blue—a summer blue where the clouds be so rawny, the blue peers right through 'em. Ivy comes over, bringin' a fresh figgity with her, hopin' you'd like somethin' sweet. You always did like raisins. Anyway, Ivy hears the confloption longs afore she gets there. She doesn't know if you and Lety is in a bit of a wrangle-gangle, but she knows somethin' be unsettled. When she gets to the door, she sees Lety, runnin' round the room like a whizgig, a broom raised over her head.

"'What you doin', Lety? I ain't never seen nobody sweep the ceilin' afore now. What you sweepin' the ceilin' fer, Lety?' Ivy asks her. Lety just grunts her reply, and Ivy has to get all the way in to see the culprit. 'There's a crow in yer house! Lety, darlin',' she says, tryin' to stay calm but knowin' full-well there's a storm brewin', 'how'd that old crow get in here? I knows you knows that you can't 'low birds inside. Ester must have warned you 'bout lettin' them flyin' things in here.'

"But Lety didn't stop," Stella explained, her rocker frozen in its most forward position. "And when she has that bird cornered, she draws back the handle of her broom and whops the life out of 'im! But she didn't stop there. She whops and whacks at that poor crow 'til, 'stead of the bird, there be feathers and straw flyin'. Then she sits down on her bed and waits 'til her breathin' comes back to normal. Ivy cleans up the mess and don't tell her that havin' dead birds in the house be bad luck. It says Lety's goin' to lose a loved one soon."

"Did Lety know that?"

"I don't think Lety thought 'bout things like that. But Ivy did. She collects the neighbors together, and we all agrees to dog Lety day and night so nuthin' happens to you. We watches her suckle you when she runs outta food in the cupboard. We watches her bathe you, fearin' that she'd leave you 'lone in the tub. We watches her sleep with you, makin' sure she don't roll over on top of you. You was nearly two and big enough to nip or bite if she did, but we sat outside her window just in case."

Stella was rocking harder now, like she was being chased by the boogeyman.

"It be Chester who was supposed to be watchin' that mornin' but he fell asleep cuz he'd been drinkin' again. He didn't want to let his wife know he was flukin' on the moonshine so he volunteered to get out of the house. You was the one who waked him up cuz you be hungry. It taked him several minutes to realize that Lety was gone. He searched high and low for her—too scared to tell anyone he'd messed up. But he had to tell us cuz there be no one to care for you. You taked us to her after nearly two days of us searchin' high and low for her. You knew where she be cuz she'd taked you there so many times afore. She was lyin' there in a small cranny in them rocks overlookin' the water. She had such a peaceful look on her, 'cept that the flies had already dined on her eyeballs. Doc Snow said she'd hit her head on the rocks when she fell—just a misstep as she quibbed from rock to rock. She must have spected to be gone but a short time or she would've taked you longs with her—must've wanted to catch one last peek at the water that taked her man away."

Stella stopped rocking, finally taking note of Sophie sitting beside her.

"She had a grand funeral, you know. Everyone whooped it up well into the night. We even 'couraged Chester to join in, him always carryin' the brew on him, you know." The old woman sighed. "But I still miss Lety, trouble that she was sometimes. She was like a fairy, dancin' longs the water's edge—a big awkward fairy."

"So who raised you?" the young man asked.

Sophie had nearly forgotten that she was still on stage.

"My dear mother passed on when I wasn't yet two. I can hardly remember meeting my Nanny Ester. But it must have been quite a shock. As soft and cuddly as my mother seemed in pictures there on my grandmother's mantel, Ester was lean and sinewy—and from what I can remember, malicious."

"Ester be a dear dear lady," said Aunt Stella, refilling her pipe. "Could be a bit crousty if you crossed her. When she gots mad, it showed in her bloodshot eyes and in her bivver, a tremble like a moonshine can just afore it splodes. I'm not so sure she wanted you, but she takes you into her house cuz you can't stay by yerself yet. She wasn't wedded then. She been married five or six times and most like feared you'd scare her suitors 'way, though I can't think there be many men left in the north of Newfoundland that hadn't knowed her. Does you 'member her, Sophie?"

"I remember that she told me what was right and what was wrong, and as long as I followed the rules, I would have dinner and a warm bed. Of course, Josie, her cook, took care of that part. Ester never spoke fondly of Josie. She just told Josie what to do, and Josie did it. I tried to get close to the young woman so she'd protect me when I was in trouble, but Josie wasn't interested. She only wanted to be with her girlfriends and eventually only came round to fix dinner. Most of the time, I was alone with Nanny, and Nan's punishment went on unnoticed.

"I found it difficult to be good all the time. I didn't like to wear shoes. I'd take them off and run on the rocks near the water. I'd sometimes play with the kids that she called rag-molls but didn't know any children who weren't in that category. If I got my clean clothes dirty, she'd make me bathe in a tub of ice cold water, so when I got to the beach, I'd remove my clothes and run naked along the shoreline. I suspected that removing them wasn't the answer, but it was all that I could come up with so I never kept it a secret. I know they were watching. At least the minister was. The Reverend Ivany used to sit on the rocks and watch me all the time. I didn't go near him because he never looked like he approved. But once he brought his daughter, Gracie, who was close to my age, and I approached them and asked her to play. I know she wanted to. She looked at her father, waiting for him to nod. He did, but when Gracie started to remove her clothes too, he pulled her away and dragged her home. He still came, though, but I didn't go near him again."

"The Reverand Ivany be a friend of yer Nan's. I sees him there when I visited more than once." Stella laughed. Her stooping shoulders shook as she remembered. "Ivy says she seen him too when she went to Tooley to visit Ester. He'd come by, bringing Ester flowers, and she had him to tea."

"Did his wife or daughter ever come with him?" Sophie asked, her voice almost a whisper.

"Not that I 'members. I don't think I ever met his dear wife. You knows more 'bout her than I do, girl. Anyway, Ivy must not have knowed he was married either cuz she thought he was surely goin' to be the next Mr. Hawkins. She said he wooed Ester when he comed over, and Ester would blush like a little girl, her wrinkled skin makin' her cheeks color a number of shades of red. We'd laugh over it cuz she had more than a few years on him. Ivy said he be blind if he couldn't see that and once asked him if he'd misplaced his glasses."

"I remember that he came over once in a while. Ester had a piano and made me practice etudes for hours. When he visited, she'd have me play one or two and then told me to go amuse myself upstairs. I was never allowed to stay nor did I want to. I was scared to death he'd tell her about my naked adventures on the beach."

"I suppose you 'members what happened. Poor thing, you was there and old enough to know what happened. How old was you then?"

"I'd turned five just a few weeks earlier. Ester was angry with me for spilling something on my good dress and had sent me upstairs. She said she'd prepare the cold bath and call me when it was ready. I was to undress and wait for her. I waited until it was dark and then snuck down the stairs. The tub of icy water was there, waiting for me to pay the penalty. The nip in the fall air and the look of the water gave me gooseflesh. I went to search for her. I found her out on the front porch, sitting in her rocking chair, not rocking, but slouched down."

"You didn't tell anyone, did you."

"No. I was naked so I went back up and put on my nightgown. Then I went to her bed. It was so big and soft while mine was so hard. At least I thought so. I'd once seen Ester there with a man. They were bouncing up and down on the mattress. Warning me the slats would break, Ester wouldn't allow me to do that on my own bed. They were making funny noises like they were having so much fun. I remember feeling slighted because she hadn't asked me to join in. Of course, they didn't expect me to be home at that time. I was supposed to have gone out shopping with Josie. But Josie had taken a girlfriend with her and left me behind. Anyway, when I first entered her empty room after I'd left Ester on the porch, I sat on the edge of her big soft bed and stared in awe at the objects on the nightstand, not only touching them but soon picking them up and rolling them in my hand. My favorite was a little crystal ball on a starched lace doily. It fit into my palm perfectly, its cool facets picking up the light from the lamp. Slowly, my fingers made their way to the drawer, and as if I had no power over them at all, they wrapped around the knob and bit by bit pulled it open—a crack at first, then wider. It suddenly popped out at me like a jack-in-the-box! I remember trying to hold my heart in place because it seemed to be jumping out of my chest. *It* was a stiff piece of white celluloid with a collar button at one end that fit into a hole at the other. I pulled it out and played with it on the bed but eventually dragged the covers up over my head and fell asleep. In the morning, the commotion downstairs roused me. Mrs. Ivany had seen Nanny from the road and strolled up the walk to talk with her."

"I hears she hated Ester and, when she found her dead, she laughed and laughed," Aunt Stella said. "I don't know if she knew that Ester be screwin' her husband, but when she sees you, she squeeges up her eyes, tellin' her husband, the Reverend, that you killed the old woman. 'That ragamuffin had her grandma's crystal in her hand! I sees it. She killed her own kin for a shiny crystal and whatever jewelry she could get her hands on. I knows it!' she'd tell anyone who'd listen. I can still hear that voice of hers like the scrubbin' of a boat against the pier."

"I saw Reverend Ivany that morning. He told his wife that they were going to take me home and fix me up before I was sent to the orphanage in St. John's. She threw a fit. I guess she thought I'd be a bad influence on Gracie. But the Reverend insisted, and because I'd be living with people from the church, no one questioned that it would be the best solution. I cried when I heard it."

"They says they finds you runnin' on the beach—that you'd removed all yer clothes and ran in and out of the icy waves. Why you taked them off, I'll never know. Ester wasn't there to punish you with that ice cold bath anymore. You was free to wear that frock anywhere, eh."

"And?" someone in the audience asked. "So then you went to the orphanage in St. John's?"

"No. I continued to live in the house of the minister, his wife, and his daughter. It wasn't a happy situation. But once the Reverend discovered my gift, he was enthralled. Ignoring the whiny protestations of his wife, he became my teacher and protector. I lived in his subjugation as he taught me about sin and about a punishment that Ester would never have thought to inflict. Like sunrise and sunset, God had created right and wrong, and I was there to learn that there were no grays. I was to live in heaven and hell until I was fourteen when he grew disgusted by the corruption of womanhood invading my body, liberating me and finally assuring my passage to that orphanage in St. John's."

Chapter 3

Black and White

Wallace Ivany, mousy but proud of her position in the community, had a voice sharp enough to cut a log. Little Sophie carried her tiny suitcase into the wood frame house and waited for her orders.

The woman stared at the frightened child before rendering her verdict. "I can't have you sleepin' with Grace. All your vulgar ways might rub off on her. I've heard stories of your mother and finds you no better. You can stay in my sewin' room 'til I clear the extra one upstairs. The Reverend can get you a mattress, I suppose. Grace be in a school. Though I'm sure you're not ready, I guess I'll have to sign you up so you won't be hangin' round the house when my committees come for tea. In the evenin's, I knows the Reverend wants to start teachin' you what you should know 'bout God. Do you understand what I'm talkin' 'bout, Miss Hawkins, when I talks 'bout God?"

"I 'tended church afore. When I visited Aunt Stella and Granny Ivy, they taked me to church. Father Mercer was nice."

"Father Mercer? Good Lord! That's not even a real church, Sophie. They don't preach God's laws like they should be teached."

Sophie learned that Wallace Lacey had been raised near St. John's and had told everyone that her parents were successful merchants. She professed to be marrying below her station when she and the Reverend Josiah Ivany of Wolfe Bay announced that they planned to wed. All the women in Tooley seemed to look up to her. She entertained them with her tea parties and formed committees to do work for the church. Sophie believed her when she talked about being related to royalty. Besides Stella, Ivy, and Ester, she had no one else to compare Lady Wallace Ivany to.

Grace was pretty. Her long brown hair fell in ringlets around her face. She wore beautiful dresses to school, and her clear ivory skin, rich dark hair, and black eyes gave her such a mysterious look. Sophie often sat in awe of her. But Grace was quiet. Overly quiet. She stared at Sophie but did not approach her. While her mother doted on her, always primping and prodding, Grace received little attention from her father. Sophie spent more time with him. She would have preferred playing with her new sister. Instead, Sophie was forced to study under his careful tutelage while Grace was left on her own.

"Well, Sophie, here's the Bible. Please read Isaiah, chapter three, verses four through seven."

Sophie stared at him, the huge book in front of her.

"Don't dawdle, girl!" he barked. "Don't play games, or I'll have to give ye the paddle."

The five-year-old squirmed but made no move to open the book. The Reverend rounded the table and opened it for her. When he found the page, he pointed at the passage. His breath stank like the carcass of a rendered pothead rotting on the sand.

Sophie stared at the tiny black letters and smiled. "Book," she said "Does it have pictures? Aunt Stella gived me a book with pictures once. Nanny Ester taked it away. She telled me that readin' that kind of book be evil."

"Can you not read, girl?"

"Only pictures."

"Then we'll start there. I'll bring some materials tomorrow, and you'll learn to read. You'll never get into school unless you speak correctly and know your letters."

"And the slapper? Will you spank me cuz I don't know the words?"

"I'll have to think about that. It doesn't hurt to get the paddle once in a while to remind ye that you must speak properly and that you have to study hard so you can read."

Ivany kept his promise and worked with Sophie until she could read and even write. He did not need to use the paddle because he had a long pointer that was even more effective.

On Sundays along with Wallace and Grace, Sophie sat in the first pew and listened to the Reverend's fiery sermons.

"I can feel the sin in this very room!" He sang out, and his cavernous voice shook the rafters. "Who among ye is followin' the word of the devil himself? I know you're here." He turned to face the culprit right there in front of his congregation. "Is it you, George? Are you spreadin' your semen in this community without the blessin' of our Lord? Does the seed you sow grow up right here under our noses?"

Everyone in the congregation turned to look at George from the fish plant, a quiet man with a wife and two sons.

"I'm waitin', George," Ivany said, starting softly but letting his voice crescendo like a swelling wave. "I'm waitin' for you to confess your ways before God and all God's people here present. I see hell openin' its doors, George. They're openin' wide—so wide it might swallow up your wife, Agnes, and maybe even your sons! We ask you to confess to almighty God!" He yelled at the top of his lungs, never once stopping to take a breath.

Trembling, George stood up. "Yes sir, Reverend. I confesses that I not always be faithful to Agnes."

Agnes let out a little scream and fainted on the spot.

"And you confess to Almighty God that you've been seein' the wives of fishermen while they're out to sea and that you've spilled your seed impregnatin' many?"

"Yes sir, Reverend Ivany. I confesses that I done so. May God forgive me."

Luckily, few of the fishermen ever came to church. Word would get out, however, as the town's two busybodies broadcasted the transgression around the pier. The couples, and there would be more than a few where the wives were not only pregnant but had children up to six years old, would pour into Ivany's home for counseling, and Wallace would serve them tea and cakes and cry with them.

One such evening, Wallace's activities took over the dining room, sending the student and teacher in search of a place to study.

"If you're teachin' the girl 'bout God, maybe it be better if you teached her that in God's house," she offered.

The Reverend's face lit up. "That's a good idea, Mrs. Ivany. Sophie and I will set up a classroom in the church. No one will interrupt us this time of night. Come, Sophie, grab your bag. We're goin' up the road to the church to study," he said, taking her hand. His voice was unusually melodic. "Hurry up now, I'm anxious to show you more lessons in the Bible. You'll enjoy explorin' Jeremiah."

Sophie was much more relaxed at the church—as were the lessons. After about ten minutes, the Reverend brought out games for them to play. He would call her "princess" and dance around the room with her on his shoulders. Sophie would laugh until she could no longer hold on, and he would grab her and twirl her until they fell in a heap on the floor.

This merriment, however, only lasted a week or two. One evening, Sophie read out loud. It was the Reverend's favorite passage, and the first one she had learned to read. "Jeremiah—chapter two, verse twenty-four," the little girl announced proudly.

A wild donkey accustomed to the desert, sniffing the wind in her craving—in her heat who can restrain her? Any males that pursue her need not tire themselves; at mating time they will find her.

He was ecstatic, telling her to come dance with him. They danced for quite a while before he announced how hot the room was. "Come, Sophie, lets go down to the beach."

"It be dark," she said. "Nanny never let me go to the beach in the dark afore."

"Ah, so you've never seen the sea after the sun goes down? The moon is full so we'll be able to see the fairies dance across the waves."

Sophie's face got serious. "Not the bibe. She comes when we dies."

"No, Sophie, that's just a story. The fairies are good. They love to play after the sun goes down."

The two tripped through the field to the beach. The first warmth of early summer blew over the rocks, and the moon shone on the rolling water, making a path for the fairies.

"I don't see no fairies," Sophie said disappointed.

"They don't come out unless we lure them with our play. Why don't we leave our clothes here like you used to do and run along the beach to show them we're havin' fun?"

Sophie laughed and quickly removed her smock and stockings. She ran back and forth, screaming at the top of her lungs, enjoying herself for the first time since Ester's death. The Reverend followed her and tried to catch her as she ran by. She slowed to a stop a few meters away.

"Why do you still have your clothes on?" she asked, trying to catch her breath.

Ivany ran back to the rocks and removed his collar. Then he pulled his shirt out of his trousers and began to unbutton it. Sophie giggled and jumped up and down.

"Hey!" shouted a voice from offshore.

Both Ivany and Sophie turned to see the small dinghy not more than ten meters beyond the first few wavelets.

"Is that you, Reverend? I can't see you in them rocks, but I hears yer voice. Who be that child with ye? Is it Grace you be bathin'?"

"It's Sophie!" announced the young girl, still jumping up and down in the shallow water. She reached down, scooping the water up and throwing it in the boat's direction.

"Hey Reverend, you must be baptizin' the young thing! Am I right?"

"Yeah, Crazy George," slurred a passenger on the small boat. "He be baptizin' her all right, but I don't think he be baptizin' the girl with sea water, hey."

George guffawed until the boat shook. "I won't tell yer wife, Josiah Ivany," George yelled. "But yer goin' to have to withdraw that statement you maked a few Sundays back. I may spread my seed to womans who ask fer it, but I don't spread nuthin' to childs." He dropped his oars into the water. "See you in hell, Josiah," he said, his voice beginning to fade. "If you don't get those pants pulled back up, I'm sure you'll get to meet the boo-man first!"

Sophie looked back at the rocks, hoping the Reverend was laughing. He was not because he was no longer there. She could see his silhouette running through the grassy field that led back to the church.

Soon after that incident, Sophie was sent to school. The classroom was usually warmed with coal, but spring was well underway, and the teacher opened the windows instead. Sophie found it difficult to concentrate with the smell of flowers wafting into the room. The desk was a two-seater, and she was able to sit with her sister at last.

The school days, however, were not easy. Sophie was still way behind, and her teacher, Mr. Slade, seemed to be irritated that a backward girl was placed among the other dozen or so school children in the one-room schoolhouse. Sophie looked around her. She and Grace must have been the youngest—and the others were mostly boys.

When the teacher rang a bell, they all tumbled out into the yard. Sophie wanted to go out too, but Grace preferred to stay inside.

"What's the matter?" she asked her sister.

"I'm not well. The sun isn't good for my skin, and my constitution is weak. I catch colds when I'm round the others."

Sophie got up to leave, but Grace still grasped her hand.

"You'll get your dress dirty outside, and mother will get mad."

Sophie tugged at her dress beginning to take it off, but Grace stopped her.

"What are you doin'? You can't do that here! You must be modest, Sophie, or I'll die of embarrassment!"

Sophie trembled, her little legs anxious to run and play. "I'll be back in a minute, Gracie. I promise."

The noisy yard suddenly became quiet as Sophie gazed out at the small groups along the fence.

"Hi, Sophie, this be Willy," one of the boys said.

She turned to a couple of older girls, but they showed their backs before she approached them.

"They won't play with you, Sophie, cuz you be the Reverend's friend," Willie sneered.

Sophie did not understand. "He's my dad," she announced.

The boys broke up laughing.

"He not be your dad," Willy said when he caught his breath. "He be your lover, silly. You and he goes out to hunt the night fairies, don't you?"

Horrified, Sophie was speechless. But not for long. "I seen a bibe out there and heard her too. She screamed that someone was goin' to die! She said, 'Where's that Willie Wabby whose dad be a wizard?' That be you, Willy? Are you the loon she be talkin' bout? She said your mama was a bloody bitch and that you was born in a whelpin' bag!"

Willy started for her but the others held him back.

"Yer dad spread his semen all over town, Willy!" she screeched, emboldened.

She wanted to go on but had run out of words and phrases that she had heard others use. Sophie turned around to retreat to the classroom. The teacher hovered in the entrance. Behind him, Grace clung to the doorframe, her face as white as bed sheets. Mr. Slade rang his bell, but Sophie wasn't sure if he did it intentionally or just could not control his trembling hand. Beside the door, rested his slapper, a reminder of the behavior he expected from those entering the classroom. As the others crossed the threshold, she watched his hand reach for it.

"Miss Hawkins, would you kindly join me aback of the shed?" he invited, his words pronounced succinctly through clenched teeth.

Her introduction to school, however, could not equal the swat of the pointer she received from the Reverend when she got home. He did not seem to enjoy the task though he probably normally would have. Wallace stood over him, a hawk-eyed scunner on a sealing ship, counting the thrashes with him and making sure the tearful child was up the stairs before taking her eyes off of her husband.

"The rest of my time with the Ivanys wasn't noteworthy," Sophie explained. "I eventually fit into both the family and the community, though never entirely. Try as I might to control it, I would lose my temper easily, and the other children enjoyed provoking me. The Reverend seemed to lose interest in finding me alone, but I'm not sure it's because of his fascination with a fiery child faded or because Wallace never let us alone after word of our beach trip got out. He continued to complain about my hair and as soon as he realized that I might harbor some sort of special knack with his parishioners, his absorption in my activities rekindled in another form."

"Are you talking about your gift?" the college student asked.

"Yes. The gift that Granny Ivy told Lety I had by virtue of my birth. I never felt like I had one. How would I know? When one is young, one just supposes everybody is the same. As the summer approached, the Reverend took me to visit an old lady on her sickbed. He didn't take me to do anything in particular, but Wallace had sent us to the store. He and I were supposed to pick up groceries, and two of us were needed to carry them back. Wallace didn't have to watch us then because she had her friends out there—scopy gobs, bottom feeders, scavenging the sea floor for juicy tidbits."

Sophie followed the Reverend up the street past the store.

"We'll come back to the store after I see Mrs. Whelan, Sophie. I hear she's sick, and I need to give her a blessin'."

The old woman lived in a house on the other end of town. The cottage was small but neat. Ivany skipped up the stairs and knocked on the door.

An old man answered it. "Come in, Reverend. Jenny be here in her chair. I didn't want to get her up, but she 'sisted."

Sophie followed him in, covering her nose as she past Jenny's husband. The old man smelled like cabbage and fish.

When Jenny saw the child, her wet eyes lit up. "Ooh," she cooed. "Who's this you brung with ye, Reverend?"

"This is Sophie, a moss child under my care," he said. "How are you, Aunt Jenny? Are you repeatin' those prayers I gave you?"

But the old woman did not take her eyes off of Sophie. "Come here, child," she said, putting out her hand. "So yer mother had a lover, hey?"

Sophie did not understand, but inched forward.

"Come here. She must've thought the world of you, yer beautiful hair and clear skin."

Jenny's watery eyes glistened in the gray room. As Sophie approached, she saw the pink cast of the woman's cheeks.

"Yes, ma'am," Sophie answered, not really listening to the conversation.

The woman took her hands, and Sophie felt the fever immediately. They felt good, like a mother's bosom should feel when a child needs comforting. Sophie did not take her hands away but knelt beside Jenny. Placing her head on the old woman's lap, she closed her eyes and hummed a tune.

"What song is that?" Jenny asked.

"It's a hymn I learnt when I lived with my nanny."

"It be very pretty. Help me learn it."

"I think Sophie should wait outside while I talk to you, Jenny. The child will tire you."

"Hush hush, Reverend. She 'minds me of when I be a child. Why don't you go and come back in a while?"

The Reverend was stunned but left nonetheless. When he returned, Jenny was serving Sophie tea on the porch. Her husband came down to meet him on the walk.

"It be a miracle, Reverend. Jenny talks softly to Sophie while the child rubs her hands and then legs, and then my wife says she wants to get up. Afore this child comes, I had to help her into the chair, but Jenny could get out of it all by herself. It be the child, Reverend. She gots the gift. I hears 'bout it but never sees it afore now."

"The Reverend never told me what Jenny's husband had told him. I think I heard it somewhere else, but I already knew what I had done," Sophie told Aunt Stella. "Jenny wasn't ready to die. In my mind, I could see her shoveling the snow some winter in the future. But the Reverend did pay more attention to me again, something I didn't relish. This time it was the gift that attracted him like a shiny new coin. He would spend hours with me—in the company of Wallace, of course—asking me questions about how I felt and what I said. It wasn't the only miracle I would perform practically right before his eyes, but one of my miracles in particular would change my life once again. I would have taken my gift underground and continued had not the minister convinced me that I was an apprentice of the boo-man himself. But as I soon learned, once my gift presented itself, I no longer controlled it."

Chapter 4

Agent of the Devil

"Word of my experience with Jenny got out. It flew on the breeze like an old hag riding in on a norther," Sophie told Aunt Stella. "You could tell where the story hit—their heads bobbing as they hunkered down to listen, noddies turned clap-dishes, nattering about Jenny's miraculous healing. This irked the Reverend no end. While he started out firking and poking me, searching for the secrets behind my powers, he soon turned on me, preaching that I had been reading the black psalm. The idea that I was actually in collusion with the big boo intrigued me. Even though I was already beginning to get along with my classmates, my rank among them took a surprising leap forward."

"Hey, cherry gob-stick," Willy whispered, poking Sophie sharply.

Sophie did not take offense at the nickname. Returning home the first time she heard her new name, she spun around to study herself in the mirror. She had to agree that the short red hair that topped her growing rangy figure did indeed make her look like a lollipop. Sophie leaned back over her chair so Willy could whisper his message.

"The Reverend really gots you in church Sunday. He gots you good."

"Yeah, but it doesn't stop 'em. They keeps askin' me over for tea so they can discuss their 'flictions."

"But you must agree that the devil takes you over when you does it. Ma says I'm not s'posed to be talkin' to you cuz you're in with the boo-man."

"Maybe, but she called me over just last Saturday. You and your dad was out shootin' ticklace, and she taked to bed with the cramp. I puts my hand right down there on her belly 'til she falls asleep. She thanked me by sendin' a cake over to the house. Wallace taked it, though, tellin' her that I'm not to have sweets 'til I confesses that I gets my 'structions from the devil."

"What's the devil look like, Gob-stick? Is he big and red?"

"He so big and red," Sophie said, her mind completely absorbed with the picture and nothing else, "he 'minds me of the zact opposite of your little bud, Willy!"

A roar broke out among the rest of their classmates. Even Grace giggled behind the little hand she held over her mouth. Sophie looked up slowly. Mr. Slade stood over her like a genie, his hands on his hips.

"Please stand up, Sophie, and repeat to me what you just said cuz I can't believe one of my students would say such a thing in this classroom."

Sophie rarely needed time to think. "I was splainin' to Willie how I made this big ol' pie out of mud, Mr. Slade. It was this big," she said, measuring it with her hands, "with mud red as partridgeberries."

Probably tired of paddling her in back of the shed and not creative enough to come up with anything more exciting, the teacher sauntered back up to the front. "Because you cannot keep from botherin' your neighbors, Sophie, I will assign you extra lessons to be finished afore you leave here."

Sophie loved the extra work. It was always more interesting to figure out arithmetic problems than go home where she and Grace would be separated.

One warm spring day, Sophie and Grace walked home together.

"You don't have to go anywhere this afternoon, do you?" the dark-haired beauty asked.

"No. I took care of Mrs. Langton yesterday. Her cat gots sick. He's goin' to die. I sat with her and comforted her."

"Did he die while you were there?" Grace asked, looking horrified.

"Lord no, but soon."

"How do you know?"

"I don't know. It just comes to me."

"I wanted to show you something. I have at my playhouse."

"Playhouse? I didn't know you had a playhouse. I thought you walked home everyday."

"I do go home. But then I go out to my playhouse."

"Wallace won't like it if she sees us together, Gracie. I'm not so sure it's a good idea."

"She won't see us. She doesn't know where it's at."

Sophie and her sister skulked through the field near the house. Wildflowers carpeted the knoll. Once over the top, they could not be seen from the peering windows of the Ivany wood frame. Pausing, they gazed at the blue sea that spread out to the horizon. The strong breezes hit them full force, making Grace's long hair billow but only skimming the surface of Sophie's cropped bangs.

"It's down here," Grace explained. "We can climb down these rocks over here. There's a hole aback of that boulder."

Sophie scuffled through the sand and rounded the stone. She stopped short at the entrance to a cave, tall enough so that she and her sister could stand if they bent their heads to one side. She let her eyes adjust before entering it. As the interior came into view, she stared at a miniature version of her sister's bedroom. A rug covered the sandy floor. For a bed, Grace had draped a bedspread over a line of crates. A small rocking chair had been pushed up to another crate covered by a lacey white tablecloth. Sophie was speechless.

"You're not to tell anyone that this is here," Grace warned her.

"Surely you've showed it to the others," Sophie said.

"No. I wanted to make certain it was done before I brought you here. I wouldn't show it to anyone else first."

Sophie took a seat in the rocking chair. "So what do you want to do? I thinks we should sneak out of the house at night and look for fairies."

Grace smiled. "I wish I were as brave as you are, Sophie. I'd be scared witless that Mama would catch me."

"What could she do to you, Gracie? I've been paddled more than you can count, and it doesn't hurt anymore."

"I'm not afraid of the hurtin'. I'm afraid I'll go to hell."

Sophie's face softened. "Bring that crate over here and sit next to me." She put her hands on Grace's cheeks. "Listen to me, girl. You'll never go to hell cuz you just can't be that bad." The image of the blessed Mary that Sophie had seen in a picture book appeared in the back of her mind. "You be a saint, Gracie. God has blessed you, dear sister, and he won't ever let you go to hell."

Grace pulled away. "I don't know if that's true, Sophie. I have something under this box over here that might change your mind about that."

She walked over and dragged a board out from under the box. It was old and scratched, and Sophie had never seen anything like it.

"What is it?" Sophie asked, barely able to contain her excitement.

"It's a Ouija board," Grace whispered. "Papa seized it from a family in town cuz it's an instrument of the devil. And since Papa says you be an instrument of the devil too, I'd thought you might be able to conjure up spirits with me."

Sophie's face lit up. "Of course I can, Gracie. Just show me what to do. I knows lots of spirits out there we can chaw with. Maybe we can even get some of 'em to do chores for us."

Too excited to sleep that night, Sophie snuck into Grace's room and slipped her toes between the covers of her sister's bed.

"Gracie, are you awake?" she whispered.

"Yes."

The moonlight through the window made Grace's white face glow.

Sophie touched the flawless skin with her fingers. "You bein' a future saint and all, I'm honored to be your sister and best friend, Gracie."

"And you, Sophie, bein' such a good friend with the devil and all those hitherto departed souls—who have no way to get into heaven because they still have sin on 'em—mean everything to me. Please don't make Papa and Ma so upset they send you away."

"I'll try to follow you, Gracie," Sophie said, her eyes heavy. "Show me how, and I will join you and the angels."

"A couple of years passed without any major incident, Aunt Stella. The Reverend continued to ride me about my healing activities, but usually it was in public. In private, his eccentricities had abated under Wallace's watchful eye. One Christmas, I had a big scare, though. Ivany brought home another young waif. She was about four-years-old and angish, her lean figure and ragged clothes giving her the look of poverty. She reminded me of me, except that her hair framed her face in soft curls, and her blue eyes drew ones gaze away from the dirt streaks. At first I trembled something awful because her appearance meant that my days outside the orphanage were numbered.

"I needn't have worried, however. I saw Wallace's face flash colors like a string of Christmas lights and remembered the Reverend's weakness. All those little games we played, like the night he came into my room purportedly bringing me a lap rock to keep my bed warm. Next thing I knew, *he* was the rock, pushing his hot body against mine and asking me to feel its heat. Luckily, Wallace was making her way to bed from the shed out back. She moaned as she scaled each rise, 'My feets be ice cold, Mr. Ivany. Please sits on 'em for a while so I can go back to sleep.' The Reverend scraveled out the door afore she had conquered the landing!

The next day, Wallace learned that Mrs. Haviland had lost a baby that winter. She suggested that the curly-haired soul be placed with that family.

"My adopted mother looked at me, now all gawky from having grown up so much in one year. 'I figured you would've thought of that solution afore I did, Sophie,' she said. 'We have to stick together here and keep Mr. Ivany from doin' us both in.'"

"Sophie!" Wallace yelled up the stairs. "You get yourself down here at once! You promised you'd talk to Mr. Weld 'bout his gout this mornin' afore school."

Sophie pulled the quilt over her head. Summer was coming soon, but her body acted like it was already here. Then she thought about Grace and forced herself out of her cocoon, hastily dressing and hobbling down the stairs.

"Is Gracie comin' to school today?"

"Yes. Yes. She's been better for nearly a week now. She was droll, feelin' odd, for two days and it gave us a scare, but she's lookin' better now. When you gets there, you can give Mr. Weld some of this here turkumtine. He should take just one of these spoonfuls each evenin'. Grace will meet you at school."

Sophie rounded the gate to the schoolhouse and scampered up the steps just as the bell finished ringing. Failing to stop and gaze at the beautiful blue sky, she headed straight for her desk. Settling into her chair, she did not look up to see if Mr. Slade was glaring at her. Sophie squeezed her sister's warm and damp hand. She gazed at Grace's yawny face. It was the color of snow blossoms.

"Are you all right, Gracie?" Sophie asked.

"I'm fine," she said, hushing Sophie with her finger.

The lesson started. It went on and on, or so Sophie thought. She had read ahead in the book and could repeat the lesson backward if Mr. Slade had requested her to do so.

Finally, the teacher turned away from the blackboard and gazed at his pupils. "You guys can't seem to sit still. You're all like worms wigglin' on the hook. Okay, we can call it a day here. Don't forget the lesson. We'll continue tomorrow."

The gang leaned toward the rear of the room, making it to the door *en masse*. Sophie wriggled between them, swearing that she would not be the last. She reached back to take Grace's hand and took Willie's instead.

"Ew!" he said. "When Slade called us worms, he didn't mean you should be grabbin' mine, Gob-stick."

Sophie let go immediately and pulled up short so suddenly three boys went down.

"Come on, Gracie. Let's go play."

"Wait a minute, Sophie. I can't get up," she said, pushing herself onto her feet.

But Gracie took only one step before falling flat on her face. Sophie ran back to help her. She felt her sister's forehead.

"Gracie's burnin' up," she told Slade who had backed up against the wall.

"Pull her out of here and sit on the steps! I'll get Dr. Wellstone."

"Why? What's she have?" Sophie asked.

"She's real sick, Sophie. She's goin' to have to go to a hospital or something. I just hope she hasn't given it to the rest of us."

The house was dead silent for days. Dr. Wellstone had come and gone. Shaking his head, he said she should be watched closely. "If she gets any worse, she'll have to go to the hospital in Gander, but until then you'll just have to watch her."

Sophie went up the stairs and opened the door to her sister's room. Wallace sat at Grace's bedside, holding her daughter's hands and sobbing.

"What is it?" Sophie asked. "What's wrong with her?"

"It's polio, Sophie. Grace's got polio and she's crippled."

Days passed. Grace was still very ill and complained that she could not feel her legs at all. Wallace had moved downstairs. She sat in front of her sewing machine. The whirr rang in Sophie's ears while she ironed and made dinner for the Reverend.

"What's she doin' in there?" she finally asked him. "What's Wallace makin'?"

The Reverend sat back, his face worn and crumpled like he had been out to sea for a year. Sophie had never seen him so old-looking. He sipped his tea and his voice sounded like there was no air to push the words out.

"She's makin' a habit," he said. "She said it was goin' to be the prettiest habit anyone's ever had."

"What's that?" Sophie asked, having never heard of such a thing in her life.

"It's her dead dress."

"Whose dead dress?" Sophie demanded, the first hint of comprehension squeezing into the denseness of her brain.

"Surely not Wallace's!" he said, frustration spewing steam from his ears. "Whose do you think, girl? Has growin' up mazed your mind? Who do you know that's sick? You with that gift of yours. God's done sent his angels to take her away right under your nose," he gabbled on, his burdensome body crunching down farther in the wooden chair.

Sophie's eyes grew large. "She's not dead yet!" she screamed, determined to stop him from having her sister buried.

The keen that followed grew louder and louder until Ivany howled like a sled-dog. His chest heaved as the sobs began, "I know you won't help her, girl. You won't save her!"

Sophie bent down and put her arms around his neck. "I'll try," she whispered. "I loves Gracie more than anyone in the world. I'll pray and pray until I gets an answer."

And then she ran out the door and through the field. She did not stop until she got to the little playhouse where she sat down on the rug and cried. Hours later, Sophie dragged herself back through the field into the kitchen and boiled water. Grabbing a full laundry basket next to the ironing board, she ripped dresses and shirts into strips, dropped them into the boiling water, and squeezed them with her bare hands until the heat made them red and blistered. Then she stumbled up the stairs to Grace's room.

Sophie followed a regimen of hot compresses and exercises, stretching her sister's lifeless limbs. In between workouts, she assured Grace that she was not going to die because Sophie herself had seen them both in a dream. They had been playing on the beach, watching the whales glide over the choppy waves and listening to the happy grunts as the potheads paraded in front of them. Tirelessly, Sophie worked with Grace until she was out of the woods.

By June, Grace looked much better, and Dr. Wellstone visited again.

"I've found a place for her in Gander. They have a rehab center, but she'll have to live there until she can get round again."

Sophie felt the blow to her chest. Never having envisioned the separation, she did not think she could survive it.

"I'll go with Gracie and takes care of her," Sophie offered, desperation eating at the edges of her voice.

"Don't be silly, girl," said Wallace. "They won't have any room for you there. It's a hospital. Even Mr. Ivany and I won't go there until she be ready to be picked up."

The Reverend did not look up, cringing by the fire as if all the life had drained from him the moment his daughter got sick.

"Will she get the may water there, doctor?" Wallace continued as if nothing had interrupted them.

"I'm sure there'll be plenty of may water there, Mrs. Ivany. I'll bring my car over in the mornin'. I'll be headin' that way anyhow."

"Why don't you get her things together, Sophie? You knows best what she'll want. She'll only be away a spurt so she won't be needin' too much, I'm sure"

Sophie trudged up the stairs, no longer considering what it would be like without Grace. The school year had ended when Grace became ill, no one fearing they would catch polio more than Mr. Slade himself. Sophie's world was about to screech to a stop.

"A week later, Dr. Dunn in Gander wrote that Gracie was showing much improvement. He was shocked that Gracie's muscles demonstrated so little atrophy after having been feeble for so many weeks. He wrote that Gracie had told him what I had done to keep her and her legs alive, adding that the Ivanys were lucky to have a knowledgeable nurse in such an isolated area and that he looked forward to meeting me when Gracie was well enough to return home.

"But that wasn't going to happen. Less than a week following that letter, I returned from the store to find Wallace interviewing a woman to help with the housework. The woman had a young daughter in tow. The little girl walked over to the old man sitting by the fire. He ignored her at first. But she persisted in getting his attention, finally slipping her hand into his and drawing a smile out of his dragging jowls.

"'What's this?' I asked, knowing I had to stop him.

"'Sophie, this is Mrs. Carberry. She's comin' to help us cuz I can't keep this place up. I'll need to be workin' with Grace when she comes home.'

"The Reverend now had the child on his lap, and she giggled as he bounced her on his knee. Wallace rose and walked over to her husband's side. She stood tall, defying my look of concern.

"'And the Reverend here has agreed to give little Amelia lessons on the Bible. That ought to get him off his arse and out of the house, wouldn't you agree, Sophie?'

"I wouldn't be there when Gracie returned although I continued to write to her for years afterward. I heard that she survived her bout with polio and was able to walk out of the rehab center with few remnants of her disability.

"I, on the other hand, carried much of the world I knew into my new home, Warfield, the orphanage in St. John's. And it wouldn't be long before I would come to realize that my former life with people I had grown to love had been heaven compared to that which I was about to enter."

Chapter 5

The Dark Room

"I don't want you in this auditorium to think that all orphanages are places of horror," Sophie told the students. "My contention is that if the objective is to raise lost souls to be productive and well-disciplined adults, you cannot forget that children need affection, assurance, and tolerance. Without satisfying these needs, you won't succeed.

"Neither Wallace nor the Reverend was home when Dr. Wellstone arrived to take me to the train station in Gander. Chatting about how Gracie was doing, he carried my suitcase to the car. We didn't talk about my destination, but he told me he had heard that St. John's was having mighty fine weather. Actually, it was mighty fine in Tooley just then. We had been approaching September with a string of clear sunny days. I thought about the cave and school starting in a couple weeks and could barely catch my breath. Before I boarded the train, I pondered making a break for it, scampering to the hospital to see Gracie. Dr. Wellstone must have sensed it. He made sure I was settled on the train and watched it leave the station!"

Sophie stepped out of the cab and faced the ominous brick building. Her legs could barely carry her over the threshold into the busy hallway. She froze, dropping her bag on the cold linoleum floor.

"What you doin' here, girl?" asked a woman in a long black robe.

Sophie stared at her strange headpiece.

"You'd better be gettin' yourself to your classroom before I report you!"

"Where do I go?" Sophie asked, her voice barely audible. "And what's that funny hat you're wearin'?"

"I beg your pardon!" the nun said, finally looking down at the bag. "Take this hall. Turn left at the corner. It's the first door on the right. Toss your bag over there by the wall afore someone trips!"

As instructed, Sophie headed down the hallway, dirty white walls narrowing as she strode forward. The door to the room the nun described was shut, and Sophie hesitated.

"No, noooooo!" the voice inside screamed.

Sophie's feet twitched like they were going to take off without her. The door finally opened, and a matronly woman dragged a little girl out into the hallway, pushing her toward the doors along the opposite wall. The girl did not seem to be crying, but tear stains streaked her cheeks.Wanting desperately to touch the poor girl's arm, Sophie's heart ached.

"What do you want?" interrupted a nun behind a large desk.

"I'm Sophie Hawkins."

"Were we expectin' you?" she asked, irritated.

"Yes. I thinks."

"Had your shots?"

Sophie hesitated. "I'm not sure."

"Any papers?"

"Pardon?"

"Did they give you any papers to bring with you?"

"No."

"No polio or smallpox vaccinations?"

"Pardon?"

"Well, we know your ears haven't been cleaned. Have you had polio or smallpox?"

"No, but my sister had polio," Sophie explained, finally recognizing what the woman was talking about.

"Come back here then. Nursing Sister Traudnot will return in a few minutes. You can't be put with the others 'til you get checked out."

"Come with me," another woman said after the fifteen minute ordeal with the nurse. "You need to bathe before we assign you a bed. Hurry up, now. Where are you goin'?"

"My things."

"Good Lord, you won't be needin' most of that stuff. You have clothes assigned here. Hurry up now if you want to get dinner."

Sophie ran to keep up with her. The woman was not wearing a funny hat, but when they got to the bathing room she donned an apron and rubber gloves.

"Get over here. Take off your clothes and stuff them in the bag by the door."

Steam rose from the water filling the large tub. Sophie thought about the steam off of Ester's bath. The water then was cold, but the tub was outside where it was even colder.

"Why aren't you wearin' a funny hat?" she asked the lady summoning her to get into the tub.

"Don't dawdle, girl," the woman said.

"Sophie. My name's Sophie."

"Don't count on me rememberin' that. There's far too many of you to remember names."

"What's yours?"

"Don't get sassy now, or I'll report you to Sister English."

"The one who gave me the shots?"

"No. She's a nurse. Sister English is a nun."

"What's that?"

"I didn't hear you say that. If anyone asks, you tell her you've been baptized. They don't take kindly to the ones who have never been baptized. They'll have you examined by the doctor when he comes to make sure it hasn't been broken."

"I been baptized! The Reverend baptized me at the beach."

"No. I mean a proper baptizin' so they know you've been wiped clean of Eve's sin."

"I don't have Eve's sin!" Sophie insisted.

"Only a proper baptizin' by Father Byrne will rid you of that. You just go along with the rest. Tell 'em you're Catholic and you'll be fine."

"Should I mention that my father was a Reverend?"

"No. Father Byrne's not married. No real priest is married. You don't talk about bein' the moss baby of a priest. They don't understand anything else, and it'll give them the heebie-jeebies if you do. Just tell them your ma was Catholic, and she had you baptized afore you could remember."

The woman scrubbed Sophie all over. The bathwater turned a shade of gray before she pulled the plug.

"There now. I'll show you to a bed and then take you to the dinin' room for food. With hair like yours, it'll dry in no time."

Three long tables filled the dining room. Sophie slipped into an empty chair as girls tumbled in through the doors. All wore the same uniform Sophie was given.

A nun stood up behind a smaller table.

"Who's that?" Sophie whispered to a younger girl sitting next to her.

"Shhh. Just look at the floor and repeat the words after her."

When the nun sat down, the girl turned backed to Sophie. "You new?"

"Yes."

"That's Mother Kearney. Never talk durin' prayers. Sister English, at the end of our table, will rap your hand if she catches you."

"Why?"

"Just do it. Now eat. Which room are you in?"

"I don't know. I don't remember."

"You'll get used to it. I did."

"What's your name?"

"Sydney," she said. "I'm leavin' soon. My mum died last year, and I'm here waitin' for my aunt to pick me up."

"Don't listen to her," said the student on Sophie's other side. "I'm Val. If her aunt hasn't come by now, she doesn't want her. How old are you, anyway?"

"I'm fourteen."

"Then you'll be here for a while. You're just the right age for them to get you to sign up to do time with the Sisters of Mercy. Pretend you're goin' to do it and you get beat less often."

"How old are you, Val?"

"I'm sixteen. I'm supposed to become a novice next month. That's fine with me. You won't catch me takin' any vows, though," Val said, hesitating. "I sure hope you're not a spy. You could get me in real trouble."

"There are spies? Why?"

"Just as I thought. You're too dumb to be a spy," Val said, visibly relieved. "Sure there are spies. Spies are here to keep the nuns informed about what's goin' on. I had a friend who was gettin' things from the outside. She had a friend afore she had to come here. A spy reported her. Haven't seen my friend since," she explained, stuffing a roll into her pocket. "Probably in the dungeon. That's where they take you to beat you 'til your dead."

"Is it in the basement?"

"No. That's the laundry and other places where we work. It's in the basement of the convent, that big white house. You must have seen it on your way in. That's where the sisters live."

Sophie shivered. When dinner was over, the girls all rose and walked to their rooms. Unsure which was hers, Sophie hesitated.

"What are you lookin' for?" a girl about Sophie's height asked as she passed by.

"My room. I'm not sure where I go."

"What's your name?"

"Sophie Hawkins."

"Follow me. I'm one of your roommates. I saw your name on your bed."

The room was packed full of beds. Sophie counted at least forty of them divided by narrow rows. Sophie's was in a corner at the far end.

"My name is Jane," the girl said. "My bed is right next to yours. Unfortunately, the toilets are at the far end. You'll sometimes have to make your way there in the dark without stubbin' a toe."

"Are the toilets inside?" Sophie asked surprised.

"Of course," Jane said with a look of confusion.

The two girls sat on their beds and talked.

"How long have you lived here?" Sophie asked.

"Since I was three. My mother and father died in a storm."

"You must still be sad."

Jane looked at Sophie as if she did not understand.

"Are you goin' to become a nun?" Sophie asked.

"Only if they ask me directly. Why?"

"Because somebody told me that you have to say you're goin' to become one if you're asked."

"It's a good idea. But if you keep your head down and don't stand out, you probably won't be asked. I stay quiet and do my lessons promptly so they don't really notice me anymore. But lookin' at your hair, I'm not sure you'll be able to hide. You stand out like a crushed thumb."

"Why are the nuns so mean?"

"Because they're brides of Jesus."

"Jesus wasn't married."

"Nuns aren't either. That's why they're so mean. If Father Byrne doesn't give 'em any, I don't see how Jesus could."

The girls giggled. Sophie was beginning to feel at home.

Religious Studies was just after breakfast. First thing in the morning, Jane and Sophie hustled to chapel in the small church next to the orphanage. After the service, Sophie was hungry. The meal always some sort of porridge, this morning's breakfast was oatmeal. Sophie suspected that it was whatever leftover grains the cooks could get hold of.

Sister English taught Religious Studies to girls of all ages. Sophie walked into the classroom and waited for a seat assignment.

"Yes. Miss Hawkins, why don't you take a seat up here in front? Before you sit down, please recite a Hail Mary for the class."

"Pardon?"

"Hail Mary, full of grace— That one," the nun repeated impatiently.

"I don't know it," admitted Sophie.

"You're lackin' in any religious education, then. Have you ever been to church?"

"Yes, ma'am."

"But you don't know the prayer. Are you Catholic?"

"Oh yes, ma'am," Sophie answered without hesitating.

The teacher approached her. "Put out your hands."

Sophie showed her palms. The nun turned them over and then slapped the backs with a ruler. Sophie's skin burned. She sighed but otherwise said nothing.

"Go to the chapel for penance. I don't want you back here until Father Byrne has heard your confession. If he's not in the nave, he'll be in the back. Tell him I sent you."

"Yes ma'am." Sophie said, walking quickly out of the room before releasing the tears that had welled up in her eyes.

Sophie entered the nave and stopped to look more closely at the statues and paintings. She had knelt among the pews that morning but was too busy trying to keep up with the prayers to pay any attention to her surroundings. With the room empty, she could hear her own footsteps on the aisle, but when Father Byrne approached from behind, she did not detect his.

"What do you want?" he asked.

Sophie jumped and spun around to face him. "I'm supposed to come here to own up to something."

"You mean for confession?'

"Yes. Sister English sent me."

"You're not Catholic then?"

"Yes I am!" she said.

"Repeat the Lord's Prayer for me."

Sophie did as instructed.

"That's the Protestant version, you know."

"Oh, that's odd," she said, "I always thought the Reverend was Catholic."

The priest was shorter than Sophie by several centimeters. He was older than the Reverend, or so she thought, his gray hair combed back neatly to cover a large bald spot.

"Don't worry," he said. "I'll keep your secret if you would like. Let me get my stole, and I'll show you what to do."

Sophie exhaled. At last she had a friend.

When he returned, he motioned her into the back room. "Sit there, girl. What's your name?"

"Sophie Hawkins."

"How old are you?"

"Fourteen."

"I like your red hair, Sophie," he said, reaching out to caress it.

Sophie froze.

"Don't worry. I'll just kneel here in front of you. Let me put on my stole. There now. Repeat after me. Bless me, Father..." he began, his breath warming her cheek. "Now Sophie, tell me your sins," he finally said.

Sophie thought and thought. "I don't think I have any, Father Byrne."

He took her hand. "If you had no sins, girl, your family wouldn't have sent you here, would they? Was it a boyfriend?"

"No. I've never had a boyfriend."

"Did you sidle up to that Reverend you're talkin' about?"

"No," she answered increasingly agitated.

He leaned closer, sniffing her hair.

"What do you want from me?" she finally asked.

"Did you tell Sister English you're a baptized Catholic?"

"Yes. Yes. That's my sin! I lied to Sister English."

"If you don't want her to know the truth, you should cooperate with me. I can help you study here in the evenin'."

"The nuns won't let me leave the quarters."

"They'll let you leave if I tell 'em."

Sophie's face felt hot. "I'll come here and work in the office if you promises not to touch me."

The priest exhaled, seemingly disappointed by the challenge waged by the shrewd redhead. "For your penance, Sophie, please say five Hail Mary's and an Act of Contrition."

"Here? Now?"

"No."

"Do you want me to come back?"

"No."

"Will you tell Sister English?"

"I'm not interested in hurtin' you, Sophie," he said, his face suddenly brightening. "Perhaps next Saturday, when you come for confession, we can talk again."

Sophie shivered.

"You had better get back to Religious Studies class before she comes lookin' for you."

Sophie got up and hurried out of the church. She had not even been at Warfield a full day and had already learned her first lesson.

A week or two later, more girls spread across the beds around Jane and Sophie. Sophie looked them over. All wore white gowns like hers. All had stringy medium-length hair, ranging from blond to dark brown. The youngest was a seven-year-old named Alice. The little girl with fuzzy curls around her face seemed more mature than she was.

"How long have you been here, Alice?" Sophie asked.

"As long as I can remember," said Alice, her big gray eyes seeming so innocent. "I'm not sure what happened. The nuns won't splain it to me, but it must have been bad cuz they keeps on tellin' me I'm headed for the same fate as Mama. I'm goin' to the dungeon tonight. Want to come with me?"

"Don't listen to her, Sophie. She just talks big. That's what gets her into trouble. She's rarely in class because they make her work extra shifts in the basement," Jane explained. "That's not the dungeon, Alice. It's just the laundry and sewin' room. Quit tryin' to get Sophie in trouble too."

"I tells you there's a passage downstairs between the basement and the dungeon there. At night when I'm workin' there all alone, I can hear the noises. The nuns be beatin' the prisoners!"

Sophie smiled. Alice reminded her of herself when she was younger. "Maybe some evenin' but I'm too tired tonight, Alice. I'm worried about gettin' up at four to work with the sewin' machine. I told Sister Josephine that I knew how to sew but I've only watched someone sew, not really tryin' it myself. If I don't do well tomorrow mornin', they'll move me to laundry."

"And beat you 'til you're senseless," Alice added.

But Sophie's eyes were drawn to another girl, a blond with bright pink cheeks and shiny blue eyes. "What's your name?"

"Victoria," she replied.

"Give me your hand, Victoria," Sophie said. "Have you been to the doctor lately?"

The girl tugged her hand away with a look of surprise. Jane and Alice both glared at Sophie.

"We don't go to the doctor if we don't have to," Jane explained. "The doctor's strange. We have to stay healthy, and if we're not healthy, we fake it."

"Victoria's sick, Jane," Sophie said. "If she doesn't get help, we'll all be sick."

"What do you mean? What does she have?"

Victoria began to cry, and Sophie put her arms around her. "Maybe I'm wrong. Maybe she's okay," Sophie said. "Don't cry, Victoria. I'm sure you'll be okay."

That night, Sophie dreamt of Victoria's death. The small group stood around a deep hole on a grass-covered hillock. The little girl lay peacefully in a box without a lid. Sophie extended her arm into the hole, trying to touch Victoria's hand, and Victoria reached back, but the grave was too deep.

The next morning, she visited Nursing Sister Traudnot's office and told her to check on Victoria. That afternoon, Sophie returned.

"What happened to Victoria?" she demanded.

"Tuberculosis turned up on Victoria's x-ray. She was sent to the hospital," the nurse said, eyeing Sophie suspiciously. "She had no symptoms yet. How did you know she was sick? I couldn't even tell."

"I just knew. What's Turbuclosus?"

"You'll become familiar with it soon enough. You'll all have to be tested now. That'll teach you to stick your nose into someone else's business."

"Will she die?"

"Probably not. I'm sure the hospital will find something to give her."

"I don't think they will," warned Sophie, backing out of the room. "I don't think they'll know what to do."

"Anyway. She's not comin' back to Warfield. We don't need TB round here. She'll have to go somewhere else cuz we won't take her back."

"I never found out what happened to Victoria," Sophie said, picking up the microphone and walking to the edge of the stage. "I had my suspicions that my dream was right, but there was no way I could find out if it really was. I swore to myself that I was going to keep my head down—that I wouldn't let myself be noticed. But I had resided at Warfield less than a month and already I stood out like a rowboat on a pond, concentric circles creating wavelets on the glassy surface. Had I chosen to keep Victoria's illness a secret, more of us might have died. But the other girls didn't think that way.

"If I saw a problem with making new friends, it was only because of the big deal the nuns and Father Byrne made of my so-called miracle. The two made me the center of their world as they waited for their little saint to perform another one. And as if on cue, my gift became a magnet, pulling me into the limelight. As in Victoria's situation, I always seemed to draw the right conclusion, but the next case would have even greater ramifications.

"At least my celebrity gave me some benefits. While I was being watched by the nuns, Father Byrne dared not approach me. Fortunately, most of the nuns also left me alone, probably fearing that God would strike them down if they interfered with His chosen prophet. But Sister English seemed to possess special powers and didn't fear using them to continue to make my life miserable. Then there was the punishment, usually inflicted by her assistant, Dr. Button. This is what Jane and the others seemed to fear so much. I was about to learn why every girl in that orphanage bowed down to the management. I was about to plunge into the hell—careen down the bathtub drain like the gray water I created the first day I arrived."

Chapter 6

Into Madness

Routine defined life at Warfield. Sophie rose at four each morning to pull on her uniform and then walk downstairs to do laundry or sewing or cleaning. Chapel was at seven, and breakfast at eight. Then it was off to classes, starting with Religious Studies where Sister English reigned with a tongue as sharp as her pointer. Each evening, Sophie returned to the dormitory room to observe forty others ready themselves for bed and catch whatever social activity they could before the lights went out.

"I hears 'em last night, Sophie," Alice whispered. "Won't you come down with me tonight and take a look?"

"Sorry, Alice. I'm so tired I can barely keep my eyes open."

"You've slept next to me for nearly two years now and still won't come."

"You don't hear them every night, do you? Why do you only hear them some nights and not others?"

"I don't go down there every night. Just when they draws me there."

"Don't listen to her," warned Jane. "She'll get you into trouble again, Sophie. Remember, they're watchin' you to see if you do any more miracles. I heard Sister Josephine tell Mother Kearney that they're sendin' you away if you do. You make people outside the orphanage take notice. Bishop Alden never paid any attention to us before. The nuns don't want anybody to know how they treat us. They don't like the attention and certainly don't want the priests stickin' their noses in and takin' over."

Sophie slid under the covers. "I'm tryin', Jane, but sometimes I don't think I can help it."

The lights went out. Sophie rose onto her elbow to survey the bodies sprawled across the beds, some already still. The feeling came upon her again. The others were like seedlings sprouting on the forest floor near Tooley. The little trees needed nourishment to grow. Sophie felt she had to supply it. Only big trees could withstand the treatment here.

"Does this look right, Jane?" Sophie asked, holding up a dress she had just pulled out of the machine.

"No. The seam isn't straight. Hand it to me, and I'll see if I can fix it. Sister Josephine will surely take notice of the error, and you'll get assigned to scrubbin' down the bathin' room."

"Have you seen Alice this mornin'?"

"No. I think she's in laundry today."

"I was wonderin' if she could show me where she thinks those voices are comin' from."

"Don't go there, Sophie. She got paddled twice last week and lost her meals for two days. I don't think you should get involved."

"She's headed for trouble, Jane. I don't believe I can just stand by and let them hurt her like that."

"She's a bedlamer. Sometimes we get them in here. The nuns have to deal with it. You shouldn't."

"I don't think she's a troublemaker, Jane. I think she's in a fruz. Good lord, do you realize she's probably never been held and loved in her life? It seems like nobody cares here when you're in trouble."

Jane looked up. "Few of us have had much lovin', Sophie, but most of us don't start breakin' the rules."

That night, Sophie rolled over and noticed Alice's empty bed. She got up and carefully snaked her way through the rows to the toilets. Alice was not there either. Peeking out the door, she scanned the quiet hallways—moonlight streamed in through the windows at the end of the main passage, enough to let Sophie easily slip out and head for the doors to the staircase. Creeping through the shadows along the wall, she slinked past the second dormitory room. When she got to the stairs, she descended to the first floor. Peering through the small window in the door, she noticed the night guard, a man pacing the hall and smoking a cigarette. The lights were on in the office across the way, but everything else appeared quiet. Blackness flooding the bottom steps, she nervously slipped down the rest of the stairs. This unexpected development forced her to use her memory of the floor plan. Feeling her way along the opposite wall, she finally found the door to the laundry and slowly opened it. Sophie froze. All was silent.

"Alice?" she whispered. "Are you here?"

No one answered. As she turned to leave, a figure suddenly jumped in front of her.

"Sophie!" she said excitedly. "I'm so glad you've come. I hears them. Come over here with me."

Alice grasped Sophie's hand and led her back into the passage. The last door beyond the laundry was supposed to be locked. Sophie had never even tried it, let alone been inside. Alice turned the knob, and the door creaked open.

"What's this?" Sophie asked. "I can't see a thing."

"Hold on," Alice whispered. "It's just down here at the end. Take little steps so you don't trip."

Sophie inhaled. The odor of moist earth filled her nostrils. "Is this a garden room, Alice?"

"Just a few more steps, Sophie," Alice said. "Now kneel down."

Sophie did as instructed, gooseflesh crawling up and down her arms.

"Do you hear them?"

"Hear what?"

"The moanin'. There! That one just asked us to save her."

Sophie looked up but could not see Alice in the darkness. "I don't hear anything, Alice."

"We have to get over there fast, Sophie. Put your hand up against the wall in front of you. There's a wood door. I've been scratchin' at it but I can't get through. You try scratchin' too, Sophie."

"No! We have to get back to the dormitory, Alice. Come with me—" Sophie started to say, but a sudden pain penetrated her head, and the shadows swallowed her up.

"I found her here! I found her!" Alice screamed, tears rolling down her cheeks.

"I'll get help," said one of the first girls down the stairs for laundry duty.

Sister Josephine and the nurse quickly approached, and the nurse bent down to study the body sprawled across the floor in front of the laundry doors.

"She's been hit on the head. We'll have to keep an eye on her, but I think she'll be all right," the nurse said. "Tell me again, Alice, why you were down here before the others."

"I gets washed up and dressed quickly cuz I sees that Sophie isn't in her bed. I rushes down when it's still dark and finds her lyin' here in the hallway."

Sophie could hear the conversation but only at a distance. She tried to move but could not.

"Girls, get to work. Nurse and I can get her up to the office. This doesn't concern you."

Jane stepped forward. "I think she sleepwalks, Sister. I've seen her walk round at night as if she were in a dream. When I mention it the next day, she never remembers."

The nun glanced up as Jane quickly retreated into the laundry. The two women pulled Sophie onto her feet. By now, she could move and only needed to be led up the stairs.

"Where's Alice?" Sophie asked them. "Did you find Alice?"

"Of course, girl. Alice found you. Nurse can patch you up, and then you can explain why you were down here."

"I was in the gardenin' room."

"The what?"

"That room by the laundry."

"Nonsense. That room's always locked."

Sophie did get some satisfaction from the incident. The nurse was a new one—Sister Caroline. Her kind face was like that of an angel. Sophie sat up on her elbows when the nurse entered the room.

"Why are you here?" Sophie asked.

"Nursin' Sister Traudnot's husband took ill. She probably won't be back for a while," she said. "Now, do you want to tell me what you remember about last night?"

Sophie paused, considering. "I must have been dreamin'. I dreamt that Alice wasn't in bed. I went to look for her and found her in the laundry. I don't know how I got into the other room."

Sister Josephine went back downstairs and checked the door. It was locked. "You were never in that room."

"I guess I was dreamin' then. May I go back to the dormitory to get dressed for work now?"

"No. I think you should stay here today. If all goes well, you can return this evenin'."

Sophie never spoke to Jane or Alice about what she thought had happened to her. A week later, she awoke again to find Alice's bed empty. This time, however, she stayed in her bed. There were plenty of other troubled young women who needed her help because a flu epidemic was just beginning to break out, and Sophie and Nursing Sister Caroline worked day and night for a week to keep the young people alive. In the end, she was finally able to sleep without interruption. When she awoke, a good ten of the forty beds in her room were empty. Within a few months, they would fill up with new children again—something that disturbed Sophie even more.

"Did you ever consider becoming a nurse, Sophie?" Sister Caroline asked after things had calmed down. "You seem to work very well with the patients."

Sophie thought about how to answer. "I'd rather be a doctor. I get the urge to help people but my powers to save them are beyond me. The powers sometimes seem to take ahold of me."

Sister Caroline laughed. "I mean that you're good at soothin' sick people and making them feel better. What are these powers that you're talkin' about?"

"I guess it's prayer, healin', that sort of thing," Sophie answered, trying to think of a way to change the subject. "Did you go to a nursin' school round here?"

"Yes, but it's easier now. There's one beginnin' at the university here."

"Miss Hawkins," Sister Josephine interrupted. "We have a class startin' for novices this evenin'. I was told you were on the list. If you don't hurry, you'll be late."

"Thank you, Sister."

When Sophie returned to the dormitory, she watched girls hurriedly prepare for bed. Even with fewer students, the people crowded her. She had already seen she could not take care of them all. Many were still not well even though the flu epidemic was over. Jane circled and sat down beside her.

"What's the matter?" Jane asked, putting her arm around her friend.

"I don't know how we can keep goin'? Do you want to stay with the Sisters here?"

Jane glared at her. "I don't think we can talk about this, Sophie."

"It's deceit, Jane. We're becomin' just as bad as they are. We fear if we tell them we don't want to join the order, they'll punish us. There must be another way."

"Sophie, I don't want to know what you think. Are you so positive I'm not goin' to join up?"

"Come on, Jane. I know you. I know what you want for yourself. We both want the same thing."

"You don't know me!" she said. "You don't, and I'll have to speak with Sister English if you tell me how you feel."

"You've become a spy?"

"Not a spy. But I must be true to myself, and you're tryin' to talk me out if it. Let's just agree not to talk about personal things, okay?"

Sophie rested her chin on her fist. "Just look at all of them, Jane. All these poor souls need something."

"You're talkin' funny again, Sophie," Alice interrupted. "Why don't you take care of yourself and butt out of everyone else's business?"

"Alice? Where have you been?" Sophie asked. "I haven't seen you for a few weeks. Were you sick? Are you okay now?"

"Don't do that to me. I'm fine. It's you guys who has the problems. I'm fine."

That night, Sophie stayed up to watch Alice. The girl tossed and turned, mumbling gibberish.

The next morning, Sophie sat beside Alice at breakfast. "Have you heard the moanin' in the basement like you did afore now?"

"Yes. I goes downstairs sometimes, and the noises are still there."

"Is it only in the basement? Or do you hear them in the dormitory afore you go down there?"

"You can't hear them from the dormitory, Sophie."

"Then what makes you go down there?"

"I feels like I have to go. I can't sleep, so I decides to take a walk. Do you want me to take you next time?" Alice asked, smiling.

"Do you want me to come?"

"It's up to you. If you're interested in what's goin' on in the convent basement, then you should come down. Why it taked you so long, I don't know," she said, shrugging her shoulders.

"Why were you gone the last few weeks? Where do you go when you're gone like that?" Sophie asked.

But Alice had turned to the person on her other side and did not seem to have heard her.

Nearly a month passed before Alice shook Sophie awake. Cold hovered like a cloud over the beds, and Sophie did not want to go. But Alice was agitated. The linoleum cold under her feet, Sophie donned some socks and trailed the girl down the stairwell. At the bottom tread, Sophie lost her guide in the darkness.

"Alice?" she whispered.

"Over here, Sophie. I opened the door and am now goin' in."

Sophie crossed to the entrance of the laundry and then followed the wall with her fingertips until she smelled the scent of damp earth.

"Alice?" she whispered as she felt her way through the doorway.

"I'm here, Sophie," the voice said.

Alice sounded like she was standing far away. The room grew colder. Sophie shivered but continued to inch forward.

"Can you hear them?" the voice asked.

"No. What do *you* hear, Alice?" The room seemed colder the farther in she went.

Suddenly an artic breeze swept through the gauzy cloth of her nightgown, and the door slammed shut behind her. "Alice!" she said. "That's not funny!" She spun around and crept back to the door. The knob, icy to the touch, turned in her hand and opened easily. "Alice? Are you there? I'm goin' back upstairs," Sophie said, her whisper turning husky.

Trying to quiet her nerves when she began to gasp for air, she slowed to a stop and listened. Then she gradually retraced her steps up the stairs, pausing on the landing to look for the guard in front of the nuns' offices. All was peaceful. Sophie scampered to the second floor and into bed, pulling the covers over her head. Chilled, it took her some time to warm herself up. What was Alice trying to do? Why did she get her kicks luring her friends into trouble? Eventually, Sophie drifted into a light sleep.

The next morning, Jane shook her arm. "Wake up, Sophie."

"What time is it?"

"We're openin' up the laundry this mornin' so it'll be ready for everyone to start work. Don't you remember? It's our turn. We have to get down there in ten minutes."

"Where's Val? Doesn't she usually go down first?"

"Not this week. The whole group rotates, remember? You and I are on duty this week. Come on."

Sophie slipped on a frock and pulled up her black stockings, combing her short hair as the two girls headed down the stairs. At the first floor landing, Jane flipped on the light to the basement before descending. Sophie had not noticed the switch before. At the bottom, Jane switched on the lights to the laundry. Sophie glanced at the garden room door. It was closed. She walked over and turned the knob. It was locked.

"Come on, Sophie. The large vats have to be filled with hot water so the towels in the basket just inside the door can soak. I'll release the heat so the room can warm up and then plug in the irons and sewin' machines."

Sophie went straight to the vats along the wall. She turned on the tap, and steaming water began to fill the tub. Then she added detergent. This would be the washing tub. She dumped the dirty towels in. The other girls would stir them until they were clean.

When she approached the rinsing tub in a dim corner along the wall, she noticed water dripping from the faucet. Someone had not turned it off all the way. She headed straight for the tap but stopped short when she saw that it was full of liquid. Her heart pumping, she looked down. Arms crossed over the breasts, the body of a young girl floated face up just under the surface. Her nightgown and hair billowed, insipid blue eyes staring up at the ceiling.

Jane found Sophie when her friend did not answer. Alice's body lay on the water-covered floor with Sophie on top of her, trying to push the water out.

When Sophie awakened, she did not recognize where she was. She tried to get up onto her elbows to survey the dim room but could not. She screamed!

A lock clicked and the door opened. A woman in white burst in and tried to calm her. She checked the young girl's constraints and then exited, again securing the lock. Minutes later, a doctor entered. Sophie watched as he leaned over her, staring at her eyes, but not seeming to acknowledge her existence.

"Where am I?" Sophie asked, grabbing his wrist when he reached over her.

He did not pull away but flashed a light in front of her eyes.

"Hello. Sophie Hawkins, isn't it? Don't you remember what happened?"

Sophie gazed at him, trying to think. "Alice. The wash tub," she managed.

"What? I mean why the nun's brought you here three days ago."

"Because they think I killed Alice."

"Alice? I'll ask them about that. They didn't mention that you had murdered anyone. They just explained you were agitated and wouldn't come to your senses. They thought you were having a breakdown, and from what I've seen so far, I think I agree."

"I just found her body. I was tryin' to bring her back," she said, pulling him toward her again.

"It might be easier if I loosen these constraints so you can sit up. If you try anything, others will come running."

"Alice. Is she alive?"

"Alice who?" He turned to the nurse who had appeared behind him and asked her to check it out. "If she were dead, they wouldn't send the body here. We only deal with the living."

Sophie began to calm down.

"Have you ever been here before, Miss Hawkins?"

"No."

"Or in any hospital like this?"

"No. My sister was in the hospital in Gander for polio, but they wouldn't let me go visit her."

"Do you take any medications?"

"No," she said, suddenly realizing that he was a doctor. "Are you Dr. Button?"

"No. Why?"

"Because that's who we go to when we're punished."

"Tell me about it," he said, pulling up a chair.

The nurse returned before Sophie could respond and whispered into the doctor's ear.

"The nurse tells me that Alice is probably Alice Butts. She committed suicide nearly a week ago."

Sophie gasped but said nothing.

"So Alice has something to do with this," the doctor continued. "She was ill, you know. She was ill for years, visiting us on occasion. Did you notice that she was missing from the orphanage sometimes?"

Sophie nodded.

"She was here getting help, though the treatment didn't always have lasting affects."

The nurse bent down and whispered into the doctor's ear again.

"What? Are you sure? That's not my recommendation," he said, looking concerned. "Excuse me, Miss Hawkins. I'll be right back."

The doctor left without locking the door.

"These are your clothes, Miss Hawkins," said the nursed. "If you can please get them on now, someone from Warfield is comin' to pick you up."

The nurse then left, but Sophie did not get up. Instead, she lay back down on the bed and curled into a little ball.

The doctor returned a half-hour later. Nursing Sister Caroline walked in with him.

"Hi Sophie. Are you feelin' any better?" she asked.

Sophie sat up.

"Dr. Robbins here and Mother Kearney and I have come to an agreement. Tomorrow, you'll visit another doctor. You can stay here for a while so you can talk to Dr. Fairbourne from the Atlantic Psychiatric Clinic. You might find him interestin'."

"I don't have to go back to the orphanage?"

"Not until you're ready. I promise I'll come and visit every day, though," Sister Caroline said. "Maybe you'll be able to tell me what's botherin' you."

"For the first time since entering the orphanage nearly four years earlier," Sophie explained to the students, "I gazed at the sunlight streaming in through the reinforced window and realized there was a world outside the gates of Warfield. I put my hand out to catch the dust particles suspended in the spotlight.

"Dr. Fairbourne would be the answer to my prayers. He would get me to understand what the gift meant, and for the first time in my life, give me something to work for. I would lean on him for years afterward, and he would always be there when I needed to talk to him.

"Years later, long after the government closed Warfield because of abuse allegations against the order by the children and young women left in their charge, I would learn that a developer had a contractor map out the buildings when he entered a bid to buy the property. A tunnel existed between the orphanage basement and that of the convent. Workers discovered the tunnel originated in a back wall of a room next door to the laundry."

Book 2

A young tree bends in the ceaseless winds
Its trunk grows upward, twisted but delighted
That the blasts chase the voluminous clouds
And scraps of humanity's squander
with its blustery discourse,
Unveiling the Golden Orb and a sparkling
path of sustenance from His rays.
Though stunted by the terrible cruelty
of daily exploitation,
The tree thrives until the Master calls

Chapter 7

Ultimate Fear

"Please sit down, Miss Hawkins," said the middle-aged man, standing over a small table and two comfortable-looking chairs.

Dr. Griffon Fairbourne did not wear a tie but a sweater over an open collar, his dark hair cropped short to blend in with his balding head. Sophie, in her uniform, sat down in one of the chairs, her ankles crossed beneath her, her hands clasped tightly on her lap.

"Let me see," he began, his voice soft and friendly, "You live at Warfield Orphanage. Am I correct?"

"I live at the hospital here," Sophie answered.

"So you lived at Warfield in the past," he said. "Do you think you're ready to return?"

"No. I still get headaches and am sick to my stomach."

"Tell me what it was like living at the orphanage."

"What do you mean?"

"Let's begin by talking about your routine. Start in the morning and work your way through the day."

Sophie hesitated, her heart thumping against her chest wall. Who was this man? Would he record what she said and report it to the nuns or file it in her medical records? "Our day starts at four in the mornin'. We get up and go to work."

Dr. Fairbourne did not write anything down. He sat back and listened to her.

"Some of us work in the sewin' room," she said, beginning to relax. "We make uniforms and altar cloths and such." She took a big breath. "At six-thirty, we return to clean up for chapel, which begins at seven. Right after chapel, we eat breakfast in the dinin' room. At nine, we have Religious Studies with Sister English. We continue to go to school until three. Then we return to work until dinner at six-thirty. After dinner, we go back to work until nine."

"Do you have an exercise period?"

"Yes. We do exercise in the gym for one of our classes."

"Do you change clothes and play games?"

"No," she said. "Why?"

"Do you ever go outside?"

"Yes. When we go to chapel and back. The chapel is outside the school buildin'."

"Are there any other outbuildings?"

Sophie began to perspire, squirming and wiping her lip. "Yes. There's the convent," she said, thinking further. "That's it. Just the convent."

"No garden shed or caretaker's cottage?"

Sophie looked down. "I don't think so. I don't remember any."

"Have you ever been to the convent?"

"No."

"How long have you lived there?"

"Nearly four years."

"And you sew uniforms and such. Are there other places to work?"

"Yes. There's the laundry. When I work in laundry, I wash, iron, and fold. There's also housekeepin'."

"No outside crew comes in to clean?"

"No. The girls with housekeepin' duty clean everything."

"But you sew. What other jobs are there in sewing?"

"Cuttin' patterns, clean up, and savin' scraps."

"Do you do anything with the scraps?"

"No. I think they go to the poor. The nuns take the scrap bag away at the end of the week."

"And during your four years there you've only worked in the sewing room?"

"No."

"What else did you do?"

"I worked in laundry and occasionally in housekeepin'."

"So everyone rotated and eventually you did all the jobs."

"No. We rotated gettin' up early to open up the laundry and sewin' room. That way it would be ready for the laundry crew."

"Then why did you do all the jobs?"

Sophie squirmed. "I was sometimes bad and had to be punished."

"That's hard to believe. How were you bad enough to be punished in such a way while the others didn't have to change jobs?"

"I talk too much. I'm defiant. I'm nosy. I sin more than the other girls."

"How do you sin?"

"When I returned to Warfield," Sophie told the students, "Nursing Sister Caroline called me to her office late one afternoon. She closed the door and sat in a chair next to mine. She explained that she might be able to get me into the university nursing school if I really wanted to go. I was aghast. I asked her if I would continue to live there at Warfield. She told me that I was free to leave when I turned eighteen. If I didn't leave, I would have to move to the convent as a novice. I was already a novice and wore a novice's habit when I went to my classes, but my year of training would officially begin when I moved to the convent.

"I had to think about it. Where would I live? What about my friends, my charges? She told me that she would make sure I had a place to stay near campus.

"I spoke with Jane. She was already planning to go to the convent, having never thought of doing anything else. My heart ached for her.

"Sister Caroline finally advised me to leave the grounds. I had to agree. Obedience was definitely not one of my strengths and that was usually the first thing they looked for in nuns. When Sister Caroline asked me again, I jumped at the opportunity. I suspect the nuns wouldn't have accepted me into the convent anyway, throwing me out onto the streets. Many of my friends had nicknamed me 'The Saint'. I can't imagine either Sister English or even Sister Josephine wanting to live with a saint."

"I noticed things that weren't apparent to others," Sophie told Dr. Fairbourne.

"Tell me about what you noticed."

"I knew when one of the girls was sick. At first I went to Nursin' Sister Traudnot to report it."

"And the child wasn't sick?"

"No. I always went to her when they *were* sick. Sister Traudnot only acknowledged it when she had to. Other times, she'd make them continue to attend classes and work. I'd stay with them at night to make sure they were gettin' stronger."

"So, in these instances, the problems did exist. Were you punished other than having to care for these girls alone?"

"Yes. Please note that I was always right. The nurse rarely checked out my claims, leavin' the girls to get well on their own. When Sister Traudnot reported that I was mistaken, I'd be sent to work in the washroom—the part of the laundry where you stir the towels and sheets and then squeeze them out. I'd work there for a few weeks and then return to the sewin' room."

"And when she conceded you were right about the other girls' health, would you be punished?"

"Yes. I did ironin' after I reported that Victoria contracted tuberculosis, and they made me scrub down the offices durin' the flu epidemic. I mean, I didn't have to leave the sewin' room. I was allowed to continue there. It was after nine o'clock that I'd be told to make sure the offices were disinfected."

"You recently returned to Warfield. Have you been punished again since you returned to the orphanage?"

"No. I'm acceptin' that I have problems obeyin' and am tryin' hard to improve."

Sophie sat in Sister Josephine's office and listened to the sermon the nun had prepared for her. At least she listened to the first few words before her mind wandered off. She thought about the beach in Tooley. She had not heard from Grace or any of the Ivanys in nearly four years and yearned to go back and make sure her sister was better.

"Remember that you represent Warfield when you go off to university, " Sister Josephine finally added. "You've had a far better education than the students who come from regular schools, and it might be a good idea to report to the priest at Sacred Heart Church there for confession on Saturday afternoons. Good luck with your secular endeavors, Sophie. Perhaps you'll be able to find a place that appreciates your faults."

Sophie stood up and reached for the same bag she had brought with her four years earlier. Nursing Sister Caroline had left to get the car. She would drive her to the new apartment.

When Sophie stepped outside, it was like a brand new day. Her mind was wiped clean of the lectures, schedules, and poverty the orphanage had branded into her mind. For at least a week, she promised herself not to think about it. But it would come back that very night. She would continue to have nightmares about the orphanage for years.

"Please come in, Miss Hawkins," Dr. Fairbourne said. "I was just working on a book. Sit down over there and tell me about your new residence."

"I live with two other girls in an apartment that overlooks some beautiful fields."

"Have you been out to the sea or to other parts of the city?"

"Yes. We've gone several places and had picnics. It's been fun."

"Do you miss Warfield?"

Sophie smiled. "I like your sweater. Someone did a beautiful job on it."

"Thank you."

"I miss Jane and a few of the others but I try not to think about it."

"Have the pressures gone away? Do you feel more relaxed?"

"Pressures?"

"When you were at the hospital, you told Dr. Robbins that you felt pressure to do things. Do you remember?"

Sophie picked up a little box on the table and turned it around in her hand. "I felt I had to protect some of them, yes."

"Did you feel as if it were your duty to protect them?"

"They couldn't take care of themselves."

"How did you know?"

"They told me," she said, concentrating harder on the designs on the box.

"They just came up to you and asked you to take care of them?" he continued.

Sophie got up and walked to the door. "I have an exam tomorrow. I need the time to study. Do you have me down for next week?"

"Yes. But think about what I said. Think about why you might feel you were responsible for your roommates."

Sophie stood in the snow, letting the delicate flakes stick to her wool hat and coat. She loved it like this. Unfortunately the weather was often worse. Some days, the wind bellowed in her ears, and a thick syrup of ice enveloped the fields outside her apartment. Weeks later, as May approached, there were periods of mauzy weather—the same field would disappear behind a veil of mist and not emerge for days. Sophie would stare out the window intently as if her freedom were still a dream.

"Do you feel as if your roommates need you to care for them now?"

"No," she told the doctor.

"How do you know?"

"They aren't askin' for it."

"The girls at the orphanage asked?"

"Yes. I could tell."

"Nursing Sister Caroline told me that at Warfield it was common knowledge you had some kind of gift," he said, changing the topic. "Is that what you thought?"

"I know I have a gift. Sister English said it was a curse from the devil."

"So you try to hide it?"

"I try to control it but I can't."

"Tell me about it. When did you first know you could do something others could not?"

"I didn't know others couldn't do it until it became a big deal. Aunt Stella told me I was born with it—that my mother had it too, but when you're young, that doesn't mean much."

"Is Aunt Stella your real aunt?"

"No. She was a friend of my grandmother. She promised to look after my mother when Nanny Ester moved to Tooley."

"You're from Tooley?"

"No. I was born in Forsey Harbour but lived in Tooley. My mother died when I was two, and I had to go live with my grandmother after she died."

"Do you remember Forsey Harbour?"

"No. Just what Aunt Stella and Granny Ivy have told me about it."

"You've never been back to Forsey Harbour then."

"No. Aunt Stella and Granny Ivy visited us in Tooley on occasion."

"And your father?"

Sophie's eyes wandered to the blue sky through the window. "My father was a famous surgeon from the States. He had to move back there. I've never met him."

"Look at me, Sophie."

She gazed into his gray eyes—they were strong, the kind that drew her eyes to his. She wanted to glance away, but once she looked at him, she couldn't turn back to the window.

"You're rocking in your chair again, Sophie. My guess is that your father isn't a surgeon. Do you know who your father was?"

"No."

"Did they ever talk about him?"

"Not much. Just that my mother loved him and waited for him all the time."

"So what's your first memory of your childhood?"

Sophie sat back and thought. A line formed between her brows.

"Do you remember your mother?"

"Yes. I think so. I have a photograph of her but it has creases in it."

"What do you remember clearly?"

"I remember the baths on the porch at Nanny's house. When I was in the tub, I could look out over the field and see the ocean. I liked to watch the boats bob on the blue water."

"That's an interesting place for a bathtub. Why was it on the porch?"

"Because I only used it when I disobeyed her, and the water felt colder out there."

"Surely you didn't bathe outside in the winter."

"Sometimes. The water would steam when she put snow on it, and I'd pretend it was hot."

"If you had a gift, why couldn't you keep her from punishing you?"

"I didn't know about the gift then, and it doesn't work that way."

"What else do you remember about your grandmother?"

"I remember when she died. I was five and found her body in a chair on the porch."

"Was there anyone there to help you?"

"Not right away. I went upstairs and fell asleep on her bed. I liked her bed because it was warm and soft."

"Do you remember anything else?"

"I remember the beach. I would run naked up and down the beach, feelin' free."

"Did you have any friends?"

"I had Gracie, but when she played with me on the beach, she wanted to remove her clothes too. When she tried, her father wouldn't let her come with him anymore."

"But her father came to watch?"

"Yes. I didn't go near him, though."

"And after your grandmother died, where did you go?"

"The Reverend took me in to make me ready for the orphanage."

"So you went to Warfield when you were five."

"No. The Reverend liked to teach children about the Bible so I lived with him and Wallace and Gracie until I was fourteen."

"Gracie? Is this the same little girl from the beach?"

"Yes."

"So you lived with the man that used to watch you run naked on the beach."

"Yes," Sophie whispered, a tear running down her cheek.

"You're feeling something here?"

"Yes. I feel guilty."

"Why?"

"Because I knew he was doin' something wrong and I still let him do it."

"Did he do other things?"

"Yes, he tried," she said, beginning to sob. "He did do other things."

"Did he rape you?"

"It's not rape if you let them do it."

"It's rape if you're a child, Sophie."

"But I didn't fight him."

"Did you even know what he was doing?"

"Yes."

"Did you know anything about sex?"

"No. I mean yes. I knew that he and Nanny used to bounce on her bed, and it sounded like fun."

"How old were you when the Reverend raped you?"

"I don't know—five or six maybe. I hadn't started school, but he was still teachin' me at the church at night. I told him I wanted to take a break from the lesson. I put a record on the phonograph and started to dance around. I took off my dress when it got too hot. He took off his shirt, mimickin' me. So I took off my panties, darin' him to remove his trousers. He took off his belt and then his trousers. Then he chased me around the room. I tried to hide behind the altar, but he found me."

"Were you scared?"

Sophie whispered. "No. He was my father."

"Where did he rape you?"

Sophie broke down again, trying to stifle the sobs with a tissue. Dr. Fairbourne was patient.

"On the altar. He lifted me up onto the altar because it was stone and cool. Then he climbed up too. I remember askin' him if he had any grape juice around. He said we'd have communion after he blessed me. I told Father Byrne that I'd been baptized on the beach, but I hadn't. The Reverend told me that he'd baptized me there on the altar, and the sacrament was so sacred I should never talk about it or tell anyone how it was done. I felt guilty tellin' Father Byrne a lie but didn't think I was allowed to tell him any details about the ritual."

"Are you saying he only did it once?"

"Yes. He wanted to do it again, I think, but there was never an opportunity, and he knew I had a big mouth. I'd get the slapper for telling my classmates about what the Reverend had done or said. But I never told anyone about my baptism. Soon after, a neighbor saw me on the beach with him. I was runnin' naked, and the Reverend was just takin' off his clothes. The neighbor spread the word that the Reverend was foolin' around with me. That made Wallace mad. She watched him like a hawk after that, and my Bible lessons at the church stopped."

"Did you ever talk to Wallace about it?"

"No, but I think Wallace knew because she wouldn't take in any more girls that were young—until I left."

"What do you mean?"

"Gracie got polio and had to go to Gander for therapy. The Reverend got down. He was so depressed Wallace worried about him. I was nearly fourteen, and except for my gift, he seemed to have lost interest in me. I think Wallace was worried about him because she decided to replace me with a cleanin' woman who had a young daughter. The little girl was able to draw him from his depression. He perked up pretty quickly when she sat on his lap. I was sent to Warfield."

"Did they talk to you about why you had to move?"

"No. They had Dr. Wellstone drive me to the train station in Gander. I never saw Gracie after she went to the hospital. She wrote me one formal note on a pretty card, and then nothin'."

"Have you written her since you left Warfield?"

"I've written her every month since I left Tooley. I have no idea if she's read my letters or thrown them away. I don't know why she would. I never told her about what her father did to me. Sometimes I think she found out."

"While I had started in the nursing program at the university, I soon switched my major to psychology," Sophie told the students. "I guess it was because I was more interested in what Dr. Fairbourne and I were discussing in his office. The first year, it was pretty much discovering why I felt so guilty about things that happened in my childhood. I'm not sure I'm convinced that nothing was really my fault but am still improving.

"Then we talked about my gift—what it might mean. In the beginning, I don't think he believed me but soon revealed to me something about himself that I could relate to. Once we established our positions, he revealed a second secret. I can't believe I didn't know or hadn't heard about it. I recoiled in horror—at first. But he had planted the seed that would give me a direction for the rest of my life, and I'm forever grateful to him. Though now a bit dotty, he's still living near St. John's, dabbling in psychotherapy with others besides me.

"Probably the most important insight I discovered during the first year and a half I worked with Griffon Fairbourne had to do with my emotional state soon after arriving at Warfield. I finally understood why I shook with trepidation at the ultimate punishment—an examination by Dr. Button that would reveal that I wasn't a virgin. That great dread allowed the nuns to manipulate me more than they did the others."

Chapter 8

Life Jacket

Sophie's appointments that were scheduled every two weeks became monthly after the first year and soon slipped to every three months.

"We've now been talking for over two years, Sophie, and I believe we should begin to think about your supposed gift."

"Supposed?"

"So you still believe you have an ability that others don't?"

"I've never met anybody else who sees events like I do."

"Is it there all the time?"

"No. It presents itself when something is wrong with someone."

"Not with yourself?"

"I don't think so."

"You said your mother had the gift too. Who told you about it?"

"Granny Ivy, the town's midwife. She'd visit my grandmother and tell me stories about my mother and Aunt Stella. Just before Nanny Ester died, she told me that Lety had the gift too, though at that point, I still didn't understand how I might be different. I mean I had instincts about certain dangers and such but thought everyone did."

"You been born with the gift, girl. Don't you ever forget that! You'll always be one of them fess people, nobody in Forsey Harbour ever bein' as busy as you."

"I feels like a queer stick, Granny Ivy."

"The gift might never come against ye, Sophie."

"Where'd it come from?"

"Yer mama had the same, you know."

"What she have?"

"She was birthed with the caul too, even if she be not so smart as you—you was always quick as a flame on a blasty fir branch. Ester didn't like Lety usin' it so she told her it be the devil makin' her do it. But Lety, bein' a gommel, God rest her soul, just saw things her own way. She told Fergus there'd be more than one of him. Fergus thought that meant he'd be good at sirin' sons like the caplain that crowd the beaches in June, but he never got round to that, and we finds him in pieces when he blows himself up the night you was birthed."

"Was that all?"

"No. Lety knowed when each of Ester's four husbands was gonna die, 'ceptin' her own father. Henry was number two. Such a bucky feller he was—a real charmer. Lety told her ma that her new da was a darby, a scoundrel. Ester didn't care, though; she used him as glitter, like you sees in the trees when it snows. She only wanted the town to stare at her on his arm. Always a showoff, she'd be gatchin' in front of all those sooky women, green as long needle pines, droolin' over him."

"But she sees what was goin' to happen to the others, right?"

"Lety warns Ester that Henry was goin' to hell for bein' so pretty, and sure 'nough, he was shot dead when he and a gunner's wife were grassin' aback of the barn. Her man comes upon 'em on his way back from shootin' ticklace so he had his gun tucked under his arm. Ester's third man was John, a preacher's son. He died from eatin' red-cap—poison mushrooms he'd picked and stewed fer himself when he was off lumberin'. Lety warned him not to eat anythin' he didn't know to be good, but no man is gonna listen to his child, let alone a mere daughter. Colin was the last husband. Lety said he'd been tapped on the shoulder by the deevil himself. The boom on his sailin' boat hot him right on the side of his head."

"But Lety didn't say anythin' sp'ific there, Granny. Did Ester know what Lety was talkin' 'bout?"

"Yeah, she knowed. We all knowed. Remember that Lety didn't talk much so when she comed out with one of them 'dictions, we all listened to her bawl like she was sermonizin' and we was in church."

Dr. Fairbourne stopped playing with the pencils on his desk and sat back. His gold sweater looked new. Sophie wondered if his wife had knitted it for him.

"Did you predict your mother's death?" he finally asked.

"No. I was too young."

"What about Ester's death?

"No."

"When did you notice you had the gift, other than this Ivy or Aunt Stella informing you of its existence?"

"I didn't see anyone's death in the beginnin'. I guess I saw when someone was ailin'. At first I didn't say anything. I just kept an eye on them. When Gracie or Wallace got pale or flushed, I'd watch. The next day or a few days later, they'd get a sore throat or stomach ailment. Then I'd touch them and notice little changes in the way the skin felt when someone was gettin' sick. Pretty soon, a picture would pop into my mind. I'd see how they were goin' to look in a few days. Mostly it was the pox or measles. If I saw them spotty, I'd tell Wallace to get saffron, sheep dung used to cure measles. At first, it was fun to see the changes. I could cure people before they got really sick. But because I wasn't a doctor, the gift soon became a problem. I'd see horrible things when I touched them." Sophie paused to think. "Sometimes it was good, like with Jenny Whelan."

"Who's she?"

"She was a lady in Tooley who was sick. One day, the Reverend took me along when he went to pray with a parishioner he said was dyin'. But I saw she wasn't dyin'. I placed my hands on her legs, twisted because she hadn't been able to walk for a long time. Then, in the back of my mind, I thought about how I saw her and tried to fuse the dream and the present ailment. It worked. Within an hour, she could walk. Of course, this upset the Reverend no end. At first, he questioned me, tryin' to get me to give him my secret. I didn't do it because I didn't know what my secret was. When he tired of badgerin' me, he told me my gift was from the devil. At first that made me cry, but I grew to ignore him. With Jenny it couldn't have been the devil."

"But you finally saw deaths too."

"Yes. I recall the cat. I didn't know how to prevent it when in my mind I saw the cat dead. There was no live picture to fuse the thing to. If I merged it to the picture in my mind, it might die right there in my arms. I guess I've seen other deaths but can't think of any right now."

"Did you know Grace had polio?"

"No. I didn't know ahead. I knew she was sick, but not aforehand." Sophie hesitated. "Maybe I did know. I could see she was fragile long before. After she got sick and they told me she was paralyzed, I knew she'd get well and also how to help her. If I kept her muscles hot and exercised, they wouldn't get weak and she might be able to walk again when she was better."

"But that was a known method being used in clinics already. Had you read about it or heard anyone else talk about it?"

"No. I just knew that heat and exercise would work."

"Did you perform any other big miracles before the Reverend and his family sent you to Warfield?"

"Not really. When they ailed, I helped a few people and was usually successful, but I'm not sure that had to do with my gift. I'd been able to see spirits but that was just play."

"Tell me about that."

"Gracie and I had a Ouija Board, something that I've since learned can be very evil."

"And the pointer moved?"

"Yes, at first. We talked to the spirits through the board. But then they would actually come into the cave and sit down near me. I could hear and see them. This would bother Gracie because she couldn't see anything at all and still wanted me to hold onto the pointer."

"Were these spirits other children?"

"No. Sometimes they were old. Some of them were mean, and my bein' scared would frighten Gracie too. We'd scream and try to run. Screamin' usually frightened the spirits away."

"Okay. Now let's talk about Warfield. Did you have any episodes there?"

Sophie let her mind wander to the books behind Dr. Fairbourne's desk. One lay on its side next to an ornate brass bookend.

"What's that book?" she asked.

"That's a prayer book," he said, slipping it off shelf and handing it to her. "Did you ever have one of these in the churches you attended?"

"No. It looks like you use it a lot."

"Yes. But we'll talk about that later," he said, taking it from her and returning it to the shelf.

"And that thing hooked on the back of the door?" she asked, pointing to a shiny cloth. "It looks like the tie or scarf Father Byrne wore when he heard confession and served communion."

"Does it? We can talk about that next time, okay?"

His compelling voice forced her mind back to their discussion.

Sophie took a seat next to Elinor, one of her roommates.

"Did you change your major again?" Elinor asked.

"No. I'm stickin' to psychology. What about you?"

"I think I'll stay in nursing. You would've made a good one, Sophie. There's something about you that makes you a natural."

"But you have the desire. You get the grades because you really care, Ellie. I wish I were good with the patients."

"Maybe it takes both. Maybe we should be both healers and soothers. I know you try to soothe them. It's just that you make such funny faces when you hold their hands. Sometimes it's almost scary—like you see that something terrible is going to happen to them."

"Oh dear. That sounds so bad. I wonder if I can make terrible faces in psychology and get away with it."

"Does your Dr. Fairbourne make faces when you talk to him?"

"Sometimes. I think I exasperate him. He's awfully tolerant though. I don't think I'd be so patient with me."

"You must think highly of him. Is he married?"

"I don't know. He never talks about his personal life. I suspect he is because he's so old and not a priest like Father Byrne."

"Maybe you should find out. He might make a good catch."

"Shame on you, Ellie Casey. I don't need any man. They're dirty and want to do awful things to you."

Elinor turned around to gaze into her friend's eyes. "I can't believe you really feel that way, Sophie. I kind of like 'em to go after me once in a while. It makes me feel like I'm attractive."

"You don't need to be attractive, Ellie. They'll go after you anyway."

"I saw lots of sickness and lots of death at the orphanage, doctor. I saw Victoria's tuberculosis even though I didn't know what TB was. I knew she was goin' to die and I knew we might catch it."

"How did you see that it was contagious?" Dr. Fairbourne asked, manipulating a paperclip between his fingers.

"I saw little bugs swarmin' around Victoria's head. How could I tell the nurse that? She would've thought I was crazy. But I had to tell her that Victoria was really sick. Otherwise they'd have made her continue to work with us."

"Did you try to cure her?"

"No. I knew she was goin' to die and didn't know how to cure her."

"Did she die?"

"I don't know. The nuns wouldn't tell me. Sister Josephine explained that no one with TB would ever come back to Warfield even if she lived. I believe Victoria died."

"And did the nuns treat you differently after that?"

"Yes. They hated me. They didn't want to acknowledge that I saw something they couldn't. They punished me harder than the others. Father Byrne claimed I was a saint. He told them that he wanted me to stay with him so he could report my miracles. Although the nuns would normally have handed me over to him and let him have his way, they adamantly refused here. I don't think they wanted any saint around them, makin' them look bad. But if I went with Father Byrne, I might report to other priests or even the bishop they were abusin' us. One evenin', the priest and the nuns had a huge fight. Everyone from the dormitory rooms sat on the stairs and listened to them yell back and forth in Sister Josephine's office. The nuns won, thank goodness. Sister English started to rattle off names, and Father Byrne backed down immediately. One of the girls told me later that they were names of virgins the nuns had let Father Byrne tutor in the chapel. They were no longer virgins when they returned to Warfield. Dr. Button had verified their loss of maidenhood."

"And the flu epidemic? Did you see it coming?"

"Yes, but we were forced to work until we dropped. I begged Sister Josephine and Nursing Sister Traudnot to let those who were sick go to bed, but they waited until half the girls had it. Then the rest of us had to work their shifts too. At night, I'd travel from bed to bed and lay hands on many of them. Most of them got well, though the flu doesn't kill often. They may have improved because they were finally allowed to take to their beds."

"What about Alice? Did you know she was ill?"

"I guess. I knew she was troubled. I didn't trust her but wanted to help. I was always torn but would finally surrender and accompany her downstairs. That said, I didn't hear the cries and moans she heard. I only know that I should've stayed and looked for her that last night when I ran upstairs because I was scared she'd hurt me. If I had, I might have prevented her suicide or murder. I don't know which."

"You didn't see the death in your mind?"

"No. Nor did I try. After the first incident where she hit me over the head with a tool that I think was a shovel or hoe, I never touched her. I avoided her. She knew I was avoidin' her and pleaded with me all the more to accompany her." Sophie sipped from the water from the glass by her side.

"I believe I saw Jane a couple of times during the third year after I left the orphange," Sophie told her audience. "She was wearing a long black habit and was getting off a bus with two other nuns. They were across the busy street, and I had to wait for the traffic to clear before I could cross. By the time I got to the other side, they had disappeared. Another time, she stood alone in a store in the mall. I walked up to her and gazed at her pale face directly. I put out my hand to greet her, but she pushed past me, showing no recognition at all. With her long habit, I was unable to see if she might have been harmed—if she were still healthy. Because Warfield had been forced to close just a few years after I left, I didn't even know where the order was now located. Her face still haunts me, and I find myself looking for her whenever I see a group of nuns walking along the street. I pray that she's happy."

"Is that it?" the doctor asked. "Is finding Alice's body what led to your being checked into the hospital?"

"Yes. But there was something else."

"Do you want to talk about it now?"

"Not really, but you ought to know why I'm still scared. I think about it sometimes at night and can't sleep."

"What is it?"

"When the others pulled me off Alice's body, I backed away from it until I stood against the walls," Sophie said, pausing to take another sip of water. "I moved along the wall to the laundry doors but I couldn't get them open because they were too heavy. They weren't usually that heavy. I just may have been too weak to push them open. I wanted so much to get out of the room because there were spirits or ethereal bein's flyin' around the ceilin' of the laundry."

"Fairies?"

"No. I've never seen fairies. They weren't just flyin' or dancin'. They were definitely not content. They saw me and flew toward me, grabbin' at my dress and hair. I froze."

"Did they make any noises?"

"Not that I remember, but they opened their mouths like they were cryin' out. They were scared, not mean."

"Your medical records say that when Jane brought the nuns downstairs, you were screaming like a banshee. Were you aware of that?"

"No. I don't remember anything after that."

"Do you have any theories about seeing the spirits?"

"No. But they must have wanted something from me. Unfortunately I was in no condition to help them."

"So do you feel that you're in control of this gift now? Have you defined it so that you can tell me exactly what the gift is—how it manifests itself?"

"No," Sophie said, her head down. "It seems different every time it comes up. I don't know when it's goin' to happen. I don't know exactly what I see that others don't. I think it's a curse."

"It's a curse because you haven't harnessed it, Sophie. Once you know what it is, you'll be able to use it for good because I think it is a gift, and there are lots of people who need your help."

Sophie relaxed. "I don't think I can do that right now."

"I don't think so either. I believe you should take a break for a couple of weeks. Think about the stories you've told me. Go to the beach or to a park and try to figure out how you would like to help people with it. Then we can talk about it and see if you can force your talent to do what you want it to."

"You didn't say anything about the incident—curin' the girls during the flu epidemic. Was it normal? I mean, most of them who lived would have probably survived without my doin' something."

"I most certainly believe you saved those girls, Sophie. I don't think for a moment that many would've lived without it. It's a manifestation of that gift that you've got to harness. There's no doubt about that."

"I don't know how you could possibly know that about the epidemic."

"I have a secret too, Sophie. A friend of mine who's also a bishop is alive today because of me. He and I were trouting on the Terra Nova River one summer. I made him wear a life-jacket even though the river was less than knee-high. He scoffed at first because he thought he would look silly. But there was no one around, and he knew me—he knew that I could see things others couldn't. He wore the lifejacket, and it kept him afloat when he fell into a hole and was swept down river nearly half a kilometer."

Chapter 9

Shedding the Burden

"The turning point of my analysis came in my senior year at university. Until that time, life swept me along," Sophie explained to the students. "Yes. I had changed. Knowledge of the world alters a person inside and immersion into the mainstream alters how one speaks and dresses. Chameleon-like, my clothes and hair changed to fit the styles and my diction and pronunciation soon reflected my surroundings. On the other hand, I still had no say in my destiny and no power over my gift. Dr. Fairbourne would quickly put a stop to that. Here I was, approaching graduation with no idea what I would do for the rest of my life. But at least on the surface, I fit into my new home.

"It was the beginning of Advent. Snow smothered the landscape in white, the transient hue of virginity. My mind was on shopping. I hoped Dr. Fairbourne didn't mind something a little less expensive than a sweater. I knew his name was Griffon but still had trouble thinking of him as a Griffon. I was drawn to the bookstore—not a surprise because bookstores call to me from all parts of town. I found a bookmark that might actually tell him how I felt.

If I have the gift of prophecy and can fathom all mysteries and all knowledge, and if I have a faith that can move mountains, but have not love, I am nothing.

"Chapter 13 of Paul's first letter to the Corinthians," he said when he opened the little present in his office. "This is a very telling gift. Am I to interpret this to mean you think you have come to some conclusion about yours?"

"I'm not sure. I only know that I want to make my gift do what I want it to do. When I was with the Ivany's, I didn't always use it for good. How can I be sure I will use it the right way all the time? Did you ever use yours for evil?"

"Probably. No matter how much I tried, there were always times when I was under pressure of one sort or another, and it would influence what I did. For example, if I knew a colleague needed medical help but he wasn't someone I liked I might not warn him so he could get that help."

"What if I can't see anything bad in those who hurt me the most? For example, the Reverend—I knew he'd do something to the new housekeeper's young daughter, Amelia Carberry, but I did nothing. That was wrong. Though I sometimes wanted to see something telling me that the Reverend was ill or going to die, I never did. And while I wasn't old enough to realize that Nanny Ester was abusing me, I never saw anything that predicted her death."

"Maybe you did but didn't want to acknowledge it."

"Are you saying I may be selective with my gifts of healing and prophesy?"

"I don't know. That's something you're going to have to think about. Why don't you break down your gift so you can analyze each piece? The first, for example, would be when you see that someone is going to die."

"I've never really seen that one except for a cat."

"What about Victoria?"

"Oh yes. I guess I saw that she was going to die, but I didn't recognize how close it was by the picture in my mind. It didn't seem like her death was imminent."

"And Alice?"

"I didn't see that."

"You didn't? Are you sure?"

"I never pictured her body in the vat of water or anywhere for that matter."

"I got the feeling you did," Dr. Fairbourne said. "But maybe you didn't accept it because if you had, you would have felt helpless. Couldn't you have been trying to protect her?"

"Then why did I let her continue to go downstairs without me? Why did I leave her down there that night?"

"Perhaps you feel guilty you did. Why do you think your own health spiraled downward when you saw the body?"

"But I tried to save her."

"That doesn't mean you didn't feel guilty. You simply may have wanted to make the outcome different than what your instinct told you—that she was going to die. You may have prayed or hoped that you were wrong, that your gift was inconsistent, that it wasn't trying to lead you down the path again."

"You're saying that I tried to deny my gift. What about the spirits?"

"What do you think the spirits were for?"

"Why do they torture me?" Sophie asked, covering her face. "I'd failed to save Alice, and they were there to harass me."

"Could the apparitions have been a sign?"

Sophie looked up. "For what?"

"Maybe a reminder that you had been led astray? That you were wasting your time trying to save someone you could never have saved?" He paused and continued when she did not respond. "Tell me about the other times you saw disembodied beings."

Sophie thought for some minutes. "You mean with Gracie when I used the Ouija Board? I'm not sure I actually saw them."

"Really? I'm positive you mentioned that they were there. Think about it."

"But nothing happened to anybody after I saw them!"

"Grace got polio."

"Yes, but not until a few years later."

"What happened right after you saw them?"

"Nothing. Nothing happened that I remember."

"Did you get closer to Grace?"

"Yes. We were very close. That night, I slept with her. Wallace would have the Reverend use the slapper on me had they found out. We weren't supposed to socialize with each other at all. I told Gracie that while I was bad, she was an angel. I promised to follow her and learn her ways."

"Do you still think those spirits were evil? They seem to have brought you and Grace closer. Maybe that intimacy is what enabled you to find a way to help her."

"And the bugs that I saw around those who were sick at Warfield? Were those good spirits too?"

"Did you know what to do when you saw them?"

"You don't believe I'm bad, do you. You think my gift is something God gave me to help people."

"Why do you see these spirits as evil? Do you really believe that crap the Reverend told you about being an agent of the devil? Sure that made you stand out when you were a child. Everyone noticed you. You scared them. But you're an adult now, Sophie. Those spirits never did anything that could be attributed to the devil, did they? Did anything happen that was bad?"

"Some people died."

"Did they go to hell?"

Sophie smiled. "I don't know."

"Yes you do."

"All right, there was no reason for them to go to hell. And if they didn't go to hell, their deaths probably had nothing to do with the devil," she said, nodding her head. "So they must have been good spirits. They must have been my 'wake-up-and-notice' spirits."

"And if they were good spirits, why do you fear them?"

"Because they sometimes come when I'm not ready to look."

"Aha! That sounds a lot like life, doesn't it? Don't most things come up when we least expect them or want them?"

Sophie's smile faded. "What about seeing if someone is going to live or die? That still scares me."

"No one said a gift was supposed to be easy. Doesn't every gift have a good side and a bad side?"

"You have that gift too, don't you?"

"Yes. I don't always call it a gift. I often see it as a curse."

"What do you do when you see that someone is going to die?"

"If God wants me to prevent it, he'll see that I succeed at saving this person. If not, I believe he expects me to ease their passage."

"But it doesn't make you feel good."

"No. It makes me feel sad. But that's where faith comes in, Sophie."

"I don't have that. God hurts. God lets people do horrible things to me and those closest to me."

"You're mad at him. At least you acknowledge his existence in your life."

"Aren't you mad at him sometimes?"

"Yes. I get mad a lot. Faith is one of those things that you have to work at. It comes and goes, and I'm not certain it's there much of the time. But I sure hope it's there when I need to pray for something. At least it's easier to communicate when it's there. I guess the hardest part is accepting the outcome."

Christmas Eve arrived without a break in a five-day snowstorm. Nursing Sister Caroline invited Sophie to dinner. Caroline was able to pick her up, but the storm would force Sophie to stay the night.

"Sophie, this is my husband, Boyd," she said, "Boyd, this is Sophie."

"Ah, the student."

"Yes," said Sophie. "I know that Caroline works at the hospital now. What do you do?"

"I'm a barrister. You get to see me without my collar. Very few people get to know me without it."

"I've never met a barrister, Boyd."

"Did I tell you I saw Sister Jane, Sophie?" Caroline asked.

"No. Where?"

"At the hospital."

"Is she all right? I'm always worried about her."

"She's fine. I found out she's at St. Francesca Salesia, a convent in Dunstin. She was at the hospital for a chest x-ray but everything is fine."

"Is she happy?"

"She seems to be. She was always quiet. You remember that. I think she always wanted to be a nun."

"Really? I thought she hated them like the rest of us did."

"What was she supposed to say when you approached the subject the way you did? She probably thought you were callin' her a spy."

Appropriately chastised, Sophie took a sip of her drink. "I think I did once."

After dinner, Boyd announced that no one was taking the car to the university because Prince Philip Drive was closed. He offered Sophie the guest room, and she accepted.

"You'll join us for Christmas Eve service, Sophie?" he asked.

Sophie was surprised. "Of course, if that's what you do."

"We go to St. James Church. Is that okay with you?"

Sophie squirmed.

"It's Anglican, Sophie," Caroline said. "Dr. Fairbourne and his wife go there. Maybe we'll see them."

Sophie smiled.

St. James Church was near the bay. The storm made the water look angry, but Sophie did not mind. She was used to it—foamy waves breaking over the rocks, shattering newly formed ice pans along the shore. Pine boughs with red and gold ribbons and candles at the end of each pew, the inside of the church was beautiful.

Sophie looked around for Dr. Fairbourne but did not see him. When the procession started up the aisle, she stared. The stole around his neck was the same one she had seen on the door.

"Is he a priest?" she whispered to Caroline after they sat down again.

"Yes. But he's only fillin' in for the rector here because Father Martin has a cold."

"No wonder he likes to talk about God."

"Does it make you feel uncomfortable?"

"A little. I haven't met one who doesn't want to hurt me."

"You know Griffon, Sophie. He doesn't want to hurt you. He's not like Father Byrne."

"Where's Father Byrne now?"

"Retired. At least closin' Warfield accomplished that," Caroline said, patting Sophie's knee. "Don't worry about it. After this service, I'll introduce you to Dr. Fairborne's wife."

"I was there."

"Where?"

"At St. James on Christmas Eve."

"I didn't see you. You didn't take communion?"

"No."

"So. Is there a problem?"

"Why didn't you tell me you were a priest?"

"Do you trust them?"

"No."

"So it's good thing I didn't tell you until you knew me better."

"I thought you were a psychiatrist."

"I am. But that doesn't mean I can't be a priest too."

"That's why you talked about faith, isn't it."

"I guess. I know I have to work at that. Being a priest helps me keep my faith."

"What does an Anglican priest do?"

"Very much the same as other people outside the Church. What do you think one does?"

"You sermonize. You tell everyone what's right and what's wrong. That's your main job."

"Oh my. That's a bleak picture of what I get up in the morning to do."

"You read the Bible and tell us what it means."

"I'm not sure I'm learned enough to do that, but I do try to tell interested people what it means to me."

"You help comfort the living when someone dies and you're there if we need to talk about religious stuff. You listen to confessions."

"That sounds like I'm pretty important. You're making me feel good about myself. Why do you think one becomes connected to the church, either as a priest or a lay person?"

"I think you want to help people."

"But I do that in this job, don't I? Why would I need religion to do this?"

"I don't know. Does it make you feel better?"

"Think about my gift for a minute, Sophie. Say I sit here in front of someone and see that something life-changing is going to happen to him or her. What do I do? Tell them?"

"Does the Church help you make that decision?"

"I think, in my case, religion helps to remind me that it's not my position to be in control. I'm here as an instrument of God. Life will continue to change whether I know about it or not. I believe I'm supposed to be here to help others accept the will of God. But faith in God's will isn't easy to hold onto when you face some of life's difficulties."

"So I should have accepted Victoria's fate and not anguished about it."

"Could you have done anything?"

"I definitely think I could have done more to protect her."

"But you were busy protecting the others, weren't you?"

"I guess. Somehow, though, I should have convinced Sister Josephine that Victoria still needed us."

"Tell me what you think of this idea. Every time someone disagrees with me, I should be able to change his mind so that he agrees."

"That's ridiculous. If that were possible, we would all think alike," Sophie said, her eyebrows arching defiantly. "But that doesn't convince me I shouldn't try."

"Did you try to change Sister Josephine's mind?"

"No. I wish I had."

"Why do you think you didn't try?"

"I didn't understand why Victoria had to be sent away."

"She didn't give you all the information then?"

"No. At the time, I didn't know TB was that contagious."

"That sounds like you and she were on the same side. You both wanted to protect the others. How could you possibly change her mind when she was on the same side?"

"I guess I sensed that. The minute I switched to side with poor Victoria, I was undermining my own argument."

"So does that make Sister Josephine evil?"

"No. Sister Josephine was actually trying to take the burden from me."

"Who do you think makes the final decision when it comes to life and death, Sophie?"

"God."

"So when you realize that God makes the final decision, does the burden feel as great?

"No."

"You seem to carry another awful burden on your shoulders, Sophie. When the flu epidemic occurred, you said that Sister Josephine and Nursing Sister Traudnot made the girls keep working even though they were sick."

"Yes. The girls would have to work until they dropped."

"How were the girls who kept working sick? Did they cough? Did they complain about sore throats?"

"Yes, but sometimes not at first. They would work all day and then fall into their beds sick."

"You knew they were sick before that?"

"No. I was too busy trying to help the girls who were already sick."

"So the obligation was too big for you to handle alone."

"Yes."

"How would you have handled it? Would you have sent them all to bed and waited to see if they were sick?"

Sophie squirmed. "Probably not."

"So if you couldn't check the girls before they went to work, and Sister Josephine and Nursing Sister Traudnot weren't blessed with the ability to see that someone was sick before she actually showed symptoms, who was left to make the decision?"

"I think Nursing Sister Traudnot should have known. She should know when someone is sick."

"So all nurses should have the ability to know when someone is getting sick before they actually do," Dr. Fairbourne said coolly. "If you agree with that, then your anger is probably justified. But if you're carrying around all this blame and hate for people that don't deserve it, I can't help you."

"But what about Dr. Button? Should he have been helping the nuns pass judgment on us?"

"No. What about the Reverend? What about Nanny Ester? What about Father Byrne? Is it okay to hate them for what they did? That's a hard one, Sophie. Are they evil? They did things that were evil. More likely, they had twisted minds. I can't tell you how the Reverend convinced himself that sex with little children is more satisfying than sex with his wife. I have no idea why Nanny Ester believed that little girls learn better in icy water. Dr. Button evidently assumes that a woman's virginity is more important than her dignity, her privacy. I don't know who influenced them. I can't tell you how they feel when they commit these ugly deeds. I can only surmise that the Reverend knows he has a problem and can't give a sermon without rationalizing what he does. Dr. Button has to live with the fact that most of the women around him aren't virgins and that most of them don't have a desire to remain so. The only thing I can do is try to teach people what I think the Bible says, what I think tolerance is, and what I believe Jesus was trying to show us. The harder I work at studying what God wants, the more I can influence these people and guide them to a more humane way of treating others."

"Some of them don't deserve your help."

"And some of the people you'll face with your gift won't deserve yours, Sophie. But does that mean you'll let them face death alone? Will you sit by and not try to change their minds? Did Alice deserve all the attention and worry you gave to her?"

"What do you mean?"

"She hit you on the head, Sophie, didn't she? Isn't that what you believe? She led you into a dark room and left you there. She wouldn't tell you what happened when she would disappear."

"But she was sick."

"You didn't know that. What would Sister Josephine or Sister English have said if they saw you in the halls after curfew? Would Alice have defended you?"

"No."

"But could you stop yourself from trying to help her? I know you tried not to, but you eventually gave in and followed her down the stairs again."

"You don't think I was just curious about the voices like I was with the Ouija Board?"

"I think you knew you wouldn't hear moaning when you got downstairs. Did you think she was evil?"

"No. I guess I knew there was something wacky going on in her mind."

"What's the difference between Alice and the Reverend?"

"The Reverend raped me."

"Who said that raping you is worse than trying to kill you with a shovel? Who told you that one is worse than the other?

Dr. Button? Is that who you're listening to? You're still here, Sophie. You are at a crossroads in your life where you and you alone can decide how you're going to make a difference. You're not messed up like the Reverend or Dr. Button. You have compassion for others."

"Are you saying I should forgive the Reverend and Dr. Button?"

"I'm not suggesting you go back to Tooley and forgive Mr. Ivany. I'm saying you should let him go. He didn't win, Sophie. He's probably still down there in his little hell if he's not dying of some sexually transmitted disease. You won. You're making big decisions. You have friends. You beat him, Sophie. Let go of what he tried to do to you."

"And my gift? How can I know what to do when I go out there? How do I know that what I'm doing is correct?"

"Remember the bookmark, Sophie? Let's look at another passage in first Corinthians. This is in chapter seven:

> *To one person the Spirit gives the ability to give wise advice; to another he gives the gift of special knowledge. The Spirit gives special faith to another, and to someone else he gives the power to heal the sick. He gives one person the power to perform miracles, and to another the ability to prophesy. He gives someone else the ability to know whether it is really the Spirit of God or another spirit that is speaking. Still another person is given the ability to speak in unknown languages, and another is given the ability to interpret what is being said. It is the one and only Holy Spirit who distributes these gifts. He alone decides which gift each person should have.*

Some of us are given the gift of special knowledge—others, the power to work miracles. You've been sent out with the gifts of both prophecy and healing. Why would he let you down now?"

"That was my last visit with Griffon Fairbourne as a break-down victim," Sophie told her audience. "He said there was nothing more I needed from him. I didn't really believe that then, and as time past, I would seek him out again. I did believe him, however, when he said that faith was important if my psychic abilities were to continue. On my own, I visited Queen's College and interviewed with the provost and other students. I continued to attend services at St. James and became close to the rector, Father Martin, and his wife. My acceptance into the Master of Divinity program at Queen's College brought great relief and joy.

"He was right, of course. This was the crossroads of my life. I was now in charge and would continue to believe that—until the next problem reared its head, leaving me wondering where my gift was hiding out."

Chapter 10

A Beginning

"Hi," the man said, turning to one side to shake hands with the student next to him. "My name's Ben Lacey. Welcome to Queen's."

"Glad to meet you," Rachel answered. "There aren't too many people here. I guess the classes aren't as big as at university. Did you go there or are you from outside the area?"

"I was there, but I don't remember meeting you. What was your major?"

"Anthropology," Rachel replied. "This is my friend, Sophie. She majored in Psychology. And you?"

"Mine was History. Behind us are some of my friends. Cyril Cummings here studied Music and is from nearby. Right behind you is Noah Lodge from the Western Diocese. Noah, where did you say you came from?"

"Marsh Cove. It's just outside of Corner Brook," he mumbled.

"Noah, this is—sorry, I don't think I caught your name," Ben said.

"Rachel, Rachel Wood. My friend, Sophie Hawkins, and I are from here in St. John's."

"I've known both Cyril and Noah since our freshman year at Memorial," Ben continued. "We all lived in the same building."

"Why did you decide to come to Queen's?" Sophie asked, noticing Ben's expressive brows crawl with excitement.

"For different reasons, I guess. I kind of like the tradition of the Church. I can't wait for the Bible studies. I'm not sure why Cyril thinks he's here, except that he's a bit sensitive and does well with people."

"Are you all going for ordination?" Sophie asked, unable to take her eyes off Ben.

"Yes. And you?"

"I am. Rachel's going for the degree, I think. She keeps changing her mind."

"Noah's a natural at the priesthood thing. He's great at influencing people. I think he'll do well at the preaching end. I'm not sure he's thought further than that. He's a bit of a rogue, so watch out."

"What do you mean?" Sophie asked.

"He's kind of a womanizer, having dated almost every woman at university. I'm surprised neither of you ever dated him, let alone ever heard of him."

"Ah. This class is Old Testament Studies?" Rachel asked. "I'm not sure if it'll be good or bad."

"I think it will be wonderful," Ben said, unable to hold still. "Ancient history is my kind of stuff."

Sophie felt a tap on her shoulder and looked around to see Noah with her sweater.

"Is this yours?" he asked. "I think it fell down."

She took the sweater and studied him. He was probably tall, his long legs scrunching up behind her chair. His face was serious, the same as it had been the last time she had glanced over her shoulder. His bleached hair with darker blond roots protruded in all directions. Chewing on his pen, Noah slouched in the seat, extending his legs under her chair. When he noticed Sophie eyeing him, his face lit up into a wide smile, an expression Sophie sensed was not very sincere. Feeling the heat on her cheeks, she quickly turned forward again, thankful the lights had dimmed for the projection machine as the lecture began.

The same students accompanied each other from classroom to classroom. By the end of the day, Sophie and Rachel had begun to become more familiar with the young men.

"I like your hair," Cyril told Sophie. "I don't think I've seen too many women wear it that way."

"No. I haven't let it grow out because I'm not sure what it would do. I'm afraid it would stick up like I'm ablaze. It certainly threatens to ignite."

"What class did you like today, Sophie?" Ben asked.

Sophie sat up, basking in the attention. "I liked the Conflict Management class. I could have used that where I lived."

"With your family?"

"No," Sophie replied, glancing in Noah's direction.

Pouting, Noah had slouched down in his seat, deftly looping a pen around his knuckles.

"I lived at Warfield."

"The infamous orphanage?" asked Cyril, leaning forward with interest. "We had an assignment on that in one of my writing courses. I wrote a ghost story. That's essentially what Warfield is known for, isn't it?"

Sophie smiled, thinking about the spirits and the noises Alice heard. "Not exactly. Unfortunately, I remember it as a slave establishment. A suspicion of ghostly apparitions would definitely have made our existence more tolerable."

"That's a disappointment. What about that underground passageway between the convent basement and the orphanage?"

"I had heard that they found something, but the doorway from the orphanage had been sealed up so none of us was really aware of it while I was there."

"How long were you there?"

"Four years, until I was eighteen."

"So you lost your parents when you were fourteen?" Cyril asked.

"No. I lived with different families until I was fourteen. I lost my mother when I was two. Are your parents still alive, Cyril?"

"Yes. They have a house in a little town on Trinity Bay. I used to think they were too close by, but having relatives around can sometimes be convenient. My dad manages a grocery store there. Ben's parents live somewhere around Conception Bay so they're even closer. They're both teachers, but his dad's retired, I think. Noah is from the west. He's the rich one with a nice truck. His dad runs a company in Corner Brook. I'm surprised he's doing this. I know his dad wants him to come home to take over the company. We'll never become rich being priests."

Sophie glanced at Noah whose brown eyes stared at her as if he knew they were talking about him. Sophie turned to face forward and gazed at her new roommate. Ellie had relocated to Gambo to work at a clinic. Rachel moved in at the beginning of the summer. Rachel was beautiful, her thick dark hair framing bright blue eyes. Sophie knew the young men were interested in her roommate who acted like she was used to the attention. She handled it with ease.

"What do you plan to do with your Masters?" Ben asked Rachel.

"I'll probably teach. I've been offered a job in Ottawa. I'm not sure. Actually, I'm undecided. I always wanted to be a priest. It was so lucky the Church opened it up to women just as we were getting out of university."

"What made you waiver?"

"I guess I'm folding under outside pressure. You mentioned Noah had pressure to do something else. My older brother is in Ontario and says I should go there to teach. I can't make up my mind."

Sophie listened to her friend talk. Rachel was a natural for the priesthood. Always thinking about it and desiring it, she had considered being a religious leader as a young girl. Sophie questioned her commitment. In fact, Sophie had not even thought about her career before Dr. Fairbourne mentioned it. She gazed at Noah watching Rachel with admiration. Rachel seemed to be a natural, but Sophie wondered if the young woman could handle him.

"At this point, my life was beginning to change," Sophie said, switching the microphone to her other hand. "Gone were the days when I fretted about my next home. Instead, I now had to worry about the rest of my life—too much to take in all at once. The difference was that I was now in charge of it. No longer did my fate belong in the hands of my grandmother, the Reverend, or a nun. I was in control of my own destiny. Unfortunately, I still doubted Dr. Fairbourne's assessment that I was in control of my gift. For a few years, at least, my abilities seemed to be controlled. I didn't see imminent illness or death. Queen's College was a safe haven where I took in everything I could. The answers were in books, and the tests were on paper. I soon learned that I could accomplish what I needed in this environment. My new friends too were open and confidant—a small group within the great walls of a university system. We learned to depend on each other and work together. My self-assurance soared as we became parts of a team, all striving toward the same end."

"Hey, Sophie, wait up!"

"Hi, Noah. I told you. I don't know anything more about her. I don't know why she won't go out with you. It couldn't possibly have anything to do with your reputation, could it?"

"I was just a boy, Sophie, but I've sown my oats and am ready for a real relationship."

"Tell that to Rachel yourself. I'm not your agent. I have my doubts about your maturity and don't think I can be convincing."

"Where are you going?"

"I have an appointment. I'll be back for study group later this afternoon."

"What do you think of this conflict management stuff? Do you like the role-playing? I get lost sometimes," Noah admitted, trying to keep up with her.

"I hear you're good at presenting the sermons. It's the same thing. What advice you give in your sermons is the same as that you can give to an individual."

"I just get up there and talk. I don't really prepare so I don't remember what it is I sermonized about."

Sophie laughed. "I have to agonize for days over a simple homily and then can't present it so anyone listens. You get up there and say whatever comes to mind and make it sound so profound. I can't believe you don't really contemplate the importance. Was your father an Anglican priest?"

"Are you kidding? I wish."

"Oh yes. Didn't Ben say your parents were rich and didn't really approve of your vocation?"

"My father's rich," he corrected. "He's paying for this now but didn't offer until my mother threatened to take him to court."

"Are they still married?"

"No. They were divorced when I was too young to remember. Since then, I've lived in two worlds. Yes, I've been rich and comfortable most of the time. I spent several weeks out of every year with my father and the rest of the time with my mother who made sure my father paid her enough so we didn't go under."

"And your mother had the power to take him back to court when he didn't pay? I don't think that usually happens."

"It is when the father wants his son around. Of course he didn't really want me around. He was a bit of a rogue, and I kind of hurt his style. But taking me from my mother hurt her, and he felt powerful doing that. She used this to her advantage. If he kept paying us, he could take me when he felt he needed me. I guess you could describe me as a pawn."

"I think you're good at playing the game. I've heard you described as a rogue too, you know."

Noah smiled, that wide smile that had attracted her the first day of classes. "You don't like me much, do you?" he said, turning to face her as they walked.

"Of course I like you. I don't think there's a person around who doesn't. You've got charisma, and the successful priest has to have something to lure his flock in."

"But I have to get through the rest of the classes."

"You mean the sincere ones? You're doing all right in the Old Testament and Church history classes, aren't you?"

"Yep. Put it out there and I'll memorize it. It comes in handy during a sermon. It's the theological ethics and role-playing stuff that gets me. I can argue both sides so easily, though I sometimes forget which side is right. I don't think there's only one answer to anything."

"Hmmm. That is a problem," Sophie said, slowing her pace.

"That's why I need your help. I can tutor you on preaching if you'll help me argue for the most ethical side—that is, unless there's something between you and Ben that I'd be interrupting. Why are you stopping? This is a psychiatric clinic. Is this your appointment?"

"I have a friend here. We're meeting for lunch if he can get away," she lied. "As for Ben and me, we're seeing each other yes, but right now we're just friends. I can tell you that Rachel is home at four if you just happen to phone after that, but I can't guarantee she'll go out with you, nor would I recommend you to her."

"Thankfully, that isn't your call."

"Nor my realm of influence since no one seems to be interested in listening to my sermons."

"Yes," he said, smiling broadly. "I can change that, you know." He backed away to cross the street. "I think I'll call her. I'm not sure it'll be so easy to teach you how to make your arguments more attractive. It may take the rest of the time we have here, but if you put in the effort—"

Sophie watched Noah make his way across the busy street and disappear around the corner. Then she turned to enter the clinic.

"Good morning, Sophie. Ready for first period?"

"Good morning, Rachel. I didn't see you come in last night. You must have been studying late."

"Actually I wasn't studying. Noah asked me out. We went to the club and talked."

Stunned, Sophie took a moment before saying, "Hope you're fresh enough for a full day of classes."

"I'm on top of the world. Noah was a gentleman, and I like him a lot."

"I heard he was a womanizer. I hope he's better now. Are you sure he wants a serious relationship, Rachel? He doesn't strike me as the type—"

"Who says I want a serious relationship right now? You guys have a few years here and then you'll spread out across the province if you're lucky enough to get parishes. Noah has the right idea. Getting serious would really cause problems down the road."

"Just so you know, Rachel. If you're both looking for the same thing, I guess it's all right. I wouldn't do it, though."

"I've never heard you talk about having a relationship with any man at all, Sophie. I guess I wasn't sure where you stood, if you know what I mean. I thought maybe you doubted your sexuality."

"Ben and I are dating," Sophie said.

"Neither of you seems that interested."

Sophie was taken aback. She had never thought about it at all. Her future life lay sprawled in front of her, but not once did the picture include a man. She knitted her brows, trying to imagine herself with a husband and family but nothing came. Was it her gift? Was the gift showing her that her own future did not include one?

"Hey, Sophie. We need to get together to study for the test in Ethics," Noah said, trying to catch up with her in the halls. "If I can make it through tomorrow's exam, I promise I'll work with you on that sermon."

"Did you forget? The group is going over to the auditorium tonight for that forum on the Koran."

"Before a test?"

"Ben asked Cyril and I to get the tickets before Father Herbert announced that there was an exam. Are you sure you don't want to go?"

"Maybe Rachel can help me."

"I believe Rachel 's coming with us too, but you can ask. I'm sorry, Noah. I told you I'd help but I didn't know."

"That's okay. Maybe Rachel's better at it anyway. She manages to pull good grades out of her hat."

"And she's really nice. Don't take advantage of that, Noah."

"What are you saying? Has Rachel been talking to you guys about our evenings together?"

Sophie did not look at his face, knowing that the brown eyes and wide smile would keep her from telling him the truth. "Just that you have a reputation. You don't seem to commit to anything."

"And you do? I thought we were going to study together."

"I mean about relationships."

"You're talking about sex?"

Sophie pushed on, trying not to show him that her muscles tightened when he said it. "I'm talking about relationships—life after sex."

"Are you saying Rachel can't take care of herself?"

"No."

"It sure sounds like it. Look at me, Sophie."

"We're late for class," she said, pulling away.

"You're able to see me as a person, Sophie. I don't think you really see me as a magnet, drawing you in to have sex with me. Are you saying Rachel isn't like that?"

Sophie stopped and turned to face him."I'm not sure how I see you. You've never approached me in any way other than as a fellow seminary student. That lets me see you as a classmate. But that's not the kind of relationship you have with Rachel. I don't know that side of you so I can't say how she'll react. I'm just telling you as a friend to be careful with her. That's all," she said continuing down the hall.

"I'm not my father, Sophie," he called after her. "And you owe me a study time."

Sophie dropped by Ben and Cyril's apartment on the way to the forum.

"Where's Rachel?" asked Ben.

"I think she's with Noah. He mentioned getting her to help him prepare for the test tomorrow. I didn't see her at home."

"Oh yeah, the test," said Cyril. "I couldn't prepare more anyway. Ben and I studied all night last night."

"So she's still dating him? Maybe she's hooked him," Ben said thoughtfully. "If anyone could make him stick to a commitment, she could."

"Oh yeah, Ben?" Sophie said, nudging him affectionately. "I didn't know you knew her that well."

"I don't. I guess it's just how I would react if she were with me."

Sophie smiled. "Cheer up. I think she's strong and has held him off this long. There's still hope she'll come to her senses before she succumbs to his charm. What do you think of the classes so far?"

"Not bad. I believe we'll all make it, don't you? Of course next year we have to go into parish administration. I'm not so sure about that one. I'm not very organized nor am I too creative."

"Remember, Ben, we're a team. We'll all study it together. I'm still scared of getting through the liturgical courses. I sure hope Noah passes me some of that charm he carries around with him wherever he goes—his gift of elocution."

"You'll be lucky if that's all he passes to you, Sophie. I'm not sure what he'll bestow on Rachel."

"Rachel and Noah managed to hide their relationship from my prying eyes after that. Neither talked about where they were going, and I never asked whenever Rachel left for a night or weekend with a stuffed bag," Sophie said. "It hurt me because I didn't see myself as a spy and felt terribly lonely when I was on my own for days at a time.

"By the end of our second year, the whole dynamics of the group would transform, of course. The changes would not only affect my associations with Noah and Rachel, but they would touch each member of the group—a ripple would readjust the grains of sand at the bottom of our small pond. My education would grow to include how the differences in our experiences and backgrounds could affect the rest of our lives. Of course, I had Dr. Fairbourne whom Queen's had willingly promoted to become my spiritual director. He would continue to be the rock to which I was anchored. The path to my future was already set out so mine wasn't about to be altered by an upheaval among the troops. It was how I felt that changed. On the outside, I was going to make it through my ordinations for the diaconate and priesthood. On the inside, I would be swept away by a hurricane created by the turmoil of emotions surrounding love and intimacy. I had interpreted my gift incorrectly. Life with the opposite sex wasn't going to miss me without making an impression. And to my consternation, my gift wasn't going to save me from its violent impact."

Chapter 11

Not What It Seems

"Standing on the sidelines had been my goal since entering Queen's, and I had been succeeding, or so I thought," Sophie told her audience. "Yes, we had somewhat paired up. Rachel and Noah seemed to be going strong. At least, she spent less and less time at the apartment. I studied with Noah because we had an agreement, but as if it were the result of another tacit covenant, his relationship with my roommate was never discussed or referred to. Noah never touched me inappropriately or spoke in a manner unbefitting a person in another commitment.

On the other hand, Ben and I became closer as our friendship grew. I loved his energy, his positive outlook, and those darned eyebrows that revealed his every thought or mood. They almost hid his hazel eyes—thoughtful eyes. I took pleasure in our long discussions about liturgy and history. The first signs of something more than friendship began in spring at the end of our second year, and I appreciated his wanting to make sure of every step before we let anything more happen. Of course, our marching orders would occur in less than a year, and our relationship might have to withstand forces that would threaten anything more than a correspondence from afar."

"Thank you for the wonderful afternoon, Ben. I loved going to the gallery and seeing all the lovely paintings. I haven't been able to do too much of that before."

"Next time, we can go to Provincial Museum. That has a lot of stuff in it that I'm interested in," he said, kissing her on the cheek before heading out to his battered 1968 Ford.

Sophie let herself into her apartment and grabbed the pile of books at the foot of the sofa. She would take them to her desk and start reading again. Sitting back, she smiled. Things were going nicely with Ben. He was so sweet and always knew what to say or do. And he was smart. His enthusiasm about becoming a priest was catching. The whole group surged forward with him when he was around. She had not expected Dr. Fairbourne's comments just a few days earlier.

"Are you sure he's the one? How does he make you feel?" he asked, seemingly unruffled by her professed love for her friend.

"I like him. He's smart and funny."

"I mean physically. Do you feel anything tingle when he's around?"

"I'm not sure I'm capable of that," Sophie replied, looking down at her hands. She hated it when he manipulated the direction of the conversation. He never let her veer off to safer ground, and she could not force herself to take control.

"Why not?"

"I'm afraid, I guess."

"But you like him. Don't you trust him?"

"I think I trust him—just not that far."

"Is he too fast?"

Sophie became rigid. "I'm not sure. We've been seeing each other, going out and studying together, for over a year. Isn't that about right?" she asked, thinking of Rachel and Noah who seemed to be all over each other just a few weeks after their first date.

"Do you want to sleep with him?"

Sophie's face turned hot. She did not want to look directly at Fairbourne. "I think I need more time."

"More time for what? To trust him? Does anything about him remind you of the Reverend?"

"No, not at all," she chuckled. "I told you he's sweet. But I think that loving someone that much means we should get married and I don't believe either of us is ready for that."

"So you still want to be a priest?"

"Oh yes," she said, looking at him for the first time. "I want to make my goal. A family can come later, don't you think?"

"That's up to you."

Sophie picked up her book. She thought about exploring her relationship with Ben more thoroughly. At least then she would be able to tell Dr. Fairbourne that they were definitely in love.

Friday evening came all too soon. Rachel was out of the apartment until Sunday. Sophie had invited Ben to dinner, their first quiet evening together since they met over a year earlier. She rushed to open the wine just as he knocked on the door.

"Hi, Ben," she said, kissing him on the cheek. "Sorry, I must look a mess. I had to hurry to fix everything up in time."

"I brought some music, soft jazz. It ought to go great with dinner. Did you finish your sermon? I haven't. I'll have to do it tomorrow. It's due Monday, you know."

"How could I forget? Noah was critiquing my writing until eleven the night before last. We didn't even start on presentation."

"Are they here? Or did they take off again?"

"They took off. I never know where they go. It sounds so romantic, doesn't it?"

"I guess. I'm not really one to hit the road, though."

The meal was quiet. Between them, they finished the bottle of wine.

Sophie took a load of dishes to the sink. "Don't mind these. I have the whole weekend to do them. Let's sit and talk."

She and Ben sat together on the couch, awkwardly kissing. Sophie nestled and soon felt her abdomen tighten up. "Maybe we should go to the bedroom," she said. "I'm not sure this is so comfortable."

Hand in hand, they walked to the bedroom. Both removed their clothes and slipped under the covers. He put his hand behind her neck and pulled her beside him.

"You know, we've been going out for such a long while, Sophie."

"Yes. I thought it was time we took the next step. I hope you don't mind."

"No. It's a good idea," he said, turning onto his side.

He played with her breasts and leaned over to put his mouth on hers. She did not know what to do and played along, hoping he would make the next move. Ben leaned closer, letting his hand wander down her back, pulling her hips toward him and rapping his leg over hers.

"I'm sorry," he finally said, leaning back.

"What do you mean?" she asked, scooting closer. She liked the warmth of his skin.

"No. I mean, I'm sorry," he said, beginning to blubber. "We really can't do this. I mean, *I* really can't do this."

Sensing panic, Sophie would not loosen her arms. "It's all right. I can wait, Ben. You'll be able to do it next time. It happens."

Ben pushed her away and sat on the edge of the bed. "I don't want to do this again, Sophie. I think there's something wrong. Not with you, you're always so sweet. You make all the guys feel good about themselves."

Sophie slid her feet over the side and sat next to him. "Are you saying you can't love me?"

"Oh no, Sophie. I love you so much. That's why this hurts me until I can't hold the tears back. You're great, Sophie. And any guy would clamber over the next to be with you," Ben said, looking into her frightened green eyes. "You know? You're right. We should try again later, maybe when we're not under so much pressure." He got up and began to pull his pants on. "I'm so embarrassed. This doesn't usually happen, but I guess I care for you so much, I've made this more than it is." Before buttoning his shirt, he chucked her under the chin. "I'll see you Monday, Sophie, when things have calmed down. We'll talk about going somewhere on Friday, okay?"

After she heard the front door close, Sophie sat frozen on the side of the bed for several long minutes. The tears did not come. Was she relieved? Sophie was not sure. All she knew was that she was lonely and found it difficult not to call him on the phone and ask him to come back and keep her company until morning.

While Sophie slept little that Friday evening, she was dead tired the following night and did not hear Rachel enter the apartment in the early morning hours. When Sophie realized she was awake, she quickly sat up and looked at the clock on the nightstand. It was only five. It was not the alarm that had roused her. The clock was still set to seven when she would have to get up and prepare for the service. Sophie put her head back down on the pillow, thinking about the last dream and trying to reenter where it had broken off. But then she sat up again. A toilet had flushed somewhere close by. Was someone in the apartment? Then she heard the door to Rachel's room close and what sounded like a sob.

Sophie got up, donned a robe, and walking over to Rachel's door, softly knocked. She heard a muffled noise. Rachel finally opened the door a crack.

"Is that you, Rachel? Why are you home so early?" Sophie asked, pushing it open.

Rachel stifled another sob, and tears flooded down her cheeks, drenching the tissue she held over her nose.

"Are you all right, Rachel? Tell me what I can do?"

"We broke up," she said, her voice hoarse.

"You and Noah? Why?"

"We just broke up."

"Weren't you two going to your hideaway this weekend? Did you go?"

"Yes. But he was different. He didn't want it," she said, haltingly. "He kept losing his temper."

"Did he hurt you?"

"No. He sort of ignored me."

"He didn't leave you there alone, did he?"

"For some of the time, but he came back late last night and told me to get packed up. He said he had to come back here to study."

"I'm not sure that's breaking up. Maybe he began to panic when he realized he didn't have his sermon done."

"No. On the way back, he told me he didn't think we should see each other anymore. He said the relationship was getting old and didn't know how to revive it."

Sophie held her anger in. She wanted to pound him and swore she would do it the next time she saw him. "I've got to go to church in a bit. Can I make you some tea?"

"Please don't go, Sophie. They won't be angry if you miss this one service. Noah has missed a lot of them, and they haven't said a word."

"Or he hasn't told you that they've warned him about it."

"I'm sure he was telling the truth about that, Sophie. He's so good at what he does, I think they overlook it."

"Well I hope you can restrain yourself. I don't think it's a good idea to rush after him until he comes to his senses, Rachel. Play it cool."

"You don't understand, Sophie. You've never had a relationship like this one."

"No, but Friday night I kind of got the boot too."

"Ben?" she asked, suddenly sitting up and taking notice. "I didn't know you two were that close."

"I thought we were. He can't make up his mind about the relationship either. It looks like you and I are both in the same boat and we've capsized."

"Do you hate him?"

"No. I just feel wretched. I guess I was deluding myself about it. Do you hate Noah?"

"A little. I sure hope he comes back, though."

With the approach of summer, the group sat around a table in a noisy nightclub, toasting themselves with each new round of beer.

"To Ethics," Ben said, raising his glass. "I'm so sick of morals having to do with biology and technology but not really explaining anything about morality and sex."

"Here, here," answered Noah. "I thought I slept through that part of the class. I didn't know they never brought it up."

"To the definition of a Christian marriage," said Cyril, raising his half-empty glass. "I have no desire to know anything more about the accepted practice of sexual liaisons between men and women."

"Here, here," answered Noah once again. "To Cyril's clear announcement of his position inside and outside of the closet."

Cyril smiled proudly. "You say that so bravely, Noah, knowing that your glittering brown eyes and toothy smile make my knees weak."

"I don't mind when anything on you goes weak, Cyril. It's the opposite that scares me," he said, putting his arm around his tottering friend's shoulders. "Where's Rachel?" Noah asked, turning to Sophie. "We can't get completely smashed before Rachel comes."

"She's probably not coming. She told me she might have to go to Ontario next week to interview for a job," Sophie said, watching Noah's face carefully.

"She can't not be here," slurred Ben. "I'll go get her. Continue the next round without me, but make sure the waitress leaves me another beer," he instructed Cyril.

"Too bad we can't escape this summer," Sophie told Noah. "Who really wants to stick around and intern? Where are you being sent?"

"To St. Stephen's in Randall Cove. I hope Ben's parents don't go there. I hope nobody I know attends that parish."

"I'm at St. Cyprian in Cape Head. Isn't that where your hideaway is?"

"Yes," said a seemingly drunk Noah. "Why don't you stay in the cottage while you're interning? You don't have a car so I don't see you having much of a choice."

"What about you?"

"I would only come round on the weekends."

"Alone?"

"Sometimes. I do go there to think, you know—think and pray."

"You mean p-r-e-y," Sophie said, unable to hold her tongue.

Noah smiled. "I don't know what you mean, Sophie. Perhaps you should stay there just to understand me better."

"I'm sure I don't want to know that part of you better. If Rachel's situation is a result of getting to know you better, I'd rather pass."

"I don't mean like Rachel. I don't think you could ever be like Rachel, do you?" he asked, watching Sophie's face. "Anyway, Rachel will land on her feet. Just watch. She and Ben will see to that."

Sophie let out a whimper. For the first time, she realized why Ben had been coming around again. She thought he was interested in rekindling the relationship, but Sophie reran the last few visits in her mind. She had been happy that he spent time cheering Rachel up. He had a knack for making people feel good about themselves, and Rachel was definitely feeling better.

But had Sophie seen more than that? Had he touched Rachel more often than was proper? Had she walked in on them once, when he had awkwardly stood up and offered to help Sophie carry some groceries to the kitchen? Had she actually heard muffled talking in Rachel's room late one night? Sophie could barely swallow. Where was her gift? Why had it not warned her? She looked over at the full glass of beer in front of Ben's empty seat. Would he come back to the bar with Rachel? When would it be okay for her to return to the apartment if he did not?

"You know, Sophie," Noah said, leaning close to her until she could smell his breath. "I'm really proud that you've mastered sermon-making."

Sophie pushed him back up until he seemed balanced on the stool.

"I know, Noah. And I owe it all to you."

"Why are you such an iceberg?"

"Am I?" she asked, not really listening to him.

"You seem so closed all the time. You've got such beautiful hair and a pretty face. Your emerald eyes are gorgeous. But you make us feel like we're leering if we watch you."

"You know how to leer. Anyway, you mean all of you discussed what I'm like—including Ben?" she asked, not giving Noah a chance to reply. "You promise to keep your thing away from me and my friends, and I might listen to what you're saying."

"Oh, Sophie. I think you should go to your spiritual director and talk to him about it. No guy is going to sweep you off your feet and into bed until you relax a bit and realize that sex is part of God's plan," he said, not seeming to notice the tears that Sophie kept wiping from her cheek. He rocked too far toward Cyril. "On the other hand. Maybe Cyril here has the right idea. Maybe we ought to just give ourselves to each other and not worry who it is at all."

"Cut it out, Noah," Cyril countered. "Even I care about my partners. I don't leave them littered all over the landscape. Some priest you're going to make, baptizing your parishioners with semen."

Sophie recoiled in horror. "Let's not talk about this now. I think you two have had too much to drink, and we ought to call it a night. Ben obviously isn't going to find his way back to the bar." She slipped off the stool and picked up her bag.

"I'll walk with you, Sophie," Noah offered, suddenly sounding sober.

"I'm fine, Noah. Thanks, but I can make it there on my own."

"I know, but I think you should stay with Cyril and me tonight."

"What are you talking about? Do you need someone to clean up when both of you vomit?"

"No, Sophie," said Cyril. "It's just that Ben and Rachel should probably be alone."

Noah braced Sophie as her knees started to buckle.

"That's awfully thoughtful of you guys. I guess it's okay if I crash on your couch tonight," she managed.

"You can use my bed, Sophie. I'll hang out on the couch," said Noah. "Don't worry, the sheets are clean."

"The wedding was small and simple. It took place in the backyard of Ben's parents," Sophie explained, holding the microphone close to her lips. "Rachel had asked me to be the maid of honor, and I accepted. What else could I do? Ben was stoic. His parents cooed over his beautiful bride, and his mother cried when Ben turned to watch his bride come up the isle. To my surprise, Noah attended but didn't take part in the ceremony. The best man was one of Ben's brothers. Cyril was in it, though, looking fine in a frilly shirt, bushing out over the cummerbund. At least Ben had insisted that Cyril pick out his own tuxedo.

"I watched Noah's face as I walked up the aisle before Rachel. It gleamed. His wide smile pushed his dimples aside, and he winked at me. We were in the same boat or so it seemed. Were we taking on water? Would we make it to our final destination?

"We would only be a group of three when we returned to Queen's for the final year. Ben and Rachel both dropped out of the program. Of course, Ben would continue his schooling later, after their life together was better defined. Rachel's face was radiant. Somehow it was fitting that she would not finish her masters. It seemed that this was what she wanted all along. If her life wasn't going to be with Noah, it was going to continue on with Ben. My Ben.

"Ben's brother got up to give the toast. 'It's such a surprise that my little brother beat me to the altar, although I shouldn't really be astonished since he was headed to the altar one way or the other. Welcome to the family, Rachel. We can see in your face that you love him and that you both will be very happy together.'

"'Here, here,' I whispered. 'And if she can't make you happy, Ben, I'll probably still be here. At least for now I still see myself as a disciple of Jesus and I promise to stay true to my vow. If I don't find love and contentment in my chosen vocation, I'll always have my gifts to keep me company.'

"I was right. Those gifts weren't going to stay hidden for long. Pretty soon, they would push to the forefront, and I would seem to be at their mercy once again."

Chapter 12

The Goal

"We were no sooner settled in our new classes and preparing for our final year at Queen's than we had to face another departing figure," Sophie said after stopping to pour herself some water. "Cyril decided that he wouldn't seek ordination in the spring. Some time during his summer internship, he had made friends with a budding movie director. When Cyril returned to Noah's apartment, he barely said a word about his new friend. In fact, he barely said anything at all. Noah and I soon began to worry about him. We took him to the movies and to some local bars, but nothing seemed to cheer him up. Suddenly, however, his mood soared. We felt like we were the last to know."

"Cyril, why weren't you in class today?" Sophie asked him after unsuccessfully hunting him down at the apartment. He was in the cafeteria, stuffing his face—something he did often with little affect to his waistline. "We can't give up now. We're so close to our goal."

"Not my goal," he said, a huge smile inflating his normally hollow cheeks.

He reached into his shirt pocket and handed her a piece of paper. It was folded so many times Sophie had trouble opening it. She flattened it over a clean space on the table.

"Who's this Kieran?"

"A friend I met during my internship."

"What's he saying? He's going to Toronto? Why?"

"Give it to me. Obviously you're having trouble comprehending what he's saying. He's a movie director. He's going to Toronto to see if he can start a production company."

"Have we seen any of his movies?"

"No. He's nineteen, for God's sake. He's just starting out."

"So?" she asked, beginning to understand Cyril's irritability.

"So I love him. He wants me to come and be a partner in the business."

"Ah," she said, unable to say another word.

"I have to go to Toronto, Sophie. Just like you have to be a priest. Just like you have to follow Noah."

Sophie squirmed. "Noah and I aren't even in the same diocese. He's going to the Western Diocese, and I'm staying around here." She smiled for the first time. Cyril always knew how to get a reaction. "I suppose it would be selfish to tell you that we need you to stay because we love you too."

"That would be very sinful of you. Priests are supportive, not clingy," Cyril said, taking another bite. "Anyway. I already told Father Herbert."

"And he was upset too."

"No. He was relieved. He wasn't sure how he was going to handle an admitted homosexual. It's against policy to turn one away, but in reality, placement can be difficult. I was last on the list to be placed even though there's a shortage of priests."

"You told him?"

"He knew. Someone had seen Kieran and me together in public and reported it to Father Bryan whom I was assisting. I guess I should have been more careful, but I couldn't help it. I love him."

A tear ran down Sophie's cheek. "We'll have to have a party, you know. Shouldn't we invite Kieran?"

"No, he's already in Toronto," Cyril said, putting his face close to hers. "Can I ask you a favor, though?"

"Anything."

"Don't let Noah invite any female strippers," he whispered. "He did it for Ben's stag party, and I had trouble holding down my liquor. I've never seen anything so gross in my life. The leather costumes were poorly stitched and didn't go at all with these god-awful shrunken-head necklaces."

Sophie smiled. "I'll miss you terribly, Cyril. The way you see things is so refreshing. I'll let you break the news to Noah. I'm sure he'll be very happy for you too."

"Do you think Cyril enjoyed the drinking party we all had for him?" Noah asked days later.

"Yes. It was nice of Ben and Rachel to come, especially because Rachel hasn't been too well."

"Now that Cyril's gone, I'm going to need a new roommate. I'm not sure I can afford to live alone."

"Neither can I. I put my number on the bulletin board this morning and can't wait to see if I got any calls."

"We're together all the time, Sophie. Why don't you just move in with me? You'd have your own room, and I promise to be a gentleman."

"That ought to go over big with Father Herbert. I don't think he's even heard of the sexual revolution."

"Who would know? I certainly wouldn't advertise it."

"Especially when you bring girls home with you and have me stay away for hours if not days."

"I promise I wouldn't do that to you. Nor do you have to worry about me going after you."

"I know you wouldn't go after me because I know all your ploys, Noah Lodge," she said smiling. "Anyway, since when don't you have the money to live on your own?"

"It's such a pain to have to go out to study when we can do it right there in our apartment."

"But I'm worth your trek to the library every evening. Someday you'll thank me, Noah."

January arrived with an eruption of snow. It was a very busy time for both Noah and Sophie because their bishops were going to talk to them about new openings in their respective diocese. Bishop Sheppard called Sophie in one afternoon in the middle of a storm. Sloshing to his office, she was not sure she was staying on the sidewalks because the snow obliterated the curb and buried the street. She must have wandered off the walkway and cut across the end of Derby Pond. Thankfully, the ice beneath her boots did not give way.

"Good afternoon, Sophie," he said, pouring her a cup of tea. "Let's sit over here closer to the fire. You're going to need to dry out some. Now, tell me about your classes. What do you feel are your strengths and please describe what you think are your weaknesses?"

"My grades have generally been good, I believe."

"Oh yes. That's why I want to hear about them from you. If I look at your grades and recommendations, I don't see any weaknesses at all."

"They're there, of course. My strengths are pastoral, I think. I'm good with people and am equipped to handle most difficulties. I consider giving sermons to be my weak point, but I find I'm improving."

"So you want to be a rector in a parish, I assume."

"Yes."

"Hmm," he said. "Well you know how difficult it is here in the Eastern Diocese. When we have openings, we have a whole slew of them, but right now we have not a one." He cleared his throat. "If you really want to work in the Eastern Diocese, I can probably place you sooner in Labrador. One of my rectors is asking to return to the east coast here. I know of at least one opening in the Western Diocese. If you would like to become a deacon this spring or summer, I can recommend you to Andrew Edmunds in Corner Brook. He'll be here next Wednesday to talk to one of his candidates."

"I see."

"There's at least one opening there. Others have mentioned that you would be well equipped for it."

"Others?"

"Other. Griffon Fairbourne is a colleague of mine. He said you had quite a psychology and nursing background. Neither of us is sure you want to pursue something along those lines, but there's definitely an opening there."

"What is it?"

"The hospital on the Northern Peninsula is looking for a chaplain. The beds there are almost always full of people with one disease or another. The hospital draws in the cases that can't be taken care of in the clinics or smaller ones. Many patients never come out. If you have a stomach for that sort of thing, I can talk to the bishop."

Sophie felt a chill. Why would Dr. Fairbourne recommend her for such a position when he knew she had trouble controlling her gift? Was it a test? What if she could not cope?

"I would certainly like to talk to him about it," she said, resigned to the possibility she would have to change her direction once again. "Are there many parishes open in that one?"

"I'm not sure. You'll have to ask him. I don't keep track of all the openings outside this diocese."

Sophie finished her tea and then stood up to leave. "Thank you. Will I meet with the bishop here?"

"Perhaps. Andrew or I will call you with the final time and place. If you choose not to stay in this diocese, I want to wish you luck."

Sophie trudged back through the snow to her next class and ran into Noah, waiting for her in the hallway.

"How did it go?"

"Not great," she replied, wiping a tear from her cheek.

Noah put his arm around her shoulder, causing the flood-gates to open. He led her to some seats in the lobby. "They don't want you?"

"No. They don't have positions for me. I guess it never occurred to me that there wouldn't be something. I thought there was always a shortage."

"Sometimes they release you to another diocese."

"Yes. He said I might try yours but doesn't know how many positions are open there."

"That would be great. We could visit each other."

"Maybe. He also mentioned my working at the hospital there."

"Would you like to do that?" he asked, handing her his handkerchief.

"I don't know. It kind of scares me."

"I'll let you in on a secret, Sophie. The whole thing terrifies me."

"What do you mean, Noah? You're great at preaching. You'll have them eating out of your hand in no time."

"What if I don't like it?"

Sophie wiped her eyes and looked directly at him. "Not like what?"

"I'm afraid it might be boring once the newness wears off."

"I thought you were called to do this. You defied your father, for heaven's sake! Why would you take the chance he'd disinherit you if you weren't called to help people?"

"You're so saintly, Sophie. I'm not talking about the money. I'm talking about the challenge."

"I can't think of anything more demanding than this. What kind of challenge are you looking for? Why didn't you become a fisherman or lumberjack if you wanted something life-threatening. Or you could have stayed with the paper mill and become a business guru. Why did you pick this?"

"This *is* a challenge. I guess I don't know exactly what I'm rambling on about. I just have doubts like you have doubts. Since it's too late to walk into this class, why don't we head downtown and get a coffee?"

"In the middle of a snowstorm?"

"The snow is slowing. The roads don't look that bad now. Come on. Tonight we can tackle the homework at the library."

"Noah's interview went better than mine did," she told Ben's students. "He walked out of the office with a job. He would become a rector of the parish of Brandy Point, including St. Matthew's and several small churches in neighboring villages, all north of the port where people catch the ferry to Labrador. I was up next and was there to congratulate him. I could tell he was ecstatic, having put his fears well behind him. He gave me the thumbs-up just as the bishop came out to invite me inside."

"Simon tells me you're highly qualified for any position I have," he began, sitting down behind the desk and motioning for her to take a chair. "I do have more than one opening. Maybe we should talk about them so you can make a wise choice."

"Thank you, sir."

"As you know, all of the western area is sparsely populated, and while the roads are good, they don't extend to the whole of the diocese. I mean that I could place you to the south between

Port aux Basques and Burgeo but some of your parishioners there can only be contacted by boat. If that kind of isolated area interests you, there's an opening there."

"I'm not sure. I had always thought I would be the rector of a parish. I've never been to the western part of Newfoundland so I'm at a loss about where places are."

"Luckily, Simon has a map on the wall over here. The distance between Port aux Basques and St. Mark where the other opening exists is about seven hundred kilometers. That one is at a hospital."

"And the hospital position would be as a chaplain."

"Yes. The patients aren't so different from members of any flock, but these would be individuals who are ill and their families. The nice thing here is that your parish wouldn't be spread over a large area. They would all be in one set of buildings and couldn't run too far—a rather captive parish."

"Noah Lodge just told me that you placed him in another town. Where's that?"

"Brandy Point—right here, not more than a two-hour drive from St. Mark. Simon mentioned that you did quite well in the pastoral ministry course on grieving. I can place almost anyone in the southern position, and for the time being, the other rectors around Port aux Basques have split the chores for the empty parish. It's the hospital position that has been so difficult to fill. That one takes someone with special skills. Evidently, your spiritual director thinks you would be a perfect fit for it."

"Thank you. Yes. I guess it would be a good fit," Sophie acknowledged, though still uncomfortable.

"I'm very pleased you've decided to join the diocese," he said. "I think we can talk about your ordination to the diaconate when you've had a few weeks to adjust to the thought of such a big move. Someone from my diocese will contact you."

"Thank you. I look forward to hearing from that person," she said, standing and taking his hand. "I'm honored to become a part of the Western Diocese."

Noah waited for her in the lobby in front of the lecture hall. "Did you take it?"

"What do you mean?"

"St. Mark is not that far, you know. Did you take the position at the hospital?"

"Yes," Sophie said, unable to contain her smile.

"So you can drive down and visit every weekend."

"I can take the bus down, yes. I don't have a car."

"We'll have to fix that. I'm not sure the bus stops near Brandy Point. We can get a used car."

"Yes? Who's going to pay for it?" she asked. "And who's going to drive it?"

"You've never driven?"

"No."

"Then that comes first. We'll start this afternoon. If you can master my truck, you can drive anything."

"But, Noah, I won't be able to get a car. Even a used one will cost too much."

"Nonsense. First you learn, and then we face the other problem.

"Noah did teach me how to drive. His truck was a manual shift so it wasn't easy, especially on all the little hills around St. John's. I also had to take a class so I could obtain my license before I went to St. Mark. When I had my license, he took me to a used car lot, and we found a small 1977 American-made car. It had little power, but he explained that there weren't many hills between St. Mark and Brandy Point. To pay for it, he sold the sleek fully equipped pick-up his father had given him and selected another smaller car similar to mine. He drove his off the lot after me, tooting the horn every time I slowed down.

Sophie pulled his alb down in back and walked around to face him. "There that's better, isn't it?"

"I guess so," Noah said, straightening the collar at the back of his neck. "You look great."

"Thanks. Are you as edgy as I am?"

"I think I'm more nervous. My parents came. Now if I can keep them from fighting up on the altar, I'll be okay. I didn't expect both of them to come."

"They live so close, I would've been surprised if they hadn't. They look nice. And definitely proud."

"Yeah. Now I have to perform. I keep having a dream that they discover what a bad deacon I am."

"Nonsense. You really shined our third year. You'll do fine," she said, retying her cincture.

"I finally met your Dr. Fairbourne. He said he was presenting you," Noah said. "Looks like a nice guy."

"You have to be a good priest for your parents. I have to be one for Dr. Fairbourne. He expects me to perform miracles without whining about it."

"That's not true. Without your whining, he'd be out of a job. Who else have you got to present you?"

"Father Herbert. I'm grateful he came all this way. I saw Ellie before I came in to vest. She was my friend at university. She's a nurse who recently got engaged to a doctor. I can't wait for the wedding."

"No relatives?"

Sophie paused. "No. I don't know of any that are still alive. Mama and Nanny died a long time ago."

"You were from Forsey Harbour, weren't you? Aren't there any people you would invite from there?"

"No," she said stoically. "I invited Gracie, my sister in Tooley—well, not my real sister. She didn't respond. I really must get in touch with that girl one of these days. I want to see how she is. What about you? I haven't met the priest from Marsh Cove yet. Is he presenting you?"

"Yes. He was my sponsor. I also got the former bishop of the diocese presenting me. God, I don't think I can live up to the expectations."

A man opened the door and stuck his head in. "The procession is about to begin. Are you two ready? Can't keep the bishop waiting."

Sophie looked into Noah's expressive brown eyes and waited for him to respond with his charming grin. Then they walked out to face their futures.

"It's difficult to remember everything that happened. I felt like I was dazed," Sophie said, leaning forward against the podium. "I remember hearing the beautiful tones from the organ. The notes still reverberate in my head, and every time I hear the hymn, I relive that day. Someone filmed the whole service so I can't pretend I don't remember it at all. Griffon was wonderful. He controlled my every move with the palm of his hand on my back, assuring me that I wouldn't mess up. I didn't intend to glance at him when I finally received my stole, but it looked so much like his, I turned to acknowledge him immediately, an error that the unforgiving camera caught. I didn't peek at Noah once. The film revealed later that he had glimpsed at me more than a few times, his chiseled face blanched. I couldn't decide if he was feeling ill, doubt, or terror. I suspect it was a little of all three. My expression was no better. I saw the doubt and concern in my eyes, though Noah told me later that I looked serene—almost like an angel. I didn't impart to him that right after the service I threw up in the ladies room off the hall. He didn't seem to notice that I barely touched my lunch at the reception. I kept myself busy by talking to many of the guests, including both of his parents who were as charming as he was.

"I spent the night in a bed and breakfast overlooking the mill sited at the edge of the bay. Smoky clouds loomed, softening the bright blue of the water. Noah went home to stay with his dad and his father's young girlfriend who thankfully hadn't shown up at the ordination. Once alone in my room, I looked into the mirror and studied my face. I didn't feel any different. Maybe I looked more humble around the mouth, but unfortunately my eyes imparted no greater wisdom, something I had counted on before beginning my long journey the next day.

"Becoming a deacon, of course, was only the first step. The priesting would come months later. I didn't fear driving the seven or so hours up to St. Mark on the northernmost tip of the peninsula. There was only one highway along the coast and plenty of signs at the end of it. I worried, however, about what was expected of me at the other end. I was beginning to fret about whether or not the gifts were going to kick in so that I could do a credible job helping my flock. Would these gifts allow me to save these poor souls by healing their bodies or would they only hurry me on to certain calamity?"

Book 3

Despite the rocks and pits that pepper its plane,
The road endures and winds through the scattering
of pine trees and boulders
Until it emerges into a clearing where
rays of sun spotlight it;
The pitfalls diminish and the obstacles scatter
And ones destination is in sight.
The rambler wanders from one shoulder to the other
Testing the road's limits,
Often tumbling over the invisible border
But the road persists, carrying him through the thicket
Until all becomes apparent and effortless
and glorious.

Chapter 13

New Life, Old Habit

The day was dark and drizzly, not atypical for northern Newfoundland in the summer. Sophie, accelerator to the floor, guided her car over the crest of the first hill. The underpowered engine sputtered but continued to inch forward. Below, the clouds broke, letting in a hazy sun. The view was spectacular. Ranging from deep blue to pale gray, the bay was busy with boats of all sizes moving in several directions. Liberally sprinkled on the hillsides facing the harbor, houses basked in the rays. Sophie pulled over to the side to walk. A soft mat of groundcover crunching under her footfall, she climbed a small hill. She grabbed the binoculars around her neck and focused them northward toward the ocean. To one side, she got her first glimpse of her new home, a massive brick building extending on either side of a round edifice. Built in the 1920's, the beige four-story hospital did not convey the drama of Warfield's Gothic structure, dark red bricks brooding over a tree-lined drive. But from this distance, the highly uniform windows, mere slits on a plain backdrop, reminded her of a prison. It had a lawn, but little else, the trees and bushes having been paved over for parking. It was then that she heard it, the wanton cry that rang in her ears. She turned to gaze toward the harbor, trying to catch sight of sea birds crying for food, but shedding droplets on her, a heavy cloud passed overhead. She hastily retreated to the car, gaining cover none too soon as the roar of wind and split of thunder tore through the surrounding hills.

Parking in front of the hospital and scurrying through the doors, she slowed to marvel at the large lobby. "Hello," she said to the receptionist. "I'm here to talk to Dr. Oliver Charles. Could you please tell me how I can find his office?"

Directed to the elevators in the east wing, she pressed the button to the third floor. When the doors opened again, she wondered where she was. Windowless doors on both sides shutting out light from the outside, the lengthy hallway was dark and deserted. The polished floor reflected the dim bulbs overhead.

A few steps along, she heard a door shut near the other end. The emerging figure's footfall echoed as it moved two doors nearer and slipped into another office. For the first time, she began to hear voices and turned to open a nearby door.

Inside, a woman sat behind a desk while another sat on top of it. A sudden quiet hung in the air. "What can we do for you, girl?" the woman in the chair finally asked.

"I'm looking for Dr. Charles," Sophie offered.

"Go down the hall ten or twelve more doors on the other side. There be a nameplate to the left of the entrance."

"Thank you," Sophie said. "Sorry to bother you."

Retreating to the hallway, Sophie continued along, trying to keep her shoes from scuffing the floor too loudly. When she got to Dr. Charles' office, she knocked. A middle-aged man came out of the room one door back, scanning a chart and conversing with a younger man wearing a stethoscope around his neck.

"Excuse me," Sophie said. "I'm looking for Dr. Charles."

The short graying man put up a finger and continued conferring with the younger doctor. Finally he stopped. "I'm Dr. Charles."

"Hello. I'm Sophie Hawkins."

"Ah yes, the minister. I don't have time to be your boss or anything so I'm afraid I can't be much help. Sister Adler on the first floor should be able to see that you're settled in."

Sophie nodded and began to walk past them toward the elevator.

"Miss Hawkins, I've been assured that you know what you're doin'—I mean, that you can handle everything without much supervision."

"I don't think I was sent here to be under any supervisor in particular, Dr. Charles. It was my understanding that I was the only one charged with the pastoral care of the patients here while the rest of you tended to their physical health. Is there something I should know that's different about this position?"

The younger doctor smiled and waited for Dr. Charles to answer.

"This position has been open for a long time, Miss Hawkins. It has remained open because the diocese has tried to send us incompetents."

Sophie smiled. "I'm sorry if the bishop's efforts have been inconvenient for you. I'd love to stay and listen to the stories, but not now. I need to locate my office and find out where I'm to live."

"There will be no one to show you round. We just can't find the time to deal with that."

"That's fine, Dr. Charles," she said, continuing down the hall. "I think I'm competent enough to find my own way around."

Reaching the stairs, Sophie skipped down to the ground floor and asked at the first nurses station where she could find Nursing Sister Adler.

"I am Sister Adler," announced a heavyset woman with a thick German accent, entering from a room off to one side.

"How do you do, Sister Adler? I'm Sophie Hawkins."

"Ah yes, the new minister from St. John's. Come here into my office. I have some keys for you, which you can take as soon as you have filled in all the proper paperwork."

A few hours later, Sophie walked outside to the parking lot. She turned her car up the street for no more than a block and parked in front of a more modern building. Keys in hand, she carried her bags to the second floor and moved into her new apartment. It would take the rest of the day to get unpacked and hooked up to the outside world. Exhausted, she would then tumble into bed.

In the morning, Sophie returned to the hospital. This time she walked through the lobby and turned west, following this hallway for only ten to fifteen steps. She was surprised the door was locked. With or without a chaplain, the chapel door should have been kept open. Gray light peeked in from behind drawn shades, but not enough to dispel the darkness of the small room. She found some cords and pulled them up, revealing two tall windows portraying a modern scene on matching multi-hued panes. Dust danced in the rainbow-colored rays.

"That's better," she said, still wondering where else families could have gone to seek solace when worrying about the health of loved ones.

Walking into her small office, she looked through the drawers of the empty desk. In a credenza along the wall, she found a dirty dust cloth and spray. She would spend the next hour cleaning and making a list of what she would need.

By the end of the following day, Sophie was free to wander the halls and get to know the layout better. The receptionist had copied a floor plan for her, and she wandered from unit to unit, meeting the staff and even a few patients.

On Saturday morning, Sophie had a visitor.

"Hi," he said when she answered her apartment door. "I believe we've met. My name is Dr. Black, Ewan Black."

"I remember you. You work with Dr. Charles."

"Yes, and I'm a bit embarrassed that I didn't stick up for you more. Oliver can be difficult. He didn't really send those incompetents away, you know. He drove them away with his meddlin'. I overheard the bishop warn him to leave you alone. I hope he didn't offend you."

"Are you from around here?"

"You mean the way I talk? No. I'm from Scotland. I'm here on loan to train the doctors on new surgical techniques we're usin' in Glasgow. And you?"

"I'm from the eastern side of the island. It feels much farther away than it actually is, I'm afraid."

"Anyway, I'm here today to ask if you've seen much of the area. I'd like to show you around. There's some beautiful countryside close by."

"Thanks, but I thought I'd go back to the hospital and organize my office. I have a list of supplies I need and was told the best time to break into the supply room was on Saturday."

"I see you're workin' too hard already. You can't do that. Not only will everyone resent you, but you won't be in good shape to face the people you're supposed to help."

"If you don't mind stopping at the store first so I can buy a few things I need around here, I wouldn't mind taking a peek at the area," she said, smiling. "I'll need to get back pretty early though. I'm really tired."

"As I said—maybe you're already workin' too hard."

"No. It's just that I'm having trouble sleeping. The racket. Do you ever get used to it?"

"Is it noisy here? I have a small cottage on the edge of town so I don't hear a thing. Is there too much partyin' goin' on in this buildin'? You should talk to someone about that if there is. I believe only those on hospital staff live here, and if others are bein' awakened too, the quality of work will be affected."

"I don't think it's partying. Come here to the window," she said, opening it up to the gentle breezes outside. "Listen. Don't you hear it? It's kind of a whine or a moan. Voices. Lots of voices all at once. I've heard the din since the first day I arrived. It's constant. Maybe it's a fluctuating buzz of equipment. Is there some kind of mining or such going on in the area?"

"I don't hear what you do. Maybe it's a pitch I can't hear myself. Oh. I heard that. Those are the boats dockin' along the pier and cranes pullin' off the load. That screechy sound? That's down at the pier."

"I'm not sure now. Do lots of freighters dock here?"

"Yes, resultin' in lots of minor accidents."

Sophie grabbed her jacket, and they both headed down to his car.

"Needless to say, I enjoyed our little outing immensely," Sophie told the audience. "Ewan was quite the gentleman. After shopping for picnic items, he pulled his car off the road not ten kilometers outside of St. Mark. We clambered over large boulders until the bay was so close, we could almost reach out and touch one of the whales in a pod frolicking along the shore. Their playful barks and grunts drowned out any thoughts of the eerie noises around the hospital.

"I allowed myself to look more closely at young Dr. Black and was pleased. His thick black hair and bushy eyebrows almost hid the most beautiful eyes I had ever seen. They were bluer than the sea under a bright cerulean sky. But most of all, they were kind eyes, reacting to everything I said. I was disappointed when he dropped me back off at the apartment, but I knew I would see him again, if not on another outing, at least at work during the week.

"My job at the hospital got easier as the weeks passed. I was able to become familiar with most of the patients in our own cancer ward, though I was sometimes sent to see those who had become outpatients at a facility down the road. I formed support groups for the families. We met in the chapel, often in the evenings after visiting hours. There were also long-term patients in the children's ward. I enjoyed visiting there whenever I got a chance. And I avoided the third floor of the east wing where I had first met Dr. Oliver Charles. The dark hallway and closed doors were troubling to me. I would have to go there once again, though, after I had been the chaplain for three or four weeks."

Sophie walked passed the door but caught something odd out of the corner of her eye. A young blind boy who had lived in the room for months was now dressed, his short legs dangling over the side of the bed.

"Jeffie," Sophie said, walking up beside him and softly touching his shoulder before giving him a hug. Then she turned to acknowledge his parents. She took the young boy's hand. "What's this, Jeffie? Are these your clothes? Where are you going? Did you plan to leave me without saying goodbye?"

"Hi, Sophie. Da's goin' home. Ma's gettin' a room near here."

"They're sendin' him to Cole House down the road," his mother explained.

"You're going to rehab? That sounds like fun."

"If only my headaches were gone," he said.

Sophie glanced at his mother.

"He still has the headaches," Jeffrey's mother said. "Dr. Bennett told us that he probably won't worry so much when he realizes he's not helpless anymore."

"But Dr. Bennett gave you medicine to make your head feel better, didn't she?"

"Yeah, but it's the same medicine I took afore I got sick."

"Before you got the measles?"

"Yes. I used to get the headaches then but took the pills, and it helped a little."

"Did you ever tell Dr. Bennett that you had the headaches before you got sick?"

"I think so. When Ma first brought me in, I could still see."

"I think we told you that we live on the mainland," his mother said. "The clinic there told us to bring him here because we couldn't control his fever. I mean, it would come down when we gave him aspirin, but it returned even worse in a day or two."

"And Dr. Bennett told you his headaches were because of the measles?"

"Yes. She said the measles often causes headaches. But then he lost his sight, and the headaches seemed to be something we could put up with."

Dr. Bennett suddenly appeared in the doorway. Her gray pageboy bouncing, she energetically swept her lean body across the room, peering over the reading glasses precariously perched on her nose. "Well, Jeffrey, are we anxious to go? Are your folks just waiting for me to give you the go ahead?"

Sophie had Jeffrey lie down as Dr. Bennett dumbly watched. Circling the bed, the young deacon placed her hands on his head.

Tugging at her glasses that now dangled on a chain around her neck, an impatient Dr. Bennett would only endure a few minutes of silence. "Sophie," she finally said. "Is this some kind of prayer?"

"If you can give me just a few minutes more, Jeffie, I'd like to steal the doctor for a moment or two. I promise we won't be gone long." Sophie dragged Dr. Bennett out of the room and down the hall. "You've got to keep him a little longer," she said.

"What do you mean, Sophie?" the doctor asked, irritation giving her voice an edge.

"I don't think his blindness is from the measles."

"What are you talking about? He came in here with a fever that the staff had to fight to get down."

"But did you x-ray him?" Sophie asked. "Did he ever tell you about the headaches?"

"Headaches are a result of the fever and often an aftereffect of the measles."

"They go away," Sophie urged. "From what I've heard, I don't think the headaches now have anything to do with the measles."

The two women had come to the end of the hallway and spun around to walk back toward the room.

"I'm sure he has them now because he's afraid to get on with the rest of his life," Dr. Bennett explained. "Of course his blindness is going to make him uneasy. Once he understands that he can overcome his handicap, the anxiety that is causing them will go away. If I were speaking with a nurse or anyone with actual training in psychology or neurology, I might listen. My advice to you is—"

"Did he ever tell you about the having the headaches before he got sick?"

"Sophie, I believe this is my patient! I don't interfere with your work. I think it's preposterous that you think you can do so with mine!"

Sophie grasped the doctor's arm. "Emma, Jeffrey has a brain tumor behind the left eye," she said, spitting out the words before the doctor could get away. "It's small and hard to detect on an x-ray but it's operable. I'm sure he's not completely blind. At least he detects movement with the right eye. I could tell he was following me when I moved."

Staring into Sophie eyes, Dr. Bennett froze. "You know," she finally said, her breath warming Sophie's cheek. "The odds of you being correct are infinitesimal. Why should I even listen to such a absurd suggestion?"

"Because you can't afford not to. Just one test and a few more hours of observation will save this kid's life, and that's what you're about, Emma. You're here because you can save children's lives."

Knowing that Jeffie would still be in his room so she could visit him the next day, Sophie strode past the doctor and out of the ward. She stopped at the nurses' station on the first floor of the east wing and waited until someone acknowledged her. "I have a question," she told the young nurse. "I have a floor plan from Sister Adler here but it says nothing about the fourth floor on this wing. I see all the other units listed. What's on the fourth floor above us?"

"Fourth floor? I'm not sure we have one."

"Of course we have one. If you walk outside and count the floors, you'll see the line of windows just like those on the west wing."

"Maybe we don't use it or it's just storage."

"Perhaps, but there are curtains on the windows," Sophie said, leaning closer. "And the lights are on at night. Hasn't anyone ever noticed them?"

"I've rung for Sister Adler. Maybe she can help you."

The supervisor emerged from her office, and Sophie repeated her questions from the beginning.

Her hands on her hips, the nurse stared back at her. "I have no idea," she finally said. "Go take a look for yourself."

"I noticed that the fourth floor isn't accessible by the elevator. There seems to be a fourth floor button, but it needs a key. There's a locked door on the third floor landing but it isn't marked. I assume there are stairs to the fourth floor because it would be a safety hazard without them."

"I am sorry, I cannot help you then. I make it a point to mind my own business and maybe you should do so too."

"I see. But if there are patients on the fourth floor of this wing, I believe it *is* my business."

"You are free to talk about it with Dr. Charles, but I do not recommend it. He often interprets curiosity as meddling. I guess that is just how he is."

Sophie climbed into the elevator for the trip to Oliver's office. Between the second and third floors, the lights suddenly faded, and the cage slowed to a stopped. After a few jerks, the light came back on and the elevator doors opened onto the dim hallway.

In his office, Dr. Charles sat languidly behind his desk, reading a newspaper and sipping soup. He did not stand when she entered, but continued to read as if she were not there. Finally he looked up.

"I'm sorry to interrupt you, doctor."

"Please sit down," he said. "How's everything goin'? I hear you've established some support groups for families of the cancer patients. That's a fine idea. Have you been able to visit almost everyone?"

"Yes. I've been with each cancer patient on numerous occasions, and the patients in the children's ward are wonderful."

"It doesn't bother you then that many won't make it out again?"

"Yes. It bothers me, but that's not why I'm a chaplain, doctor. Through prayer, I accept what God has planned," Sophie explained. "But I haven't been to all of the wards yet. I haven't been on the floor above us here. Can you explain to me who are in the rooms on the fourth floor?"

"Yes. Yes," he said, seemingly annoyed. He wiped his face with his napkin and sighed. "Those used to be rooms. We had a psychiatric ward up there. It was purely experimental because in Canada the association doesn't usually put psychiatric patients in medical hospitals, and as you know, we've been part of Canada for nearly thirty years."

"So the rooms are empty now."

"Yes. They've been empty for twenty years."

"But surely someone is up there."

"No. I guess we could expand the hospital and redo the ward but there hasn't really been a need. With the new hospital in Happy Valley and one in Corner Brook, ours seems to have enough beds," he said, taking another slurp of his soup. "Is that your only problem, Miss Hawkins?" he asked, rising and walking her out into the hall.

"I suppose, Dr. Charles. I appreciate your taking time from your lunch to explain to me what's being stored upstairs."

She started to turn away but heard the buzz from the lights in the ceiling over her head. The already dim lights faded momentarily, making the hallway almost completely black. Then they crackled and the faint intensity returned.

"Tell me, doctor. Why do you keep the lights so faint in this hallway?"

"Money. I can't believe Dr. Black didn't explain it to you. We have to economize to keep this place runnin'. While the nursin' sisters and patients need light in the wards, there's no need for a lot of illumination in this hallway. We have windows in our offices that give us good light, and in the dead of winter, we do have lights like these we can turn on directly over our workspaces if we lose the sun before we go home. We must all think of economy so we can make our guests as comfortable as possible."

"And why does the power surge like it just did?"

"I have no idea. I have a committee lookin' into that. Until they solve the problem, we'll just have to put up with it."

Sophie decided to take the stairs down. The chill she felt after talking to the odd little man made her head for the cafeteria to get some tea. She had the feeling that there was more to the electrical problem than a closed ward. Was it her gift? If so, she knew it would eat at her until she faced the problem directly. But Sophie also wondered if the gift might be urging her to take the next step and if she would be able to survive it once again.

Chapter 14

Brand New

Noah turned the car into the parking lot of St. Matthew's Church. It was a fine day—too fine to begin the task of moving into the rectory or meeting with his assistants. He got out and walked across the road to the pebbly field in front of the beach. This was still his sea, even if it had been a while since he had been home. The slate-colored rolling waves that threatened the shore only to peter out at the last second, the swish of the wavelets harmlessly splashing over the rocks, the lonely call of the raucous sea birds, and the salty odor of rotting seaweed—he missed it all. At one end of the coarse beach, huge stones grew out of the sand. Noah sprinted over and scrabbled onto the tall platform.

The mass was a collection of boulders, sandstone brown veiled in a mat of life—multi-colored lichen and shells already drilled by beaks and left to weather in the deep cracks and crevices. Meters away from the waterline, Noah sat on a carpet of short grass, little purple flowers poking up through a collection of sand and dirt. Only the eyes of the seabirds could spy on him here. This was the peace he had known as a child, hiding from a fractious family life, parents who each tried so hard to shield their sheer revulsion of the other with smiling derision. Hoping to return later and find a crevice into which he could stuff a blanket for future visits, he noted the place. This would become his spot, his hiding place.

Knowing that he had to face his first job eventually, he climbed down and retraced his steps through the field. A man met him in the driveway and led him up the stairs to the rectory.

On Sunday, the church was full. The whole town and neighboring villages had come to listen to him at the one prayer service he could manage his first week. He would add the other five church buildings over the next few weeks, but for one Sunday at least, they were willing to gather in a single place and meet the young deacon who would become their spiritual director. His first sermon was fiery, extolling the virtues of one popular interpretation of the gospel one minute only to rip it to pieces the next. Then he threaded through the bits and wove them together in a novel way, convincing his listeners that his new explanation was the way everyone should see it—the only viable interpretation of the lesson. Mesmerized by his animated voice, his vigorous gestures, his direct eye contact, and his compelling smile, no listener seemed to be left out. Why had they not seen it that way before?

Noah greeted them at the end of the service, grasping each hand in his two, repeating each name, trying to file it in the back of his mind. His attention would not be drawn away from any of them. He would understand them, each age group where the dialect and pronunciation recast itself over the decades. Language here was upset only slightly by the influx of teachers from other parts of the island, but little else bonded islanders with the rest of North America. He did not have to talk like they did but only had to understand the words, the intimation. And he did that well.

"Yer much younger than we spected," one older woman said. "Not too many young women round here to keep you tied to these parts, ye know."

He smiled, making sure she understood that at that moment her very presence engrossed him. He must have felt her hand melt into his.

"Ye knows anything bout boats, Fader?" a man asked, his face tanned, even in the deep creases that surrounded his eyes and mouth.

"Yes. Yes, Mr. Abbott. I've been watching the fishing boats pull away from the dock each morning. There are some fine-looking crafts among them. Is one of them yours?"

"No sir, but I brings her round from Black Inlet each mornin' to pick up bait. I jest painted 'er a bright green so she'd feel pretty out dere 'mong dose otter pealin' 'traptions. Ye look after dat, Fader. Look on de bright green one tomorrow in de mornin'. It'll be me and me crew."

"How many do you take out with you, Mr. Abbot?"

"Sometimes four, maybe five. Times be changin', you know. Don't need so many as we used to, do we? Lately, I jest takes me grandson longs, but he be hankerin' to move on now. He'll probly move inland wid de rest of 'em, drowin' demselves in de cities like caplain gadderin' on a beach waitin' to turn into somebody's dinner."

"Hi, I'm Millie Bellows. I hopes you plays cards, Father," a middle-aged woman said. "We plays cards in church hall on Thursday nights to make money for church repairs and activities. Sometimes the hall be the only place for the youngsters to go, you know. We lets the older ones have dances and parties there."

"Thank you, Ms. Bellows. Are you our youth group leader? We'll have to get together and talk about how I can support you."

"The teens will love that, Father Noah. They rarely gets someone so close to their own age to talk to. You might even be able to pull 'em into church on Sunday. I can't wait for you to meet 'em."

The service over, Noah ambled across the street to the small rectory. Removing his surplice and cassock, he relaxed with a cup of coffee in front of the window that overlooked the bay. There were whitecaps on the choppy water, but the sea was always in some kind of turmoil. Reminding him that it was still only early summer, icebergs crept southward. He would grab an old blanket and clamber over the boulders to the spot he had picked out. He could take a notepad and fill in the dates on a calendar. He certainly had a lot of work this week, still having to meet with his vestry and the outreach committees. He could make appointments with the parishioners who were sick and get to know families in all five of the surrounding churches who probably needed his attention even more than those in Brandy Point. On a sheet of paper, he could begin next Sunday's sermon. Noah got up to grab a blanket out of the linen closet and walked down the front steps of the rectory without the notepad. He would handle that tomorrow.

It had come upon him as he lay on the rocks listening to the waves. He needed to be out there on the water, to feel the roll, confront the whim of nature, and remind himself that he was not afraid of it, that he was in control. It was not the same as being in charge of a parish. He did not really dominate here. He was an administrator and a preacher. His parishioners went home after the service and hopefully learned something from him. But they were already angels—trying to get through a purgatory here on earth. He could influence them, make them feel better as they all marched toward the hardship—that downward spiral of age that forced them all to endure excruciating hardship before the sweet day they would face their gentle maker. The fact that his job scared him more than the powerful force of the ocean did not occur to him. Was it a lack of faith? So toward the middle of the week, Noah got into his car and drove down to Marsh Cove.

"Ma, are you here?" he asked, letting himself in the door.

"Noah, is that you?" she replied. "I'm in the kitchen. Come tell me why you're here in the middle of the week."

"I'm here because I work weekends," he said, kissing her on the cheek.

"That doesn't tell me why you're here," she said, getting up from the table and reaching into a cupboard for another cup. "Tea?"

"Yes," he said, sitting down and letting her coddle him. "I'm here for my boat. The trailer's still in the garage, isn't it?"

"I don't touch your stuff. You had better seal the boat before you take her out, though. I don't know what condition she's in. How's Brandy Point?"

"Nice. The people are real nice. You would like them."

"Are you saying they're all old?"

"Pretty much. There are some young people. Some go to the high school and a few in grade school. If they go to college, they disappear."

"Sounds like a challenge. I can't see how you can do it. It must be difficult being spiritual director to a bunch of aging ladies."

"Not really, at least so far. They love to coo over me and teach me how to play bridge. Their sons have all left for greener pastures, and I'm the only one left. They've adopted me."

"You could have left too. I don't see what you accomplish hanging on here. I think you just never grew up."

He smiled, knowing she could not resist his charm. No one could, for that matter.

"All right, I know," she continued. "You just want to be close enough to take care of me."

"I wish I could trust you to get help, Ma. I can't stand seeing you sitting around, too feeble to get up out of your chair. Are you sure you don't want me to move back in with you?"

"Heavens no! It took me too long to get you out of here. Why would I want to give up the privacy I earned?"

"Just as I thought. I feel guilty not being around to discourage your active promiscuity."

"I refuse to talk about what I do here—especially after you decided to go into the priesthood, dear," she laughed.

"I hoped you'd feel more uncomfortable sharing that with me because I'm your son," he said. "Thanks for the tea, by the way. You remind me that I have a job and should finish what I came to do. Then I'll roll back up to Brandy Point."

She walked out into the yard with him.

"You're going to pull the boat with that? Where's your truck?"

"I had to help a young damsel in distress. She needed a car for her job, and I couldn't resist."

"So your next trip down will be to the mill to get your father to buy you a new one."

"Mother, I'm going to be a priest. It doesn't look good for a priest to drive around in a brand new truck."

"But a good dinghy won't have the same effect?"

"The boat is a necessity in Brandy Point. I have to have something in common with my parishioners so they'll know I'm one of them."

"Ah. I understand then. Just put the stuff that's inside the dinghy along the wall and don't hurt yourself. I hope you'll visit again, Noah. I miss you."

"As long as you continue to behave yourself," he said.

Noah sat beside Mrs. Clark. "How does this differ from bridge?" he asked, taking a sip of the fruit punch he was served and grimacing at its tartness.

"Sorry, the crop last year didn't get sweet enough," she whispered to him, her face close to his. "I thinks Millie doesn't know when the partridgeberries are ripe. That information gets passed down from generation to generation and the fact that she 'longed to an orphanage means she never really learnt any of that important stuff."

"I see."

"Don't let Effie tell you that I never learnt how to pick partridgeberries, Father! No way did I ever live in an orphanage. My father died at age ninety, and my mother, rest her soul, will be one hundred this next year. I likes the juice tart. Effie has to throw extra sugar in hers, and it be bad for the teeth. Most of my teeth be the originals, Father, while she takes hers out at night."

"I do *not* take my teeth out at night!" Effie said emphatically.

"Nobody listens to Effie. She exaggerates everything. If she comes to the church and tells you to hurry home with her because her husband, Angus, be dyin', it means the TV's broke and he has nuthin' to do."

"And the game?" he asked. "Do you want to give me some of the rules?"

"No. If you knows bridge, you'll be able to pick it up quick," Millie said. "Hurry and put your loonies in so we can get to biddin'!"

The second weekend, Noah made the rounds of all six churches. The number of parishioners at St. Matthew's dropped. It was essentially the same crowd that had attended the service the Sunday before, but they were now disseminated among six separate buildings. The following week he would have to sit down with the warden and vestry to see how they managed the upkeep.

"Dis be summer," said one of the parishioners in neighboring Black Inlet. "Dere ought to be more come de fall when fishin' be full over. Can't stop fillin' the hold just cuz it' be Sunday, can we?"

"No, Mr. Dawe," replied Noah, looking longingly out over the bay. "You have to fish when you can since the number of cod is decreasing."

"I be here cuz I be waitin' fer de ice. I likes sealin' better' dan fishin'."

"I understand, Mr. Dawe. Glad you're able to attend on the Sundays when you're not out on the pans."

He was dressed and ready to take his boat out on the calm water when he had to answer a knock at the rectory door.

"Oh, Father," she said. "I didn't know you was goin' anywhere on a Sunday afternoon. I hope I'm not interruptin' anything."

"No, no, Millie. Please come in."

"It's just that my daughter be home now, and she won't listen to a word I says. I was wonderin' if you can talk to her. She be a little older than you, I think, Father, but not much, maybe a year or two."

"I would be happy to talk with her in my office in the parish hall. I have a few hours free tomorrow. Send her to my office at say ten."

Noah sat at his desk with the phone to his ear, trying to get his warden and vestry together for one evening that week. She entered the parish hall, and Noah immediately put the receiver down. She was big. Very big. In fact, Noah panicked, worrying that she might have the baby that very minute. He stood up and looked for a chair big enough for her before offering his own.

"Just a minute. I know there are some folding chairs in the closet. I'll get one for myself."

"Yes, Father," she said, a silly grin crossing her face.

"I'm sorry, I don't think Millie ever gave me your name," he began after sitting down on the wrong side of the desk.

"It's Rose, Father. Rose Whiffen."

"Ah, Rose," he repeated, not knowing what to say next.

"Mum told me that you be wantin' to talk to me. I s'pose it's 'bout me boyfriend, Patrick."

Noah's head whirled. "Your boyfriend, yes. Then you two aren't planning to marry before the baby is born?"

"Patrick's not wantin' to get married at all, Father. He be scared of what might happen."

Noah watched as she shifted her massive trunk. When the bulge moved on its own, he worried that Rose's abdomen might explode. Mesmerized by the warped lump, he could not take his eyes off of it. "Does Millie want you and Patrick to get married? Is that the problem?"

"I don't know. Mum doesn't talk 'bout it much. She just wants me to be happy I s'pose, but I be happy already."

"Perhaps you two should think about the child."

"What do you mean?"

"Perhaps Millie thinks the child might be happier with two parents and that's why she's worried. The Church believes that matrimony is appropriate before a couple decides to have children," he said, unsure how he was going to explain it further.

Rose turned her head, leaning forward to look at him from head to toe. Noah squirmed uneasily.

"Yes. Mum thinks I should get married too."

"So—do you want Patrick to come in and talk with us?"

"Why?"

"Because he and you need to talk about marriage."

"No. Patrick and I don't want to get married."

Noah leaned back, nearly tipping the chair over. "Then I don't understand."

"Mum's tryin' to get me to meet other fellows round the Point. I have to report back to her what you looks like so she knows I talked to you."

Noah felt sick to his stomach. "I can tell her you were here if you would like," he offered.

Rose beamed for the first time. It was an attractive smile, pushing her swollen cheeks off her jaw line. "I thinks Mum's sweet on Patrick. She says I'm too young for him."

"How old are you, Rose?"

"I be thirty-two."

"And how old is Patrick?"

"Patrick be fifty, I thinks—maybe more."

"What does Patrick do?"

"He gots a good job. He works construction when the weather be good and clears snow in the winter."

"Then why doesn't Millie want you to marry him?"

"You see, he be married up 'til Mary, his wife, died nearly a year ago now. I thinks Mum figured he wanted to move in with her. He kept comin' round the house, and Mum cooked for him and cooed over him. She told me she felt sorry for him."

"Isn't Millie married?"

"No. Her last man died when I be eighteen. He be a skipper and 'ferred chancin' it on the sea than to go 'bout the house all day. His boat sank up near Nain. Anyway, Patrick comes over and eats her food and lets her wash his clothes, but he starts touchin' me under the table and says I makes him feel like a bedlamer. He'd work all day and needed me to rub his achin' muscles. I goes with him to his work, so when his muscles gets stiff, I'd be there to rub him down. In no time we be gulchin' in his truck or jiggin' on the beach. But as soon as Mum finds out my barrel's up, she says she wants nuthin' to do with any baby of his and chases him out of the house with a broomstick."

"But you still love Patrick?" he asked.

"I likes Patrick. His pride makes me bivver right here," she confessed, caressing the bottom side of her bulge.

Noah fought to keep his composure. "And does Patrick love you?"

"He keeps comin' back for more, Father."

"Then it's my belief that you should marry the father of your baby. Do you really think Patrick would object to that, Rose?"

"No. Maybe I should talk to him. Maybe he'll want to get married now. It's just that Mum keeps bootin' him out of the house when he comes round."

"Why don't I talk to Millie for you. Would you like that?"

Rose smiled. "Yes, Father."

Noah told Rose to have Millie come in and see him the next Monday. In the mean time, she would tell Patrick that they should come in to talk about the wedding. Rose looked very pleased. She hoisted her heavy body out of her seat and waddled toward the door. A minute later she returned and kissed Noah on the cheek.

"If something happens to Patrick," she said. "Maybe you'd like to come over. I loves to watch ol' movies on the TV. I be a good cook too, and you wouldn't be so scrawny after eatin' some of my meals."

"You just get Patrick here so you two can be married before that baby comes, Rose."

"Yes, Father."

Noah watched her scrawl out the door. He was proud of himself. Talking the woman into marriage when the couple obviously loved each other was the right thing for everyone, including Millie. He just had to figure out a way to make sure Millie saw it that way too.

Unfortunately that would not happen. Late Friday night, Noah was roused by a loud rap on his door. It was Millie.

"Come quick, Father. She's bad, real bad. The baby's come, but Doc Delacour from the clinic says there be something wrong. You gots to come, Father."

Noah pulled on his pants and followed the women up the road to the cottage she shared with her daughter. He entered the bedroom to find a small group of people, including the doctor and a man he presumed to be Patrick, circling a bed, and blood-splattered linens and towels piled on the floor. Patrick could not seem to stop moving. Continuing to cross back and forth at the end of the bed, the anxious father opened his mouth to yell, but nothing came out. The doctor bent over, working on something at Rose's feet. When he looked up at Noah, Patrick moved back, suddenly revealing a bluish-black doll of some sort stretched across the blanket.

At first, Noah did not understand. He tried to comprehend, but his mind went blank. And then it hit him. The whole scene was surreal. Patrick's jerky movements seemed to play out in slow-motion. The doctor, panic chiseling his face, stared in Noah's direction. The black-faced baby doll, did not cry, did not inhale, and the umbilical cord still attached to its belly, hung over the edge of the bed. Rose lay quietly, her knees flopped open, her face porcelain-white. Where moments earlier, she must have grimaced with pain, she now appeared almost saintly. All this came to him like the rush of a flock of pigeons. Noah did not reach for his stole to pray over the bodies. He did not even think of why Millie might have summoned him. And if

Millie screamed or wailed now, he could not hear it over the buzz in his ears. Instead, Noah retreated. He turned and ran out the door just in time to vomit all over Millie's carefully tended flower garden.

Chapter 15

Payback

"Ewan and I continued to enjoy our free time together. I never thought I would find someone who was so confident and still thoughtful. I spent more and more time seeing the countryside and ending up at his cottage. He was right about the noise. The voices I heard near the hospital were all but drowned out by the crashing of waves just meters away from the front door of his little house. Love on my part didn't arrive all at once. It would take months for me to trust anyone after my experiences with both the Reverend and later with Ben. But Ewan was ever patient. He never demanded passion from me and relished any token of affection that I offered. Love did eventually come as well as profound respect and trust. I knew he would ask me to marry him and planned to remain by his side for a lifetime."

Sophie washed her face and donned a t-shirt and a pair of jeans. She was ready when she heard the knock.

"Hi," she said. "Are we going to your place?"

"No, not tonight. I have to go back to work."

"Do you need some dinner?"

"No, I can pick something up at the cafeteria," Ewan said. "I just wanted to be with you for a few hours before I went back."

"Then why don't we take a walk? There's something I need to show you. I realize you don't hear the noise, and if you don't see the lights either, I'll know I'm going crazy. Do I need a sweater?"

"No. It's beautiful out there. What lights?"

"Come with me. I'll show you."

The two strolled down the gravel road hand in hand.

"We're walkin' back to work," Ewan said. "I was tryin' to escape it, and you're draggin' me back."

Sophie smiled. "See the stars? There are no clouds and no moon tonight. Look how clear it is."

"All right," Ewan conceded, nuzzling her neck. "You win. We can make out on the lawn in front of the maternity ward."

"There. Do you see that?" she said, pushing him away. "What time is it?"

"A little after nine. What are you lookin' at?"

"The light on the fourth floor. Oliver said it was an old psychiatric ward that has been closed down, but someone's up there."

"You mean that one light? Have you ever seen it off? It could be on all the time."

"Why would that one be on full strength when there are no people there? Oliver's trying to save money by keeping the lights dim on the third floor. I don't believe he'd let that one stay on. He would have made sure it was kept off."

"Whoops, it's off now. Maybe he discovered it."

"It'll be back on," Sophie said.

"How do you know? You haven't been spyin' on the fourth floor, have you? Maybe they accidentally left a psych patient up there when they closed the ward up. I wonder how old he would be now?"

"I'll admit I'd have had to take a lot of walks to see the changes that go on up there," she said, playfully elbowing him in the side. "But if you think you can scare me, you're mistaken. I'm not the one having to go back in that building tonight."

Ewan turned her around and kissed her on the lips, and she responded. The voices being louder than ever near the hospital, she did not admit that she was frightened. She let him put his arms around her, making her feel infinitely better.

Sophie passed through the children's ward, only to find Jeffrey packed up and ready to go again.

"Hi, Jeffie, you're not leaving, are you?" she asked, tousling his hair.

"Hi, Sophie, yup. I can't wait to get home and see my dogs."

"I can't thank you enough, Reverend," said his mother, giving Sophie a hug. "He's goin' to be fine now. They'll fit him for some corrective glasses in Corner Brook tomorrow, and then we'll head for the ferry like nothin' happened."

"It's Sophie," she corrected. "It was you and your son that made me question the diagnosis. I only wanted to keep him here longer because I'm basically selfish. I knew I would miss him too much if he left." She turned back to Jeffrey who cuddled a stuffed husky someone had given him. "And now he's leaving anyway. I guess I wasn't meant to keep you, Jeffie."

"I'll come back. I promise," he said, suddenly a little sad.

"I only want you to visit if you're healthy," Sophie told him, walking toward the door. "You all have a good trip."

A cluster of rooms through some doors at the end of the hallway were new. Sophie did not know what the new section held so she had to investigate. Swinging the doors open, she stopped at the nursing station that sat in front of six doors, each leading to a room.

"What's this?" she asked. "Are these all full?"

"Not yet," said one of the nurses. "We have three so far. They're transferin' more from Happy Valley."

"Look at all this monitoring equipment. What do these patients have?"

A doctor stopped and looked at a file. "These are polio patients," he explained, shoving a pen behind his ear and holding out his hand. "Hi. I'm Dan Ellis. I don't think we've met. I take it by the collar you're some sort of chaplain," he mumbled.

"Hello, I'm Sophie Hawkins. I thought we had controlled polio. Where are these cases coming from?"

"We've almost beaten it," he said. "These aren't new cases, though. The transfers are PPS patients mostly—that's post polio syndrome."

"I haven't heard of that. Is it common?"

"More common than we would like to admit. Follow me. I'll introduce you to the three we have so far. Good morning, Mr. Flood," the doctor said to a middle-aged man sitting on the edge of his bed. "This is Ms. Hawkins, the chaplain."

"Sophie," she corrected, shaking the man's hand.

"Mr. Flood had paralytic polio as a child, age seven or eight, wasn't it? He had splints on his legs for two years, but the therapy enabled him to walk on his own for several more," Ellis explained. "About five or six years ago, he began to experience numbing in the lower legs. The symptoms came and went but got progressively worse. He's returned here for therapy. We're hoping we can get him back on his feet."

The doctor continued talking in the hallway. "It was thought that PPS hit mostly women, but obviously that's not true. We also supposed that it was due to overuse of the larger muscles the patients needed to develop in order to make up for polio damage of the smaller ones. There are also questions concerning that theory. By placing some of these people together, we might be able to come to better conclusions. Across the hall here is Mrs. Gleason. Her polio at age ten ran the gambit—bulbospinal polio. There was permanent damage to the legs muscles but also inability to breath on her own. Believe it or not, a few years ago, symptoms returned with a sore throat that gradually got worse. She's now back on a modern equivalent of the iron lung. It's hard to stop the downward spiral once it starts."

Sophie had intended to drive to Brandy Point on Friday for a first annual reunion with Ben, Rachel, Cyril, and Noah.

Unfortunately, plans fell apart. Ben and Rachel had had their first baby just after Noah and Sophie's ordination to the diaconate, and the trip would have been too much for both mother and child. Noah was still very busy trying to get control of his new parish. It was better for everyone if the party were put off until spring. She still took the day off, however. Upon seeing the PPS patients, she vowed that she would drive to Tooley and see for herself how Gracie was doing.

She did not think that it would be possible for Tooley to have changed so much. It was a shock when she first spotted the deserted and rundown buildings of the fish plant, and now quiet and empty, the once-busy pier. The church still stood by the field she used to cross over to the beach. The fresh white paint gleamed in the late September sun. The Ivany house was newly painted too, smoke pouring out of the chimney. Sophie pulled the car up in front of it but could not convince herself to get out. Her heart raced. What would she find? Would the family look the same? Would they be glad to see her?

Instead of heading up the walk, she crossed the street and marched into the church, much smaller than she remembered it. Slowly making her way up the aisle, she stared at the stone altar and shivered. As much as she tried to concentrate on Grace, the past pushed its way to the front. She mounted the steps and touched the stone, tentatively at first. Then she wiped it with her palm. It was smooth and still cold, unfeeling. She thought about Ewan's warmth and smiled.

"Hello," came the voice behind her. "Can I help you?"

She turned and faced someone she had not met before. "Hello," she said, putting out her hand. "I'm Sophie Hawkins. I was looking for the minister."

"I'm the elder. You're with the church?" he asked, noticing her collar.

"I'm with the Anglican Church, yes. I'm sorry, I'm looking for the Reverend Josiah Ivany."

"The pastor, Ivany, left the church several years ago. May I ask why you would like to see him?"

"The family doesn't live in the house any more then?"

"No. My wife and I do."

"Oh," Sophie said, sounding somewhat disappointed. "Do you know where the Ivanys live now?"

"I'm sorry. I don't think I caught the reason for your inquiry. Perhaps you would like to talk to someone with the authority to give out that information. My boss lives in Gander."

"I see," she said, debating whether or not to open up to him. The two of them walked out onto the front steps. "I used to live in the Ivany house. I was a foster child raised by Josiah and Wallace. Do any of the family still live around here?"

"Then you would know about the scandal."

The look in Sophie's eye would have given away her ignorance had he not been looking dreamily out to sea.

"It caused quite a ruckus in town," he continued. "Bishop Gibbons quietly tried to convince him that he should step down. It's been ten years now. I've only been here three. He refused to leave, and the police had to be called. There was to be a trial, but he had a breakdown before it took place and was sent to a sanitarium. I don't remember where. I'm not even sure he's still alive."

"And Wallace?" she asked.

"Oh. She died long before that. I guess her suicide nearly eleven years ago is what caused the parishioners to start looking into it. I can't believe you weren't called in as a witness."

"I was in St. John's. I don't remember reading about a trial either. What did he do?"

"I hear he was arrested for rape. There was a child under his care, and someone, a caretaker at the church or hired hand, caught him. I mean, there had been rumors for years that he molested little girls, but no one took it seriously because none of the children spoke up. As it is, Miss Carberry refused to testify."

"Miss Carberry? Where is she now?"

"She lives on the other side of town. The little house is the one that faces away from the bay."

"The Whelan house?"

"Yes. I think I've heard it called that."

"Thank you. Maybe she can help me."

"She's an odd sort, you know. The town has given up trying to get her to go to school. She's sixteen or seventeen and has never been. She might not be willing to help you at all."

"Thank you. I remember her and knew the Whelans," Sophie said, rushing back to her car.

She drove through town and slowed in front of the path to the little cottage about two hundred meters from the road. Trudging slowly down the trail, she looked out past the rocks to the beach and recalled cutting through the field adjacent to the Ivany house to get to Grace's cave. When she got to the front steps of the cottage, she navigated carefully, avoiding some of places where the treads had decomposed.

Sophie hesitated as the door opened almost immediately after her first knock. The shades all down, the front room was dark and stuffy.

"Are you Amelia?" Sophie asked the young woman who answered the door. "Do you remember me?"

Her brown hair cut short, she looked like a boy. She opened the door farther to reveal a hunting rifle in her other hand. "No. You from the government? If you knowed me you'd call me Amy."

"I knew you when you were very small—when your mother brought you here to Tooley. Is your mother well?"

Amy stuck her head out the door and looked more closely at the visitor. "You're a minister. We don't want nobody from the church round 'ere. I'll give you a runnin' start afore I shoots you."

"I'm not that kind of minister and not from a church around here, Amy. May I come in?"

"No."

"I would like to speak with your mother."

"No. She be too busy to talk."

There was a faint voice behind her, saying something Sophie could not make out.

"Is that your mother, Amy?"

"No."

"Amy, I know about the Reverend."

"Everybody knows bout 'im if theys knows 'ow to read the papers."

"No, I know about what he did because he did it to me too."

Amy looked confused. "Where was you for the trial?"

"I lived in an orphanage in St. John's. I had no way of knowing what was happening here. I wrote Gracie but she didn't answer. I guess she never got the letters because she no longer lived in the same house."

"Sophie?" the voice called.

Amy opened the door farther. The stench inside the house caught Sophie by surprise, and she almost covered her nose.

"She be in there," Amy said, finally gesturing for the visitor to come in.

Sophie walked through the musty kitchen to the open bedroom door, and expecting to see Mrs. Carberry, peered in. The room was dark. Sophie crossed it to draw the shade, letting light stream in over the mussed bed. There lay a young woman, crunched down on some crumpled pillows. The face did not look the same, the dark hair was cut short, and the cheeks were pale and swollen. But the light hit the dark lashes and mesmerizing black eyes behind them, and Sophie recognized her sister.

"Gracie, dear Gracie," she said, her voice breaking. "Why are you in bed?"

Grace smiled and put her thin arms out to gather Sophie in.

"I sent you letters. I wanted to hear from you." Sophie cried, tears flowing freely.

"I'm not too strong," Grace finally confessed. "I can't walk."

"I thought you were better. They told me you had recovered almost completely."

"I had, at first. But with mother's death and the trial, my health went downward. What about you? Why did you become a minister after you hated my father so much?"

"I didn't even think about him. I had another friend who was a minister in another church, and he impressed me so much I decided to help others that way too."

Sophie glanced back at Amy, standing in the doorway. Grace noticed Sophie's hesitation.

"It's okay. Amy helps me. When Mama died and Father had to go away, Mrs. Carberry moved us here. Havin' a bad heart, she died a while back. I believe the trial and Amy's testimony were too much for her. Amy is the only family I have left."

"But the trial—Josiah didn't make it to trial?"

"No. He wasn't right after Mr. Howley found him and Amy in the church. And no one wanted Amy to testify anyway. She was too young and didn't understand."

"Mr. Howley?"

"You remember him. He and Mrs. Howley ran the grocery store. When he retired, Father hired him to keep up the church grounds.

"Have you ever visited your father?" Sophie asked.

"No."

"And your health. Is it getting worse?"

"Sort of. On good days I can sit up, but most of the time, I just lie here.

"Listen, Gracie. I'm a chaplain in a hospital on the Northern Peninsula. They've just opened a ward for people who have symptoms like yours. The patients had polio and recovered at first. Then they started to get the symptoms all over again. I want to help you. I want to get you to a clinic that is studying this. There must be one in St. John's. If I can get you in, will you go?"

Grace glanced at Amy. "I don't think I should leave. Amy needs me."

Sophie looked around at Amy, appearing younger than her years. "I don't think either of you should stay here. It's not healthy living in this isolated spot."

"Remember the cave, Sophie?"

"Is it still there? Do you go to the cave?"

"No, but I think about it. I loved it there. I don't suppose you'd understand, but I don't want to go far from it. I want to stay here."

Sophie could see that her sister looked better already and sensed that Grace would collapse, exhausted by the visit, as soon as she left. "Would you let me get you someone to lend you a hand here? It'd be easier if another person helped Amy keep the place up."

"Who'd come?"

"There's an Anglican church just up the road in Kydd's Harbour. Let me go see what I can do."

"No minister in this 'ouse!" Amy suddenly interrupted.

"What if the minister is a woman like me? Would that be okay? Gracie needs assistance, Amy. Gracie is sicker than you know."

"I guess, but I won't get my 'opes up. Nobody's ever come to 'elp us afore now."

"I was able to get someone belonging to the parish in the next town to visit the cottage," Sophie said into the microphone. "At first, I paid her a salary, but soon the parish was able to take over and make sure Gracie and Amy were taken care of. I sent letters to Gracie through the woman, but she soon had Amy trekking to the post office and picking up my correspondence there. Gracie always wrote back promptly, and I relished reading her letters when they arrived. We never mentioned her father in any of our correspondence. He was already dead in our hearts. Unfortunately, we were close for only a few years after I first visited. Grace died in a hospital in Gander of complications from her polio. Amy, a poor tortured soul having to live alone, shot herself a few months later. Both girls were buried in an Anglican cemetery in Kydd's Harbour by the poor woman who cared for them both, closing the book on that part of my past."

It was late fall in St. Mark. Winter had held off but would soon clobber the town with snow. As she did not trust driving the car, Sophie would not make the trip to Brandy Point until spring, and the snowmobile was something she had never tried. Unfortunately, she missed Noah's ordination to the priesthood. He had explained in a letter that he had to be ordained as quickly as possible as over the winter there was no one in the surrounding area who could consecrate the bread and wine for communion. In another letter, he informed her that she had not missed much. The bishop drove up from Corner Brook, his parents making the trip too, but it had been a quiet affair otherwise.

Sophie spent most weekends with Ewan on the edge of town, and because of him, did not mind the cold beginning to seep into the areas of the Northern Peninsula. She was comfortable sitting with him in front of a roaring fire. Maybe too comfortable.

"I've got to go on the road for a while, Sophie," Ewan said one day.

"Why? Where are you going?"

"Until November or December when the ferry shuts down for the season, I'll cross the strait and then drive up the Labrador coast. There are patients that the hospital released in the last six months that we'd like to monitor. I can go from clinic to clinic visitin' the patients and examinin' records."

"Do you think it will take that long?"

"Actually not. And I won't do it in one trip. I'll be back several times. Do you want to stay here while I'm gone?"

"No. It's easier to walk to work from my apartment. I can visit here and water the plants and such if you'd like."

"That would be good. I'll call often," he whispered, nuzzling her ear.

"When do you leave?"

"Tuesday. I have surgery scheduled for tomorrow. I'm sure you won't miss me much."

Sophie smiled. "You're right. My patients satisfy me just as well."

"Now that I don't believe. I'm pretty hot and you know it!"

Icy winds buffeted the coastal communities after the first dusting of snow. Sophie worried that the relentless battering of storms would affect Ewan's trip, but every few nights, he called, assuring her that it did not. He returned from his first trip north within a week but was in consultation with Dr. Charles for much of the time he was at home. Sophie was unable to spend the first few nights with him at all. On the third night, he came to her apartment, exhausted. Sophie held him close as he fell asleep in her arms. The next day, he was on the road again. It was on that day that she went to the cottage to clean and water the plants.

Sophie was careful to dust around the articles on his desk, not wanting to mix any of his important documents, and almost did not notice the ring of keys pushed back under the stack. Sophie recognized the ring, having seen him use the keys to open cabinets in the hospital. She began to slip it into a drawer when she suddenly stopped. There were several keys on the ring. The cabinet ones were different from the door keys. She could identify the ones to certain doors because they matched those she had. But there was one that was different from all the others, and Sophie examined it closer, wondering what it was for. Instead of leaving the keys in the drawer, she slipped them into her pocket. It was probably nothing, but she could not wipe the nagging image from her mind.

The next day, she made a point of visiting the east wing elevator. Waiting until she was alone in the cage, she inserted that key into the keyhole. It turned. But she would do nothing then. She would wait until late at night when the hospital was least busy. Then she would see for herself what was causing the lights to go on and off in the rooms on the fourth floor.

Chapter 16

The Building Project

A group sat around a large table in the basement of the church in Sandy Rock. Early autumn along the coast was still warm, and those in the group hoped it meant a late start to the winter.

"I don't understand this expense," said Noah. "The church in Black Inlet needs new steps? Are the old ones falling apart?"

"Yes, Fader," explained Samuel Abbott, squirming in his seat. "How does it feel to be a real priest now? You be 'dained by de bishop last Sunday, right? Millie telled me dat dey made you permanent rector."

"Yes, Sam, I'm a real priest now."

"I knows who can fix dem steps, Fader."

"How much?"

"He be real cheap. Includin' lumber, it be less dan a dousand."

"Ask him who it be?" Lemon said, playing with his empty paper cup.

"Ye jest don't like him, dat's all, Hugh," said Sam. "But he be a member of the parish and a good builder."

"And Eunice's brother. I think he'd pose too great a risk, Father."

"What's the problem, other than the fact that he's Sam's brother in-law?"

"He be a caudler—well-meanin', but lewardly. What I mean is—"

"I know what you mean, Hugh. You're afraid he'll muddle the job. Do you have any examples?"

"Tell him 'bout Eunice's toilet, Abbott," Hugh Lemon said, turning to face the older man. "Tell Father Noah what happened afore she even flushed it."

"Now, now, Lemon. Dat had to do wid a build-up of gases in de line. Poor Eunice doesn't do well by dairy, 'specially milk and cheese."

"It blew up while she was still on the pot, didn't it? She got her pipes thoroughly cleaned out like a stogged horse connected to a hose. I'll bet she whinkered good for you, Abbot."

"My wife don't neigh, Lemon!" Sam said, beginning to get angry.

Noah tried not to laugh at Hugh's description of Eunice, but found it difficult to sound angry. "Why don't we get back to the issue here? What's his name?"

"Gilbert, Fader. Gilbert Minty," Sam offered.

"And does he have references other than Eunice's toilet?" Noah asked.

"Yes, Fader. He helped erect Nicky Nichols outbuildin' fer his skidoo."

"Hugh, is that acceptable to you?"

"It's still standin' though it only be built last spring and hasn't been tested by snow yet."

"He 'structed de stairs to May's front door. Dat be six years ago now."

"Yes, but he missed the door," Hugh said.

"And he did a good job of movin' dat door, didn't he?"

"Are there any other recommendations?" Noah asked. "I would hire Patrick, but no one's seen him since the funeral."

"I hears Millie chased him out of town," Abbot said. "I'd be gone too if Millie comed after me."

"Since we don't have that much time left before the snow messes up the project, I suggest we accept Gilbert on the grounds that he start immediately."

"So we be goin' with wood?" Hugh asked.

"What do you suggest, Hugh? I don't think we have time for cement. It's getting too cold for that."

"It'd last longer."

"And cost a whole lot more, and if not done professionally, would crack in a season or two. I think nice wooden steps will do. Sam, can you set it all up and get back to me by Friday?"

"Yes, Fader."

That out of the way, Noah had the rest of the day to fish. He collected his gear and headed for the dinghy tied to some rocks at the foot of his boulders. Starting to push his boat away from his makeshift pier, he heard Angus Clark come running toward him. The man was out of breath. He carried a pack on his shoulder and a pole in his hand.

"I needs to talk to you, Father Noah. I have an idea that would help us all out. You don't mind if we talks, do you?"

"No. We can talk softly while we fish," Noah said, letting Angus push off from the rocks while he primed the motor. "How's Effie?"

"She be good. Our son, Richard, works in Labrador, and she wants to go visit him afore the snow."

"What does he do?"

"He works for the government—something havin' to do with the native people north of Goose Bay. We have a daughter too, Father."

"Oh?"

"Marina's in Ontario. She majored in fashion at Memorial and gots a right good job there. Effie misses her something awful."

"I'm sure she does," said Noah, circling the end of the point. "What did you want to talk about?"

"The fishery been 'stributin' cuckoo pots to test the waters round these parts."

"Catching whelk?"

"Yup. Jacob and I be thinkin' we all might profit if we teamed up with the boys in Black Inlet, Sandy Rock, and Daisy Cove."

"What do you mean?"

"If Jacob Pearce and I offers to collect the catch each day from the other villages, we could get a pick-up and delivery from the plant in Port Newman. He and I would assemble the catch for the fish plant truck that comes here in the afternoon and then deliver needed pots and bait in the evenin'."

"That's a lot of boating for the two of you. Wouldn't it be better if Hugh or the others brought their catches to Brandy Point?"

"That's just it, Father. We charges for our services so that they can spend the time fishin'. They'd get a percentage, but Jacob and I would get more cuz we does so much of the work."

"How old is Jacob?"

"He be twenty. He has a girlfriend, Tulla, and they wants to get married at the church here. I thinks they be needin' the money."

"When does this trapping start up?"

"Oh. Not 'til spring."

"I can't see where it would hurt to try. You get the others to agree. I don't see any harm," Noah said, turning the boat into a quiet cove. "Why don't we throw the lines out here and relax, Angus. I think you can tackle the planning of this new company tomorrow."

Angus smiled proudly as he pulled out his pole and tore open the bait's wrapper.

The following week, Millie approached Noah about the school dance. Noah told her that he needed to supervise the church building in Black Inlet and would leave the parish hall and the planning to her.

"I hears you hired Gil Minty."

"Yes. Is there a problem?"

"Only that I'd be able to supervise twenty teens better than you can do over Gilbert Minty."

"I've talked to him on the phone. He seems really easy to get along with. I told him how much was in the budget for the wood, and it's all set to be delivered next Wednesday."

"Good, you be free this Friday evenin' to chaperone the teens. They looks up to you, Father."

"I'm sure you don't need me to help you do that. I've met them all, and I don't see what they could do that's wrong, Millie."

Millie stopped and stared until he looked back. "You don't see what a young couple could do to get into trouble? I knows you be a minister and all, but I can't believe you never took a glutch of rum when your Ma wasn't round or never jigged a girl behind a rock, Father."

Noah felt his face go hot.

"You just thinks 'bout what you did and you can be sure as the deer beat to the south afore the first snow them kids will have already tried it."

The fellow knocked on the rectory door. Dishtowel in hand, Noah did not hesitate to answer it.

"Gilbert Minty?"

"Yes, Father Noah. You wanted to talk over the plans for the church in Black Inlet?"

"Come in, come in. I was just finishing in the kitchen."

Minty followed him in and waited in the hall as Noah returned to wash and dry the last few dishes. Minty wandered over to the photographs, hanging on the wall. "Who's this?" he asked.

Noah sauntered in, still wiping a dish. "That's my ordination in Corner Brook."

"No. I means the looker."

"The woman? She was ordained with me. Her name is Sophie."

"You must have jigged her a time or two, eh?"

"No. She's a chaplain in St. Mark"

"How could you not? She be a beauty—that red hair and all. If I didn't have my Martha, I'd head my truck north and see what I could do myself. What's a matter with ye, Father? Don't you have eyes? What's wrong with her?"

"There's nothing wrong with her, Gilbert. I just never asked her."

"Since when do you ask 'em? You gots to make a move on 'em," Minty said, rocking his hips to show Noah how to do it.

Noah smiled. "I did. It didn't work."

"I can tell you be sorry 'bout failin' with her. I can see you still want her."

"What?"

"You hanged the picture on the wall here so you sees her every time you comes in the door or climbs the stairs. Go there and get her afore it's too late."

"Maybe I need a reminder of why I'm here doing what I'm doing," said Noah, smiling as he thought about why he really hung the pictures there. "I agree something's wrong. I guess I have my parents' genes. Anyway, in her last letter, she said she had a fellow."

"Did she tell you it that way? I mean, the way you puts it, she didn't say they was serious. Do you 'member zactly what she said?"

"I don't expect her to turn down someone who's sincere about a relationship. I'm not sure I'm marriage material," Noah explained, looking through stacks of papers in his living room. "Where did I put those figures? Did you bring an extra copy of the bill for the lumber?"

"Yes. I gots that and a buildin' plan. The total be six hundred dollars. I drew on the print to show you how I 'tend to support the steps and hook 'em onto the buildin's brick facin'. Sophie you say?"

"Yes. She'll be here in the spring. All my friends from seminary are coming in the spring."

"So I'll get to meet the sweet young lady?"

"Yes. I'll introduce you but only if you promise to leave her be. Do you want something to drink while we go over the plans?"

"Rum," Minty said. "I'll leave her be if you promises to make a move. I could give her a night of fireworks she'd never forget. Wouldn't want that one to go to waste, would we?"

"Like the one you gave Eunice? I doubt she's forgotten it," Noah said spreading the plans out on the dining room table. "Now, lets see what you have here, Gil."

"I never tells anyone I be a plumber, Father. I'll splain each step here as soon as you fill her up again," Minty said, handing Noah the empty glass.

Noah arrived at the parish hall late. The noise already blasted into the moonless fall night. A young deejay had hooked up a microphone in front of a tape machine, and the volume was pumped up so high, the party-goers could not hear each other speak. Noah was tempted to go to the front and turn everything down but did not. There was not a big crowd, just about a dozen couples, more girls than boys. Passing a few smokers standing near the entrance, he strolled inside to look for Millie. She emerged from the kitchen carrying an empty punch bowl.

"What happened?" Noah yelled over the din.

"It be already spiked. I gots extra soda here to refill it clean. There be twenty-five kids. You has to keep countin' heads and check behind the stage curtains. If a couple disappears, you gots to look for 'em. I made sure the church be locked. Then there be the beach. One of us has to make the rounds, you know."

"I don't think you have to worry that much, Millie."

She gave him the eye.

"But I'll try to see how I can help you," he assured her.

"There. I just sees one go out to pee. That be Nan. She be dancin' with Adam. Now we gots to watch Adam so he doesn't head for the toilet too. When the music gets slow, it be worse."

"They're slippery. I don't know who is with whom."

"That's why you counts heads. There be fourteen girls and eleven boys. One girl and two boys be out smokin', Nan be in the toilet, and Adam just slipped out the door," she said, her eyes darting. "I'll go check the toilet, and you find Adam outside."

"Who'll watch the dance floor? I always made my moves during the dancing."

Millie stopped and turned around, letting him know that his comments were not appreciated. "I has my spies," she finally said. "You don't think I could do this by myself, do you?"

The dance wore on. Noah stifled a yawn. It was taking forever for the hour hand on the wall clock to reach eleven. Millie was as vigilant as she was hours earlier. Except for the spies who remained invisible to Noah, Millie managed the group single-handedly. She would bark her instructions to Noah, and he would obey without question. Twice, he caught couples sneaking away. He was not sure what to do with them once he caught them. He would clear his throat, and let them know that he was watching them. Somehow they understood and returned to the hall. Not a dancer left before eleven, probably because Millie would not have let them leave. And when they had all headed home, Millie handed Noah a broom and told him to sweep the floors. She would wash the dishes and sponge the tables. Not a spy remained in sight to help with the clean-up. The parish hall would be sparkling before he left after midnight.

"How do you know they all went directly home?" he asked.

"The parents be spectin' them by eleven-ten. It not be our problem. It be up to the parents to make sure they gets home," she replied.

"Was it like this when you went to school?"

"Heavens no. We didn't have year-round schoolin' or church when we was young. We be so bored, we'd all meet in groups on the beach with no one to watch us."

"So you guys were pretty experienced, eh?"

"There'd be lots of weddin's when the preacher showed up in the spring cuz all the girls carried the evidence in their bellies and the boys had no wheres to run."

The morning was frosty, a haze suspended between the trees like a line of freshly extinguished campfires. It would be a few hours before the sun peeked over the uppermost branches. Another car pulled up beside his, and Noah reluctantly got out to see how the project was going. Hugh Lemon jumped out of the other car before two or three more pulled into the parking lot.

"Hi Father, come to see the unveilin'?"

"A little early, Hugh. I think he's just got the supports up. I sure hope the cement holding the posts has set properly in this cold."

"Don't worry." Lemon said, "I doubt the thought has even crossed Minty's mind."

Noah turned to glare at him and noticed who was getting out of the other cars. "What's this, a rooting section?"

"You didn't spect us to stay home when the steps are finally bein' fixed," said Effie. "Angus, here's your tea. Do any of you want tea? I brought toast too, if you be hungry."

The others, including Lemon, circled the Clarks' car. Noah approached the church and inspected the work.

"This looks pretty good, Gil. What did you use to attach the frame to the wall?"

"Three by fives. They'll never pull out, Father. They be stuck fast to the wall with screws every meter or so."

Noah pulled on the crossbeams and then jiggled the posts. "When did you put in the cement to set these?"

"Monday afternoon. The weather be warm for several hours on Monday. It be quick dryin' so it was set afore I leaves the site."

Noah turned around. The crowd had grown, all standing around their cars talking and eating. "When's the lumber delivery?"

"Any time now, Father. He said he'd be here by nine, and I thinks I hears the truck now."

There was not enough room in the parking lot for the truck to pull in and turn around so Minty directed the driver to back in. The minister, the driver, and Minty helped pile the load in the far corner of the lot.

"Do you want me to get help from your fans to lug those boards closer to the church?" Noah asked.

"No. I gots a truckle back home, a two-pronger. I'll go get her. Mind ye, she'll make quite a roaration in 'mong these trees cuz this be a heavy load. I'll go get her now."

Noah turned around, noticing that the audience now numbered more than a dozen. Millie had brought sandwiches. He searched for the tea lady to see if there was anything hot left.

"What's he doin' now?" asked Lemon.

"He's got a fork-lift at home and is going to get it."

"Really? How's the framework look?"

"Fine. Go check it out yourself. Nothing's going to pull these steps down."

A half-hour later, the engine of the fork-lift sputtered and backfired as it turned off the highway into the lot. Minty pushed down on the accelerator as he passed the crowd. The engine roared until many had to cover their ears. Black smoke blew out of an exhaust pipe affixed to a crossbar beside his head, but the homemade contraption did not seem to move any faster.

"I'm jest goin' to prong the boards closer to the church, Father," he announced.

The crowd that was not choking on the smoke, howled in encouragement. Noah looked at them disapprovingly. The whole thing was beginning to look like a circus. He walked over to the pile and watched Minty prong some of the long boards, haul them over next to the new deck, and then return to the pile for more.

On the fourth lap, the unthinkable happened. Losing interest in the repetitive work, the crowd had gone back to serving themselves breakfast, leaving Minty and Noah to finish the job. Noah watched the crowd in disbelief but turned around in time to see Minty, a load across his prongs, bend over to work on his accelerator pedal. The truckle was heading in the wrong direction. Noah started to run after the fork-lift, waving his arms and trying to yell over the roaration of Minty's souped-up engine, but Minty had his back to him. It was too late when he finally turned the wheel to correct the problem. The exhaust pipe of Minty's truckle slipped under the secured frame of the landing and began to tow it away from the wall of the church. The sound of the fork-lift could not erase that of the wall crackling as the sturdy support board wrenched away from the rest of the building. Particles from the disintegrating bricks, mortar, and inside drywall, produced a billowing cloud. The crowd stood and stared at the gaping hole, revealing the interiors of both the basement and the nave above it. Bending down in an attempt to restore some composure, Noah had stopped looking. Minty turned off the engine of his truckle and climbed down to appraise the situation. The silence echoed among the tall trees of the forest that encircled the parking lot.

The inevitable visit from Bishop Edmonds came on Friday, not even a week after Noah's ordination. Noah did not dare go fishing or sit on the boulders when he knew the visit was imminent but did make sure anyone else that might exaggerate the offenses was not around. Certainly Millie had every right to complain even though Father Noah was not directly responsible for the deaths of her daughter and grandchild. The warden in Black Inlet would grumble, no doubt. The loss of the building fund, and more notably, that of the community's beloved church loomed big in light of the doubts the bishop most certainly had about Noah's ability to run the parish.

"Noah, how are things going here? Do you trust they are moving along smoothly? Is there anything I can help with?"

"Yes, sir. I feel like I'm making a difference here. Of course, there have been a few incidents—"

"I would be surprised if there weren't. You're not only a new priest but still inexperienced in life. I suppose seeing a dead baby might make one feel so strongly that he has trouble controlling his stomach."

"I didn't expect to find the baby dead, sir. It caught me by surprise. If I had understood, I'd probably wouldn't have forgotten to say a prayer over the bodies. I returned minutes later and led the family in prayers."

"You must remember that you wouldn't have been called to the home unless it was for a passing. You must always prepare yourself, but I won't belabor the point."

"We have an economic problem. I don't know how I'm expected to request money from the diocese."

The bishop smiled. "If you know where in the diocese the extra money is kept, I would like to be told. The truth is, we don't have a slush fund for this sort of thing. There is insurance. You can apply for that. If it isn't enough, you'll have to try to make up the difference through a fundraiser of some sort. I'm not really here to go over your injudiciousness, Noah. I know you are well aware of your weaknesses and expect that you'll make sure you don't repeat any of them. I do think, however, that you could use some help."

"I can handle this parish, sir. I don't think you need to waste resources by sending in another ordained priest to show me what to do."

The bishop laughed. "You're correct, Noah. I don't have resources like that to waste by putting two of them in this parish. I do have someone that can be a personal resource to you, however. His name is Mathias Gabriel. He has a parish, St. Augustine in Corner Brook, but he's also a psychologist. I have used him as a spiritual director for others when it was necessary. I've already told him you'll be visiting. Maybe the two of you can decide what's best for you and for your parish."

Noah stood up. "Thank you, yes. I was just wondering—"

"No, your father doesn't attend St. Augustine. I don't think your father attends any of the churches around Corner Brook at all. Nor does Mathias know your mother," the bishop said, walking with Noah to the door.

"Thank you, sir. I promise I'll try harder."

"I'm not sure trying is what's needed, Noah. It's wisdom. Sometimes it comes with age and at other times with experience. You're certainly getting the experience. Take advantage of it, boy."

Chapter 17

The Big Gun

Winter arrived with ferocity. Snow piled up on the roads and parking lots, and the road-clearing began. Mounds grew by the roadside, and hillocks swelled along the edges of the lots. Sish, a slushy ice, formed in the bay, and boats hissed as they slogged through it. Hopefully, the light snow would come and go until Christmas, leaving the hard freeze until later. The ice did not usually seal St. Mark off from the rest of the world until mid-January. Of course, if they could, they would try to clear the roads. If not, the skidoo would become an important form of transportation.

Sophie did not really have time to think about the changes outside. She was busy trying to keep her patients healthy. Just two weeks before Christmas, when everyone was busy assembling ornaments for a big tree in the lobby and hanging decorations in each of the wards, one of them did not make it. Post-polio syndrome victim Lizzy Gleason, now a close friend of Sophie's, was taken off her respirator. When Dr. Ellis turned off the machine, the minister stood beside her bed, stroking her hand. Both she and the doctor sat there for nearly a half-hour until he declared Lizzy dead.

"Thanks, Dan. I appreciate your staying."

"I feel devastated. I'm sure she won't be the last we lose. We're sending the body to St. John's so they can examine her to find out what happened. I hope you can get the family to sign the papers. I know they've talked to you about a service in the chapel."

"I'll try. I think there's time. I'm not sure the cemetery is still open for business. We may have to wait until spring to get a plot prepared. If the ground isn't yet frozen, it will be pretty soon."

"I hear you, but this has to be sooner. The tissue will break down even if the body's frozen. In fact, it should be today or tomorrow."

"I understand. I'll get on that immediately, but they'd be here already if they could. They're coming from St. John's, and the roads haven't been too good. I know we couldn't have waited longer to let her go but I think they would've wanted to be here."

"I told them a week ago and the airport's open. I'm not sure they were that close or they would've visited when Lizzy was first admitted."

The family arrived the next day, and Sophie gave them the bad news. "It's important that the body be flown to St. John's right away. Post-polio syndrome is something we know very little about, and there are victims out there who need to be helped," Sophie explained.

"I don't mean to sound disrespectful, Reverend Hawkins, but our religion tells us to bury the body in a cemetery. The body is a temple, you know. I can't stomach takin' out pieces and only buryin' part of her."

"It's Sophie, by the way. I understand your fears, Mr. Olding. It's just that I don't think God wants us to ignore the suffering of others," Sophie said, pausing. "It was my understanding that she had children. They didn't come with you?"

"Lizzy had a son, Billy, but he's in England and can't come. He's asked me to make the necessary decisions."

"We can have that service tomorrow morning then, Mr. Olding."

"We want to get back afore the weather changes again. Can't you have that memorial thing this afternoon? We're all ready to attend."

"I'm rather busy. If you sign the papers to transport her body to St. John's, I might be able fit it in so it can be taken immediately. You wouldn't be able to stay for the burial anyway."

"What do you mean?"

"I don't think she can be buried before spring thaw, Mr. Olding. And that being the case, St. John's could be finished and have her shipped back in time to be buried here. If you would like, we can wait for the burial until spring."

"For that matter, I guess she could be buried in St. John's. We have a family plot there."

"That's sounds perfect. After a study at the laboratory, she'll be buried in the spring. I'll set up a memorial service for this afternoon. Do you want to celebrate communion with that? If so, I'll have Father Theo at the church here consecrate some bread and wine."

Sophie ate dinner in her apartment and waited. Just after midnight, she donned a jacket, grabbed a flashlight, and headed for the hospital. As she approached the door to the east wing, the hum she usually heard got louder. She checked the fourth floor windows for lights. The rooms were all dark. A small emergency ward flourished at the end of the west wing, but the rooms in the east had settled down for the night. Sophie marched directly to the elevator.

When the doors opened, a nursing sister emerged. "Oh, Sophie," she said, her hand over her chest. "You scared me. I didn't see you in the dark hallway. Do you have work tonight?"

"Yes," Sophie lied. "Mrs. Ridley on the second floor wanted a prayer. I totally forgot to deliver it to her earlier and thought I might leave a copy at the station so she could get it in the morning."

"That's so sweet of you, but when you go to bed so late, I don't see how you can get up in time in the morning to work."

Sophie entered the cage and let the doors slide shut. The thought of meeting someone else in the elevator scared her more than what she was about to do, but the cage stopped at the third floor and the doors opened without incident. The hallway was completely black and deserted. Her heart thumped vigorously, but she carefully inserted the key, turning it with shaking hands. Then she pushed the button. When the doors reopened, the darkness hit her once more, and she bravely stepped into the chasm. The buzz she had heard for months now sounded more like voices eerily calling out her name.

Sophie turned to face the length of the wing and flashed her light down the hall. On either side, open heavy doors revealed gaping holes. The passageway was narrow, but she managed to take a few steps forward. When Sophie reached the first door, she shone her light through the opening. Inside, a stripped mattress rested on top of an old coil-spring bed. Relieved the chamber was empty, she entered, touching the bed and metal cabinet beside it. Opening the cabinet doors, she flashed the light inside and tugged at a handful of leather straps, dropping them immediately when her hand began to shake again.

Feeling her way back out into the corridor, she continued her march toward a set of double doors at the end of the passage. The voices bellowed. Sophie imagined the incarnations of ill patients emerging from the rooms and flashed the light in the direction of each voice. Suddenly the flashlight dimmed, and when she looked up, ethereal creatures soared above her head. Her first instinct was to run. But she feared the elevator would not respond quickly enough to her summons and allow the specters to surround and corner her. Her feet frozen, she shook the flashlight, but the beam did not get stronger.

Then she remembered what Griffon had told her so long ago. The spirits were not there to attack her but probably wanted to tell her something, to warn her about a pending danger. She reflected on Alice at Warfield. Dr. Fairbourne had pointed out that the apparitions were benign, probably trying to convince her that she could not save the young girl and should not feel responsible for her death.

"What do you want?" she asked, her voice more bold than she thought possible.

The moans cut the dense air and the spirits swirled.

"What do you want of me?" she asked again.

Her feet still tingling and knees wobbling, she inched forward, pushing on the doors and entering the next ward. This one had equipment.

"An old lab," she whispered, studying an antiquated Bunsen burner by a window through which the full moon conveyed a wide swathe of light.

There were test tubes and even a microscope but not enough light to see what was being studied. The cupboard on the wall above held syringes and bottles of iodine. Ignoring the vortex of twinkling stars that caromed off the top of the wall and ceiling, Sophie gained confidence. She tugged at a notebook on the shelf, but pages began to fall out, dust billowing around them. She pushed it back.

Spinning around, she detected a door on the other side of the room. Her curiosity grew as she crossed it and urged the door open. The flashlight strengthened when she entered. Along the far end, a table beckoned her. The entities chattered and swooshed at her hair. She batted them away.

"Wait!" she whispered as she studied the table with the flashlight. At its foot, a red light on the face of a box flashed erratically. It crackled and buzzed. "Hush!"

Pointing the flashlight at the box, she slowly drew near it, tripping on some wires that had tumbled from the table onto the floor. Her attention diverted, she bent down to pick up the earphones that lay at her feet. The voices went wild, and the spirits, flying in front of her face, blinded her! Swatting at them, she stood up again.

"The box," she whispered, shining the light on it once more.

There seemed to be a dial that had been set on high. She turned it down. The voices continued to rant, but the specters began to retreat into the corner. She continued to turn the dial until the light went out. The chatter became a moan. When she bent over once more to gather the headset from the floor, the flurry did not repeat itself. Holding the device steady under the beam of light, she examined it closely.

"My dear God," she whispered, noticing the web of wires growing out of the frame.

Setting the lighted flashlight on the table, Sophie scrutinized the earpieces, which were round and flat. These were not designed to send sound to the ears. The round disks fit onto the temples. This must have been a table used to treat patients with electro-convulsive shock therapy. Sophie's stomach spun in disgust. The electricity flowing through the wires would have given her quite a shock, if not worse.

"You saved my life," she whispered quietly to the fading souls. "I'm so sorry you had to endure such pain from people that were supposed to help you."

She gazed up toward the ceiling. The hands that had earlier grasped at her head disappeared. Only clouds of light, like the undulating vapors of the northern lights, circled overhead. The remaining moans mimicked the rolling waves on a summer day.

"You were right, Griffon. I'll never fear them again."

Sophie smiled to herself but not for long. The resonance of footsteps was unmistakable. The ghosts above her head began to circle cautiously. She was sure the sound came from the next ward over. Not only that, but the footsteps were getting louder!

Sophie did not pause for a warning—did not wait to hear the voices build up again. Whoever had turned on the power to the box would probably not hesitate to use it on someone who had inadvertently discovered a secret. She reached for her flashlight only to have it slip from her fingers into a dark corner of the table. Unable to take the time to feel for it, Sophie ran out of the room through the double doors toward the elevator. Repeatedly pushing the button, she finally pressed her face against the cold metal and listened to a conversation in the cage below. The doors opened somewhere, but the talking continued. They did not shut again. She wanted to call out for help but did not dare. Above the button, her fingers traced a lock, and she fumbled in her pocket for the key.

The footsteps were now in the next ward over—the laboratory. She could see the reflection of the moonlight slide across the surfaces as the doors leading from the old lab began to swing toward her. Slipping into the dark recesses beyond the elevator, she fell against another door, closed but not latched. The knob finally turned in her sweaty hand, and not more than three meters away, a dim lamp glowed faintly up the stairwell. Racing down the stairs, she quickly reached the door leading to the third floor landing. Light from the landing flooded in when she opened it. She did not stop there but stumbled all the way down to the street floor.

Instead of leaving through the side entrance to return to her apartment, Sophie walked down the west wing to the emergency room. Pausing at a machine, she bought some tea and then sat among the patients in the waiting room. When she had calmed down, she exited the ward and walked swiftly up the road on the west side. Before turning onto the first street and disappearing behind a line of houses, she gazed back at the east wing. Though not so distinct, the voices were there. And a light shone through a window on the fourth floor.

Ewan came to the chapel just as Sophie was preparing to go home. Luckily, she was alone. She ran into his open arms.

"I'm so glad you're back!" she said.

Ewan smiled. "Me too. I hate havin' to travel all the time. Hopefully this will make some of it up to you," he said, pulling a little box out of his pocket. "It was my grandmother's ring. It's not as spectacular as I would have liked to get you, but it means a lot to me."

Sophie let him put it on her finger. "It's beautiful!" she said, "I love it."

"And?"

"And yes. I'd be happy to marry you, Ewan," she finally said, tears streaming down her face.

She did not think about his key to the fourth floor or about the way he dismissed her concern when she showed him the lighted window. She only felt joy that such a wonderful man wanted who to spend the rest of his life with her.

The day was cold. As he walked out of the rectory, Noah could see his breath. And the icy air made it difficult for his engine to turn over right away. Once he was on the road, however, the five hour trip was smooth. The scenery around St. Augustine was gorgeous. He walked into the nave and spun around to admire it's beauty. Light broke through some of the panes of stained glass. The pews were polished from years of use. Magnificently carved designs adorned the pulpit.

"May I help you?" a voice asked.

Noah turned to see the tall man in a long black cassock. His dark hair flopped boyishly over his deeply chiseled face.

"Mathias Gabriel? How do you do? I'm Noah Lodge. I hope you were expecting me."

"Yes. Andrew mentioned that you were coming to see me today. He said something about you having questions about your calling."

"I know I've been called but am not sure why everything gets mucked up so badly."

"Ah, please have a seat. I just have to see if I can get these little windows above the stained glass panels closed. It's starting to get cold and damp. Your muscles probably tell you as much as mind do about the time of the year," he said, trying to loop the end of a pole through a latch above his head. "I can listen while I do this. Tell me why you chose the priesthood to begin with."

"I'm pretty good at convincing people about faith and God."

"Ah, yes. I think Andrew mentioned that you had a knack for giving wonderful sermons. And you didn't run for office because you didn't want to move to Ontario?"

Noah looked surprised. "I don't enjoy politics. I suppose I never got into it."

"When did you feel you were called? How old were you?"

"I guess I was pretty young. I was a server in St. Ambrose on the peninsula outside of Stephenville."

"Go on. Convince me you had some sort of calling to become a priest."

"I didn't then. I was just drawn to it. I loved Sundays, especially when Father Timothy performed high mass with incense and glorious organ music. I was good at public speaking at school. I just figured God gave me the talent so I could use it to serve him."

Mathias turned to face him. "Did you have many friends while you were growing up?"

"No. When I was young, I was sort of ferried between parents. Whenever I made a friend, I would have to move to the other house before we got close."

"So your parents were divorced?"

"Yes, when I was young. I don't remember the big split. I don't even remember them fighting. By the time I was old enough to realize what had happened, they were living apart."

"What had happened?"

"Pardon?"

"How did it happen?"

"I don't know. I told you that it had already occurred before I knew that married people were supposed to stay together."

"And you never asked your mother or father about it?"

"No. Why hurt them by dredging up the past? They were happy living separately."

"So they never complained to you openly."

"No. It was all very civil. I was to go with my father when he wanted me and to stay with my mother the rest of the time."

"Were there times when your father didn't want you?"

"He was a very busy man. He manages the paper mill here in town, you know."

"I've heard the name, yes. When you visited, how did you know when he no longer wanted you to stay?"

"I guess he just told me that it was time to pack up, and I did."

"You didn't say that you wanted to stay and finish the school term or tell him that you had a date with friends the next week?"

"No."

"Why not? Were you afraid of him?"

Noah squirmed. "Why make a scene? Things go smoother if you let it go."

"Would your objection to leaving create a scene?"

"I don't know."

"And your mother. Why didn't she get mad when he wanted to come and get you at inconvenient times? I suppose sometimes she did want you to stay, didn't she?"

"I guess."

"But she didn't say anything?"

"No."

"Why not? Was she afraid of him?"

"I think she might have been afraid of losing child support."

"I understand. She feared losing the money that made you two comfortable. Do you believe your father would have taken away the money if she had objected?"

"Yes."

"Then your mother did ask at least once."

"Yes. I was four or five, not yet in school. Grammy and Grampy were coming from Halifax. My mother was from Halifax. She told him they wanted to see me. He refused, and shattering the glass, threw a chair through a window. I suppose I forgot about that. When I came back after my grandparents had left, the window had been fixed."

"That's pretty serious. I mean, if he would throw a chair through a window in anger, what else might he do? But your mother wasn't worried that he might hurt her or you?"

"I don't know. Maybe."

"Do you still see him?"

"Yes. But not very often."

"Does he see your mother?"

"I think so. She says he comes over now and then."

"Why? Do you have younger siblings?"

"No. I'm an only child."

"What hold does he have on her now that you're gone?"

"I would think he still pays her something."

"But you don't know if he threatens to take it away," Mathias speculated, sliding into the pew in front of Noah and turning to face him.

"No. My mother doesn't talk about it."

"Did he want you to become a priest?"

"No. I was to go into the business."

"Did your mother want you to become a priest?"

"Not really. She didn't expect me to follow through on that."

"She expected you to work with your father?"

"Yes. I think so."

"I guess what troubles me is why, when you wouldn't question your father on anything he did concerning you and your mother, you all of a sudden decided to go against his wishes."

"It wasn't sudden. I had planned it for a long time."

"Did you tell them?"

"No."

"So what made you defy them after letting them run your life until then?"

"I guess I grew up and moved away to university."

"But you still haven't asked your mother why she and your father split up."

"No. That's her business. Why should I hurt her again?"

"But that's not you hurting her, is it? Don't you mean, make her unhappy by reminding her of distressing things that occurred in the past?"

"Yes."

"Have you had any relationships since you moved away?"

Noah blushed. "Yes, plenty."

"You've been in school for seven and out for let's say one year. How many is plenty?"

"I guess it depends on what you call a relationship," Noah said, clearing his throat and looking around for water to wet his dry mouth.

"Two people love each other and not only show it intimately but ponder a deeper commitment. Most people have two, maybe three, in that period of time if they're lucky. How many have you had?"

"What has this got to do with my ministry?"

Mathias rose and slid toward the steps leading to the altar. "I would think anyone who has lived through a childhood as wretched as yours might have trouble with commitment."

"I don't see what you mean."

"Your father was obviously a tyrant, and your mother, extremely weak. What a way to grow up!"

Noah sat back and crossed his arms.

"Aren't you going to get mad at me? I just insulted your family. I can't believe you're not up here ready to punch me out, Noah."

"I don't think you're worth the effort."

"So you are able to use sarcasm," Mathias noted.

Noah stared back at him.

"That's a start," Mathias said, his elbow resting on his knee.

"You haven't told me what my past has to do with being a priest."

"Haven't I? You vomit when a woman meets a violent death and you let this hick builder walk all over you when others have recommended you not use him. What'll be next?"

"I didn't think the vomiting was so strange. I'm not used to seeing women die during childbirth. I'm not used to the blood."

"Aren't you? Maybe your mother didn't give birth to a child in front of you, but don't tell me you never saw a woman being treated violently. Did you throw up when you saw your mother bleeding?"

Noah stood up.

"Sit down, Noah. I'm sorry if I'm expecting so much out of you."

"She hit her head on the floor! She didn't bleed when he hit her."

"But there was blood on her head and maybe even on the floor after he threw her down. Is that why you never questioned your father when you lived with him?"

"I think I can help these people, Gabriel."

"You can call me Mathias, Noah. You're pushing me away when you call me that. I think you can help these people too. But I believe you have to help yourself first."

Noah uncrossed his arms and leaned forward. "The bishop didn't say these minor incidents at Brandy Point happened because I had problems, you know. He said I was inexperienced."

"These minor episodes, as Andrew described them, are just the beginning. If he thought you were going to learn from them on your own, he wouldn't have sent you to me. I'm the 'big gun' in this part of the province! I handle the priests who need help before their muck-ups lead to permanent damage!"

Chapter 18

Reunion

Sophie did not want to leave him. After all, she had not seen him much all winter. But spring was upon them, and the others were all coming to visit Noah and celebrate his becoming a priest and official rector of the parish of Brandy Point. She had to go. After making sure her patients could tolerate the few days she would be gone, Sophie drove out of the noisy din toward the coastal town of Brandy Point.

"There she is," said Ben, coming down the steps of the rectory and running to give her a hug. "We can't wait to find out about your job at the hospital."

"Oh, Ben. It's seems like forever since we've talked. Is Rachel here too?"

"Yes, we brought the baby. Since we're all staying here, I'm not sure we'll get much sleep."

"How old is Jessie?"

"Two and a handful."

"Which one of you does she look like?"

"Mostly Rachel, thank goodness. Can I help you with your bags? When are you going back?"

"On Sunday after the service. I wouldn't miss that for anything. What about you?"

"I think we're leaving Saturday. That gives us two good days. This thing is hard on Rachel."

"Oh?"

"I don't think she likes traveling with Jessie. You can understand why," said Ben, pulling the bags out of the trunk of Sophie's car. "They're out back. I'll take these inside if you want to walk around."

Sophie strolled over the rocks in the side yard and discovered a small patch of grass behind the rectory. Beyond, a field with long stalks and wildflowers framed the shimmering sea. She stopped to watch the hazy sun reflect off the waves and a couple of icebergs linger near the shore across the Strait of Belle Isle along the coast of Quebec.

Suddenly, Noah came around the corner of the house to meet her. "Hi. Want a beer? Come join the crowd."

Sophie gazed at him.

"You look good, Sophie," he said, kissing her on the cheek. "It seems like we've been doing our jobs for years, doesn't it? Come round here and talk to everyone. Don't be shy."

Sophie let him take her hand and guide her to the others. Rachel sat in a folding chair with Jessie on her lap. She did not stand but let Sophie give her a kiss and examine the baby.

"She's beautiful!" Sophie announced. "And look how big. Ben said she looks like you, but she's big and healthy like her father. She looks like she'll have his fair hair."

"Sophie, I can't believe I'm finally seeing you again. What has it been—over a year?"

"It seems like forever," Sophie replied. "Hi, Cyril, what are you up to? Are you still planning to go to Ottawa?"

"I came from Ottawa so I guess so."

"What are you doing?"

"Kieran and I teamed up with a start-up production company. We're working on the technical stuff, which is integral to most of the movies produced these days," he announced, pulling the cap off another beer. "And you—I can't believe how you look. That sundress is so stylish."

"I'm fine if I don't take off the sweater. It's still too cold. The icebergs reminded me of that. I might have to go into the house and change into something warmer."

"I'm sure you'll look great in anything."

Noah asked Ben to take over at the barbeque. "I have to retrieve rolls. Cyril, will you bring the condiments out?"

Sophie ran up the steps, hoping to put on some long pants. "Where did you put my bags, Ben?"

"In your room. Upstairs to the right. You and Rachel are sharing. Hope you don't mind the baby in with you. I thought it might be better if Rachel, Jess, and I got the downstairs, but Rachel thought you might object to sleeping with Cyril."

"The baby's fine. Rachel and I can talk about you guys after we go to bed," she said, following his directions.

At the bottom of the stairs, she stopped to look at the pictures.

Noah came up beside her. "I should have made copies for you."

"I'll say. I appear so nervous though. And sick."

"I think you look great. I, on the other hand, seemed to have taken a dive into the bishop's lap."

"I know he came for the ordination last fall, but have you seen him otherwise?"

"Unfortunately, yes."

"Why, what happened?"

"I'll discuss it with you when the others aren't around. I don't think they want to listen to shop talk. You'll be here until Sunday, won't you?"

"Yes. And the others are leaving Saturday. That means we should get the tour tomorrow before it's too late."

"Tour?"

"Of the churches in your parish. I want to feel what it's like to be a rector. We could do it this evening, but I don't think you want a bunch of drunks smelling up the naves. We might just run into one of your assistants."

"Sounds like you're planning some fun. I hope you brought more alcohol with you. I believe we'll run out before we get that sloshed."

When Sophie returned in her slacks, she grabbed a hamburger roll and sat down at the small picnic table. "Oh, I nearly forgot! I have an announcement," she said, holding the back of her left hand in front of their eyes.

"You're excused," Cyril said, reaching across the table for a handful of fries.

"Oh Sophie!" cried Rachel, noticing the ring. "I didn't know you had a boyfriend. When did this happen?"

"Just this week. He's been on the road and sprung it on me when he got back."

"What's he do?" Ben asked. "I hope he lives in St. Mark."

"He's a hospital surgeon visiting from Scotland."

"When does he plan to go back?" asked Cyril. "Are you going with him then?"

"I suppose," said Sophie, concerned "I hadn't really thought about it."

Ben turned to watch Noah, standing over the burgers. "Did you hear that, buddy? Sophie's getting married."

"Yes. Wonderful. He's a lucky guy."

"I'll take that last beer, Noah. I do believe you're past the happy stage."

"I'm fine, but you and Cyril can fight over the last one. Did anyone bring wine or something even stronger?"

"Isn't there a bar or store here?" Cyril asked.

"There's a liquor store along the highway," Noah said.

"What's strong enough for you, Noah? How about scotch?"

"Maybe you ought to get something the ladies can add mix to."

"I'll get something I like, then. Anyone else want anything?"

The sun sank over the water, the surface taking on a silvery glow. The group sat around the small living room, continuing to talk. Rachel was the first to get up.

"Well, I'm taking Jessie to bed and will probably not be down again. If you want that talk, Sophie, you're going to have to come up soon because I'll be dead asleep shortly after my head hits the pillow."

"I'm coming, Rachel. We're getting up early tomorrow so we can take the tour, right? Do I have breakfast duty?"

"I thought you'd be better at dish duty, Sophie," said Ben. "Noah and I can fix the toast and eggs."

"Sounds good to me. I don't mind letting you guys do most of the work. Good night."

Sophie pulled the blankets up around her neck and waited for her friend to climb in. "Just like the old days, isn't it?" she whispered to Rachel.

"Yes. Now tell me more about that hunk you're going to marry. Are we invited to the wedding?"

"Of course," she said, trying to talk about Ewan without missing him more. "What can I say? He's got dark hair and blue eyes if that's what you want to know. He's smart and treats me so well."

"Is he good in bed?"

"What do you mean?" Sophie asked, laughing. "Sure, I guess. I'm afraid I've nothing to compare him to."

"Compared to Noah, for example."

"Lest you forget, Noah and I were never lovers. We've always been friends."

"I don't believe that."

"Did Noah say we did anything?"

"No. I didn't ask him. I just assumed—"

"You're the one who attracted Noah. You and he had an affair, remember?"

"Yes, and he and I had the best sex I've ever experienced."

"I'm sure Ben is quite good in bed, Rachel."

Rachel did not answer.

"I don't think I want to know about your conquests anyway," Sophie continued. "You've got a beautiful baby to show for it."

"He wanted you, you know."

"Ben? I know for sure he didn't want me. He kept talking about you when you and Noah were off on your jaunts."

"No. Noah."

"Really? I think you're mistaken there. He never approached me our last year at seminary. Not once did he even kiss me, unless we're talking about a peck on the cheek. No. I don't think Noah has time to think about that anymore."

"He told me."

"When?" Sophie asked, deciding to go along with the charade.

"That last weekend."

"When you two were breaking up? I think he probably wanted to hurt you."

"No. Before we broke up. Even before we went to bed—when he was happy and relaxed and held me in his arms. Then he suddenly asked why you didn't want to be with him."

Sophie laughed. "That's funny, Rachel. I can't believe you're serious."

"No," she said, clinging to Sophie's arm. "I asked him what he meant. He said you were the most wonderful woman he had ever met. That's why we broke up. I started to argue with him because he hurt me."

"Dear Rachel. I thank you but am not sure I believe you."

"Sophie, look at me," she said, waiting until Sophie looked directly into her blue eyes. "I'm serious. I should have told you but I was so upset. He wanted you the whole time. He was going out with me to be around you. I'm sorry. I should have told you right away."

Sophie rubbed the ring on her finger. "Does he know you didn't tell me?"

"I told him last night that I hadn't. That may be why he was so quiet after dinner," Rachel said, starting to sob and covering her mouth with her hand. "I'm so sorry, Sophie. Please forgive me."

Sophie held Rachel close and rocked her. "You're forgiven, Rachel. Noah and I were never intimate so I don't know what I missed. I'm marrying a wonderful man and don't want complications to ruin that now."

At about three, Jessie began to cry. Sophie got up and carried her downstairs to the dining room. She could hear the snores, emanating from the room across the way. Once they settled into a rocking chair that Ben had moved there earlier, Jessie quieted down.

"You're such a beautiful little girl," Sophie cooed. "I'd let you down but I'm afraid you'd run around and wake everyone up."

Jessie did not squirm but smiled as she studied Sophie's face. The feeling came suddenly—the one that Sophie dreaded. She hugged the tot, fighting back the tears. Jessie whimpered, unable to get her thumb to her mouth, and Sophie placed her across her lap, continuing to rock her until Jessie's eyes closed and her breathing became regular.

The morning came all too quickly, especially since Jessie had been up twice during the night. Rachel begged out of visiting the churches after Sophie sat next to her at breakfast and talked about her concerns.

"Listen, Rachel, this is important."

Rachel looked up and smiled.

"You've got to watch Jessie," Sophie told her. "You've got to compare her to other children when she plays with them."

"What are you going on about?" Rachel asked, a line forming across her brow.

"You've got to make sure she has the energy the others do."

"Sophie, you're scaring me. Why don't you tell me what you think is wrong?"

"You have to make sure the doctor tests her for blood-related diseases every time you take her in. It may not show up when you get back or two years from now, but some day the doctors will find something."

Feeling relieved and hoping to face the beginning of a beautiful day, Sophie got up and went upstairs to put on her sundress.

The small group sauntered across the pothole-studded road.

"This is the church where I have my office," Noah said.

"It's beautiful," whispered Sophie, walking up to the pulpit and looking out at the empty pews. "You must be so proud when you stand up here and talk to your people."

"I thought you might like to give one or more of the sermons tomorrow."

"I haven't given a sermon in over a year, Noah—not even at a funeral."

"It's good practice," he said. "Unless you plan to move to Scotland and have lots of children."

"Bite your tongue, Noah!" She laughed. "Until I saw Jessie, I didn't even think about having any. Things are changing so quickly."

"Do you pack 'em in, Noah?" Cyril asked.

"If a dozen or so per church is packing them in, then yes," he said, smiling. "Before we go to Sandy Rock, let me show you the parish hall where we hold the high school dances. I'm still in shock that the kids saw me as an old man," He opened the double doors of the neighboring structure. "As you can see, even my office is spotless."

"This isn't the Noah I roomed with," Ben noted.

"I have a lot of help here. If I don't hide my sermons in the drawer, Millie Bellows throws the papers away. She's a tyrant, but a necessity."

The party then visited the other parishes. Noah introduced them to Hugh Lemon and the Abbots, who invited them in for tea and sandwiches.

"Did you show 'em de church here, Fader?" Sam Abbot asked.

"Not yet," Noah said. "It'll take a lot for me to confess that I'm not the perfect priest, Sam."

Suddenly, Eunice's brother walked in the door as if he lived there. "Hi, Father. I didn't know you were comin' for a visit. Martha's droppin' over in a few with a crisp if you all wants something for dessert. She'll be askin' you when we'll be rebuildin' the church. Her friends have been fundraisin' for years to keep that church in Black Inlet and would be disappointed to suddenly find out that the Anglican church didn't want it anymore."

"Yes, Gil. I suppose you told her that you had something to do with the accident too? Gilbert Minty, may I present my friends?"

Gilbert spotted Sophie right off. "It be her!" he blurted out. "You be Sophie," he said, taking her hand in his. "Did Noah show you the framed picture of you hangin' on his wall?"

"You mean the one with the bishop, Mr. Minty?"

"Yes, the one he stares at when he comes into the rectory and again when he goes to bed."

"What's this about one of your churches, Noah?" asked Ben.

"I'll show you as soon as Martha lets us taste her crisp. She bakes for the church, and I must say, she's very good at it."

Noah finally pulled into the lot of the Black Inlet church. The bishop had hired someone to cover the hole in the wall to protect the interior from the winter snows, but the neglect certainly showed up on the inside.

"What happened?" Sophie whispered to him as the others examined the damage.

"Gil screwed up. He pulled the wall down with his truckle."

"His what? Isn't a truckle a toy truck?"

"This was sort of a toy forklift that was quite noisy, having a souped-up engine and all."

"I'll bet the bishop was rory-eyed. From what I hear, he gets pretty angry when there's a problem that takes money to correct."

Noah smiled. "I would say his breeks were a bit tight. This probably wouldn't have happened if you had been here."

"I don't know what I'd do, but I assure you it wouldn't have been much different had I made the decision."

"Good. I was kind of worried about what you'd say."

"Really? Maybe I should tell you a few of my horror stories."

Noah took her hand, but she withdrew it immediately, her face feeling hot. "Why don't we all go back and see what Rachel's up to?" Sophie suggested. "I don't think we should let her have so much fun taking in the sun."

"And changing diapers and cleaning up after Jessie's feeding frenzies," said Ben. "I wouldn't worry, Sophie. I know she's enjoying it and am sure I'll hear every detail."

"Sophie," Noah said softly as the others trundled back to the car.

"No. I don't want to talk about it now, Noah! We can discuss it on Sunday."

"Do you know how to play cards? Millie expects me to play cards with them tomorrow night, and it'd be more fun if you came too."

Sophie smiled, hoping he did not notice her flush.

Saturday was busy. Sophie helped Ben and Cyril pack their cars and endured the tearful goodbyes while Noah performed three services in one afternoon. After dinner at a restaurant, Sophie and Noah headed to the parish hall.

"Sophie, this is Millie Bellows and Effie and Angus Clark."

"I seen your picture on Father Noah's wall," Millie suddenly blurted out. "You're the brindy young thing who Father Noah's been hidin'."

"Sit down, you two. We needs something in the pot," Effie said. "Eunice telled me yesterday that we owes money to fix the Black Inlet church, and if we don't pay, we'll need to hire a barrister!"

Sophie picked up her hand and played the first game well.

"Ooooh! This girl knows her cards," said Millie. "I hopes you understand we're expectin' you to contribute your winnin's to the Black Inlet buildin' fund."

"Then we all win no matter what happens," Sophie said.

On Sunday, Sophie listened to Noah's sermon at the church. He glanced at her when he finished preaching. She silently applauded. And when the service was over, he showed her his little spot among the boulders. The two sat side by side and watched an iceberg inch southward.

"I figure you'll leave when the iceberg gets over there," he said, pointing to the south. "Then you can head home."

Sophie smiled. "That means I'll be here until Tuesday."

"Oh, and I guess you want to go right away and be home for your Scot."

"Noah, we'll still be friends. I promise."

"I know," he said. "But I'm not sure that's going to be enough for you. I'm certain you'll head back to me when you tire of him."

"And you'll still be here. I know you're a great success. Seriously, I can count on you to come to the wedding, can't I, Noah? I need you there."

"Of course, Sophie. I'll be there to give you away."

When Sophie returned to St. Mark, she discovered that Ewan was on the road again. He had left flowers and a note in her apartment. She was disappointed, having wanted to be with him to make sure of her feelings for him. He came back the next day. She ran into him walking up the west wing from the emergency room.

"You're back? You were away last night, weren't you?"

"Yes, love. I returned because I cut my hand on a scalpel at one of the clinics. I thought I'd cleaned it thoroughly, but it got infected. I believe the hospital has fixed me up."

"I can't see the wound, but by the look of the bandages, it must have been serious. I'm going to have to make sure you keep it clean," she said, giving him a kiss.

"Tell me about your reunion," he said, walking with her toward the cafeteria.

"It went well. I got to see Rachel and Ben's little girl. Jessie was such a doll. I hope you want children because I'm starting to think it might be fun."

"I love them. What about this Noah? How's he doin'?"

"He's fine. I believe it was a good idea that I didn't become a rector. It's hard work. He's already had a few problems."

"Listen, I have to go back to work now. Duncan needs to talk to me. How about we hook up at dinnertime? We can relax better then."

"Duncan?"

"Yes, Duncan MacLeish, my research assistant. You've met him, haven't you?"

"I don't think so," she said, confused. "Anyway I can't wait for dinner. I missed you." She squeezed his good hand.

It was not until she saw him push the button for the elevator in the east wing that she remembered. She felt for the key in her pocket. It was not there. She had removed it from the key ring and put the rest of the keys in his drawer. The one for the fourth floor must have been in another pair of slacks. Maybe he would not notice. This Duncan probably worked with Oliver. Ewan was going to the third floor to talk to them both. She would go home and get the key before dinner and make sure she replaced it before he noticed. By the time she had finished her coffee, she knew he would not need it. He undoubtedly did not even know what the key was for.

Chapter 19

Encounter

The irregular hum of a motorboat fighting the waves pierced the peaceful beach like a sandblaster. At Angus's command, Noah turned his boat around and retreated.

"How far back?" he yelled at the man in the other boat.

"They still be too close together!" Angus called out. "Keep movin' back!"

"Is this okay?"

From a rolling boat fifty meters away, it was difficult to read the thumbs up sign Angus gave him, but it certainly did not look the same as the exaggerated arm-waving that Angus had offered when Noah erred. Slowing the engine until he idled in one spot, Noah pulled a pot from the pile in his boat, attached a buoy, and tossed the pot as far away from the side as he could. The rope, coiled on the boat's floor, quickly unwound as the pot sank. Angus roared past him, disturbing Noah's dinghy in the wake and nearly sending the priest overboard. He watched Angus repeat the process before passing him again. When both boats were empty, the two returned to shore.

"Is Hugh sinking his own pots or did you offer your services up the coast too?"

"He do his own dunkin' or maybe he be hirin' Dawe. I don't know. Lemon be a scutty man, ye know. He be drinkin' pinky or screech or other cheap stuff at the bar in town cuz he can't get the pennies out of his pockets."

"But he will pay for the deliveries, won't he?"

"Yeah, but only cuz he claims Doc Delacour tells him his heart's weak, and he doesn't want to do more work. He'll jest sting others for the loonies he needs to pay me. I don't care as long as they ends up in my patch-bag."

"When's your first run?"

"This afternoon. The others leaving them on their piers at 'bout three, we all yaffles—collects the cuckoos. At four, me and Jacob will be coastin'. We should have the load here for pick-up by six."

"You really have all this worked out, don't you. In the morning, you'll deliver bait to everyone. Will you be keeping all the pots on shore overnight?"

"I will. If we don't have to pull 'em up, it be easier to bait them and throws them in again," Angus explained. "If Lemon wants to get his share, he'll have to beach his own boat and pile his catch on the pier. Now all we needs is civil weather and we be all set."

"I'd like to go out with you and Jacob so I know the route. Do you mind if I follow you in my dinghy?"

"That be good, Father. If the catch be big, we could use more room."

Noah heard the scrape of a boat against his boulders. He sat on the rock, trying to come up with a sermon for Sunday, but the noise piqued his curiosity, and he had to get up to see who was about. "Hello?" he called out, pulling himself up and peering over the edge of the rocks. "Who's there?"

"Are you talkin' to me?" she asked, standing behind him.

"Is that little boat with the green stripe yours?" he asked her. "Why didn't you beach her?"

"Why do you want to know?"

He looked her over, shocked that such a young beauty would live in Brandy Point. "Are you from round here?"

"That's my question to you. I don't know you, do I?"

He smiled to himself. She was not only pretty, but sassy. He could definitely handle that but was not sure he wanted to.

"Hello. Noah Lodge. I live here in Brandy Point," he said, putting out his hand.

"Cynthia Hodder," she said. "I live in Toronto but used to live in Black Inlet. I'm here for a visit."

"Was this your rock?"

"Yes, but only when I was a child. Are you sure you're not too old to be playin' on rocks?"

"One is never to old to seek peace and quiet."

"Oh, is this your stuff?" she asked, sitting down beside his books. "My, my, what's this?"

"I was working but could use a break. What do you do in Toronto?"

"I work for a law firm. I'm a paralegal right now but am goin' to school at night. I want to be a solicitor."

"That's nice. We could use some around here."

"Oh heavens, Noah. I don't plan to come back. I like the city. This is too slow. If you were from round here, you wouldn't talk 'bout stayin' here. You'd say you were stuck here."

"Really. I think it has its advantages."

"Where are you from?"

"I grew up south of Corner Brook but lived in St. John's for a while."

"And you wanted to come back here?"

"I had to come back to get my boat."

"That little dinghy tied to the rock?"

"Little? I wouldn't say—"

She smiled at him, a toothy smile. He lost his train of thought. Her short light brown hair blew across her face, and she brushed it aside. Her clothes were stylish, a short T-shirt over low-slung shorts, revealing a tanned belly. She pulled her knees up and hugged them to her chest.

"So how long are you here?" he asked.

"For a week," she said, looking at her watch.

"Do you have to get back?"

"No, I'd planned to come here to sunbathe. I didn't expect to see you," she said, standing up and tugging at the back of her shorts. Then she walked over to the edge of the boulder, bent over, revealing a tan line that mesmerized Noah, and finally pulled a tote from the rocks below. "Do you mind?"

"Mind what?"

"If I sunbathe here closer to the edge. I promise I won't interrupt what you're doing."

"Uh, no."

She turned away from him and pulled her shirt up over her head. If she had turned aside out of diffidence, she would not have spun back to reach for her tote. The breezes blew over Noah, leafing through his Bible and sending his notes flying. Cynthia looked up and smiled, and he chose to watch her rather then retrieve them. She unzipped the front of her shorts and pulled them down as far as modesty would allow, and completely ignoring Noah's presence, lay face down on her towel. He rose, picked up the papers he could find, and sat back down. Then he tried unsuccessfully to work on his sermon.

About twenty minutes later, the young woman suddenly roused, sitting up to look through her tote.

"Do you mind?" she asked.

Feeling the heat on his face Noah looked away.

"No. Do you mind puttin' some of this sunscreen on my back, dotterell? It feels hot."

"Oh no," he said, getting up.

She lay back down and let him apply it to her shoulder blades. When his hand got to the small of her back, she scrunched her shorts down further and let him explore the tanned tops of her buttocks. His hand slowed, and she turned over, getting up onto her elbows.

"Does that make you nervous?" she asked.

He smiled, trying to demonstrate his control.

She looked around. "No one can see us from the beach here. I know. I picked this place for the isolation."

"Ah," he said, staring at her erect nipples.

"You can touch them if you want."

He lay on his side, his head on his palm. "I'm not used to being approached this way."

"Do you always have to play the wolf?" she asked, turning onto her side to face him. "In Toronto, we take what we want."

"And I'm a minister, which makes it more difficult if anyone sees us."

"I know who you are."

Cynthia reached over and put a hand behind his head, pulling him toward her and kissing his lips. Noah, his mind numb, let out a sigh and willingly followed her lead as she lay back down. The salt of the sea having dried on her skin, she smelled good. That and the subtle odor of sunscreen made her smell like summer—something he ached for as winter slowly retracted it claws. He inched closer and tasted her mouth. He had dreamt of doing this with Sophie, but the sting of rebuff was still too painful, and he did not think about Sophie now. Cynthia slipped her hands under his shirt and tugged the hem up until he could feel the hardened nipples against his ribs. He slid his hands under the waist of her shorts. The reaction was quick.

"Come up here," she said, trying to catch her breath. "Back here under the trees."

Standing up, she quickly removed her shorts and tugged at his pants. Not wanting to insult her, he took over, dropping his trousers. He held her writhing body close, trying to regain control, but she buckled, bringing them both down hard on the rock. If he had achieved some kind of domination, he lost it here. She had a condom out and on him so quickly he did not have a chance to make sure it was right before he entered her. Minutes later, she rolled away from him, seemingly satisfied. She pulled on her panties, and still trying to catch her breath, grabbed for her shorts. Noah could not get up.

Cynthia turned to smile at him. "That was wonderful. I usually come to the boulders at about ten each morning."

"Oh?" he uttered, not knowing what to say.

"Perhaps we'll meet again," she said, crawling toward her towel and donning her T-shirt. "I have to get back home for lunch. See you later." She stuffed her towel into the tote and then disappeared over the edge of the rocks.

Only then did Noah pull his trousers back up. He sat there, listening to the wavelets slap against the boulders. He could hear his boat scrape against them. But he did not work on his sermon. An hour or so later, he got up and made his way back to the rectory.

At three-thirty, he stuck his head through a sweatshirt and pulled on some boots. Then he splashed through the shallow water to untie his dinghy. At ten minutes to four, Angus and Jacob circled his boat and gestured for him to follow. The two crafts skipped over the waves though not efficiently because neither motor had much horsepower. At Black Inlet, the two entrepreneurs pulled up to the pier that supported three large buckets of whelk. Noah slowed his dinghy and let his eyes survey the shore where several boats had been beached. At one end he saw it, a little boat with a washed-out green stripe. He smiled, wanting her again, wishing it were already the next day. When the two men pulled away from the dock, he followed them on to Daisy Cove where they would repeat the previous steps. At Sandy Rock, they asked Noah to pull up alongside them so they could place the buckets into his dinghy. It was five-thirty. He wondered if they would make it back by six. At full throttle, they arrived in time to wave to the truck parked along the street by the church. The three of them gingerly carried the buckets up the beach and across the field.

"Next time we should start at a quarter to four so we don't keep him waitin'," said Angus.

"Do you think you'll need two boats?"

"No, Father. We could've fit it all in here if we'd filled all the buckets up."

"This be a good start, eh Father?" said Jacob. "We're goin' to be rich."

Noah roughed up the boy's thick hair. "We'll have to talk more about the wedding, Jacob," he said, turning back to tie up his boat before it got dark.

"Yes, Father Noah," he said, excitement showing all over his face.

At a quarter to ten the next morning, Noah still sat behind the desk in his office. Millie and Effie sat across from him, reporting on the funds they had raised and asking for his suggestions on the distribution.

"Is that enough to satisfy Eunice Abbott?" he asked.

"No," answered Millie, defiantly. "Nothin's goin' to suit that woman, Father. She spects us to pay to fix her church cuz she can't 'semble her neighbors for a good card game. I thinks we're givin' 'em too much. It's not our fault her brother acts like a stunned whooper."

Effie nodded her agreement.

"Actually, some of it was my fault. That said, the money should come from the parish, which is a collection of all six churches."

"If it be your fault, Father, mind you I'm not sayin' it is, but if you be 'sponsible, than you should rouse yerself over to each place and organize 'em so they can take care of 'emselves."

"You're correct, Millie. If anyone can get to the point, you can," he said, standing. "I'll get right to that first thing this afternoon. For the time being, we'll split the money as I see fit. It can always be adjusted later."

Noah walked out the door. It was five minutes to ten, and he had no intention of missing Cynthia if she happened to tie her boat up near the boulders. After all, he had slept very little, thinking about how he would approach her this time, how he would dictate their actions.

At ten-thirty, he put his book aside and looked out over the water. Perhaps she had changed her mind. Hopefully, she had not felt remorse for what had happened. He would have to show her that he cared and make sure she would be able to return to Toronto without bad feelings.

"Hello," she said, sneaking up the rocks from the other direction.

Noah jumped. "I didn't hear your boat."

"That's because I tied it up an hour ago so I could walk the beach first. Are you workin' on your sermon?"

She wore a bright red extra-long T-shirt as a swimsuit cover. His eyes fell to her long tanned legs, directly blocking his view.

"No," he said. "I was just reading. Sit down."

She squatted beside him, hesitantly.

"I-I'm sorry," he stuttered. "I didn't mean to go that far yesterday."

"I did," she said. "I thought we might be a little bolder this time."

Noah shuttered. "Right," he mumbled under is breath.

"I'd love to see how your boat takes the surf."

"You want a ride in the dinghy?"

"Yes," she said, pulling him to his feet.

The two climbed down the boulder, and he helped her into the boat just before he untied it. Her tight buttocks outlined through a damp spot on the back of her shirt, she pushed off. He pulled the boat out and turned southward.

"Where are we goin'?"

"Down toward the ferry. There are some sandy beaches down here."

"I want to go north."

"Don't you think someone might see us? You're wearing red, for God's sake."

"Does that make you nervous? I can sit on the floor," she said, slipping off the thwart. I really want to go north."

Noah turned the dinghy around and headed back toward Black Inlet. Just beyond the village, Noah circled an outcropping of rocks and slowed the boat at the back of it.

"Is this good enough?" he asked, yanking off his shirt and sliding down beside her.

She pulled the swimsuit cover over her head. Noah was taken by surprise. She wore nothing underneath. Sitting up, she slipped over the side into the cold water.

"Follow me," she said, as she stroked toward the outcropping.

He slid out of his pants and dove in to swim after her. She must have let him catch her. When he caught up, she rolled onto her back and frog kicked into the shallow water. Though he certainly could not see her clearly in the foaming water, the image of her pumping legs was branded in his mind. As a wave receded from the gravelly beach, he pulled her body onto the pebbles and crawled on top of her.

"Where's the condom?" she asked.

"In my pocket," he said, a sinking feeling in the pit of his stomach.

Giggling, she pushed him to one side. "That was dumb."

Letting one knee drop to the side, she gazed directly into his eyes. He could hold off no longer. He mounted her and was in her before she could stop him. When he rolled away, he could not look at her.

"Are you all right?" he finally asked.

She smiled, getting up to run into the waves. He knew he had to follow so she would not leave him naked on the beach, but was spent. Weakly, he dragged himself through the choppy sea. It was getting colder. Why had he not felt it before?

He was relieved when Cynthia, her red cover back on, helped drag him into the dinghy. He quickly donned his clothes and started the motor.

"Ten o'clock tomorrow?" he asked.

"Maybe. I'm not sure I'm free."

"Ah," he said, almost relieved.

He had taken control this time and should have felt better. As the hours passed, however, he still feared she had orchestrated the whole episode. He knew she would leave at the end of the week, and promised himself that if he did not see her before then, it would not bother him. But time would change that feeling too, and before the sun lighted a swathe across the restless strait, his needs would call him again to go to the boulders, and he would listen for her boat to scrape against the rocks below.

The next day, he talked her out of making love in the empty church with the hole in its side. Though her expression showed some doubt, he told her there would be builders working on the wall. Instead, she locked the door of the ladies room in the Brandy Point parish hall, and they did it there. On Friday, they took the dinghy past Black Inlet and made love in the bottom of the boat as it trawled past Daisy Cove. Facing the bow, she hung one long leg over each side of the boat. Noah had to choose between taking her and guiding the dinghy further away from the shore. Urgency forced him to his knees.

On Saturday afternoon, he saw her again. She and a woman were attending the service at the church in Daisy Cove. Afterward, he waited for her at the back of the nave.

"Hello, Father Noah," she said. "May I present my mother, Louise Hodder from Black Inlet."

"Hello, Mrs. Hodder. I don't think we've met. Have you attended services here before?"

"No, Father, I goes to the United service, but Cynthia insisted we comes here today so she could say good-bye."

"Are you leaving us this weekend?" he asked, hardly able to hide his disappointment.

"Yes," she said, taking his hand in both of hers. "I have to work. It's been fun, though."

Noah felt his face redden. Her mother looked surprised. Hugh Lemon came up behind the two women.

"Hello, Hugh," Noah said, pulling his hand out of Cynthia's grasp to shake his warden's.

"What's this? I don't want to interrupt, Noah."

"It's nothing. It seems that Cynthia Hodder here has to return to Toronto."

"Oh Daddy," she said, turning to Lemon. "The time has gone by so quickly."

"Daddy?" Noah uttered, his ears beginning to buzz.

"Yes. Louise be my ex-wife. I need to talk to you, Noah. Cynthia dear, please wait for me at the car."

Lemon stepped back to let the others shake the minister's hand before they dispersed in the parking lot. Noah removed his stole and started to follow them.

"Just a minute, Noah."

The priest began to feel the sweat gather under his collar. "Yes, Hugh?"

"At ten-thirty on Friday, Sam Abbot and I were on the pier baitin' the pots, a routine that we do twice daily as you are well aware. All I saw is your dinghy scuttle through our bay toward Daisy Cove. Gil be in Daisy Cove about to take his boat out to distribute the pots there. He tells me this fantastic story about a boat—your boat—beatin' by. Trouble is, no one was scunnin' the damn boat," he said, his fingers pinching down on a fold of Noah's alb. "In fact, he didn't see anyone sittin' up in the dinghy at all. If I ever catch you with my daughter, or anyone's daughter again, not botherin' to wait for the bishop to come and save your arse, I will string you up myself! Do you hear me?"

Noah did not answer right away. When he was able to exhale, he threw his shoulders back and said, "I certainly did *not* know Cynthia Hodder was your daughter, Hugh. Had I known,

I would've visited you here earlier and told you what a kind and helpful daughter you've raised. She was very generous in helping me procure a thousand dollars more to be deposited into the Black Inlet Building Fund."

Chapter 20

The Unthinkable

The thaw continued. The patches of brown grass in front of the hospital grew as the white vanished, and green sprouts emerged from muddy furrows. Sophie donned a light jacket to walk to work. Existing in suspended animation only weeks earlier, life emerged in a chorus of sounds, effectively drowning out the buzz that had filled the silence of Sophie's winter. Ewan had left on another trip nearly three days earlier. He said he would be back in a week, maybe two. Sophie was not sure if she was lonely or relieved. A brisk walk in the clean air would erase any worry for now.

Crossing over the back lawn of the hospital where Ewan had suggested they make out in front of the windows of the maternity ward, she smiled. Deciding to lengthen her jaunt and further clear her mind, she hesitated as she approached the entrance. Circling back across the spongy grass, Sophie turned left at the end of the east wing, hoping to reach the front parking lot and eventually the main thoroughfare through town. On the other side of the road, a long path would wind down to the pier, now bustling with both workers and seabirds.

To her surprise, the east wing did not end here. She turned the corner only to find a bank, sloping downward to a driveway that presumably allowed delivery trucks to maneuver directly up to the basement doors. On the other side of the drive, a fence extended to another small outbuilding, blocking her access to the lobby entrance of the hospital. Her stroll would be longer as she tried to get to the front lot. Why had she not noticed it before?

It caught her eye, as she turned to follow the line of the wooden fence. On the other side of the drive, someone had parked a car. Caked with the sand and salt used to clear the roads of winter snow, a '74 Volkswagen square back had been parked off to one side along the fence. It looked like Ewan's car. She carefully stepped down the embankment for a closer look. The dark green paint under the shroud of grime resembled his, and when Sophie peeked through the dirty window, she recognized the tan upholstery, taped in places where the plastic had split. Was he back? Why had he not called? Hoping to catch him in his office on the third floor, she turned around and retraced her steps.

The elevator was busy. Too impatient to wait, she skipped up the stairs, and at the top, eagerly scrambled through the dim third floor hallway. She hoped he was there and not in surgery. To her disappointment, his door was locked, but Dr. Charles was just emerging from his office.

"Miss Hawkins, how can I help you today?"

"Hello, Oliver. Have you seen Ewan? Could he be in surgery?"

The older doctor stared back. "I thought he was out of town, but you'd know better than I," he finally muttered.

"You're right. He *was* out of town, but I just saw—" she started, unsure if she should continue.

"I haven't seen him since before the weekend, I believe," Dr. Charles repeated, locking his door. "I'm goin' down for coffee in the cafeteria. Would you like something to eat?"

"No thank you," she said, walking beside him. "I've got to open the chapel. Then I have a few patients I promised to visit."

"Suit yourself," he said, summoning the elevator.

"Oh, by the way, is Duncan around?"

"Duncan?"

"Yes. I forget his last name," she said, straining to think of it.

"His assistant?"

"Yes."

"No. I don't see him often. In fact, I think I've only met him once or twice. I don't know where he goes when he's assistin' or whatever he does with Dr. Black."

"Oh. I thought he worked here in the hospital."

The elevator doors opened, and they both got in. But there was nothing more to say. Silence dominated the ride down.

Though she kept an eye out for him, Sophie did not see Ewan the whole day. Making her way home for dinner, she walked past the basement driveway. The car was still there. How did he get to the ferry without his car? Did someone else drive?

The answer would come later that night when she least expected it. The bell rang twice before she realized that she was being paged. Jumping out of bed, she ran for the phone.

"Hello?" she said, trying desperately to sound awake. She glanced at the clock on the kitchen wall.

"Sophie?"

"Yes? Who is this please?"

"This is Dr. Brewer, an epidemiologist from St. John's."

"Can't this wait? It's two-thirty in the morning."

"Dr. Charles is here. He asked me to call you because he couldn't get free."

Sophie's stomach turned in anticipation.

"I'd like you come over here right away."

"Is it Ewan?"

"Dr. Black, yes. Dr. Charles said you should be summoned."

She heard the click. He had hung up without telling her what he was calling about. Where was she supposed to go? Where was Ewan? Somewhere in Labrador? She sat on the edge of the bed, pulling on some socks, and realized that Oliver would be at the hospital. She was right. Ewan's car was parked in the driveway because Ewan was back. Rushing to don the rest of her clothes and brushing her teeth, she was out the door and on the street within fifteen minutes, half-walking, half-running, not stopping until she pushed through the doors to the surgery.

She recognized Oliver right off. His mask, still tied around his neck, hung down over his chest. Blood blemished his gown, stains that would brand themselves onto Sophie's memory.

"Where's Ewan?" she demanded.

"Hello, Sophie," he said. "This is Dr. Brewer."

"How do you do, Miss Hawkins?" Dr. Brewer began. "I'm afraid I have bad news."

She could see his lips move but could not hear him. What was he saying about Ewan? What happened? He accompanied her to the recovery room and opened the door for her. The shades were drawn, the room dark. She did not even consider that it was still the middle of the night.

"I'm afraid we couldn't save it," Dr. Charles said, entering behind them. "I took off as little of the arm as I could, but I had to make sure I got it all, you understand."

"Did you?" she asked.

"What?"

"Get it all?"

"I'm not sure. Only time will tell."

"The beta hemolytic Streptococcal infection that he contracted through a cut in his hand isn't that common," Dr. Brewer said softly. "It seems to take a combination of the Strep and other bacteria to become septic. Somehow the combination produces a toxin that eats away at the protective tissue that keeps the Strep from spreading into the bloodstream. Beta Strep has been around for years, and we can control it with antibiotics. But if we don't get to the patient in time, the bacteria breaks down the red bloods cells. Without the blood cells, the tissue dies and becomes necrotic. As the bacteria spreads, the gangrenous tissue extends. Evidently, we didn't get to Dr. Black's infection in time. There was a lot of tissue affected, and now all we can do is wait and see if the antibiotics work."

"What?" she asked, pulling up a chair and sitting near Ewan's head. "That must mean it's in his bloodstream. If you can't do anything, why are you here?"

"I'm here to find out where he picked it up. Do you know where he's been?"

Sophie closed her eyes and stroked Ewan's cheek, but she felt nothing. Were her healing powers gone? "He had a cut on his hand two weeks ago, before I went to Brandy Point. He said he had taken care of it here because they couldn't do it in Labrador."

"Where in Labrador was he?"

"I don't know where he went. Oliver, you know, don't you?"

"No. He was doin' that himself, I think."

"Who took care of his wound here?" Brewer asked.

"I don't know," she insisted. "Did he tell you, Oliver?"

"No. I didn't even know he had a cut."

"What do you mean you didn't know?" she asked, her voice high. "He wore a large bandage and told me this hospital took care of the wound. Please ask the doctors in emergency. What about Duncan? Duncan might know."

"Who?"

"Duncan MacLeish, his assistant," Charles informed Dr. Brewer. "I don't know where he is though. I told Miss Hawkins this afternoon that I don't often see him."

"I understand," Dr Brewer said. "But you have saved the tissue samples for me. I still need to identify the bacteria."

"Of course."

"And you'll call me as soon as he wakes up."

"Yes, doctor," the surgeon said.

"Then I think I'll head back to Dr. Black's house."

"Why his house?" Sophie asked, startled.

"I have an assistant there, looking to see if there's any evidence of the bacteria in the house. You'll be all right?" he asked, placing a hand on her shoulder.

"Yes, thank you, doctor."

At daybreak, Sophie walked to the window and opened the shades. The deep hues of the hills to the east ran together as the sun rose behind them, and the bay shimmered in the cool rays. Then she walked back to her seat and took his hand. He roused slightly, and she assured him that she was not going to leave.

"What's happened?" he whispered hoarsely.

Sophie poured him some water and lifted his head so he could sip some of it. "You have a Strep infection."

"Oh God," he said, his head sinking back into the pillow.

A sweat broke out on his forehead, and Sophie got a tissue to wipe it, but he grabbed her wrist with his good hand.

"Listen to me," he said, his voice getting stronger. "You've got to help me!"

"Quiet down, Ewan. You're taxing yourself. I'll help you after you've rested."

"Listen to me, Sophie. That'll be too late. You've got to get Duncan."

"I don't know who Duncan is, Ewan," she said, trying not to break down.

"Is there a doctor here to help me?"

"You mean Oliver?"

"No. He's not competent enough."

"There's an epidemiologist, Dr. Langley Brewer. He came when he learned of your problem."

"Good, I've heard of him. Now listen. In the lab, there's a file. I have spent months workin' on my notes. You have to get them to him!"

"I want to stay here with you," she said, tears filling her eyes.

"You have to save me, Sophie. You have to get those notes!"

"Where's this lab?"

"On the fourth floor of this wing."

Sophie caught her breath. "There's no modern lab on the fourth floor, Ewan. You have a fever. It's your fever that's talking."

"Yes. The file should be there on the fourth floor."

"It's a damn psychiatric ward, Ewan. There isn't a lab!"

Ewan suddenly bellowed as if he were in pain, his head falling to one side.

"Ewan?" she cried. "Ewan, wake up!"

He didn't respond. She got up and looked around for his clothes. In a cabinet by the wall, she discovered his trousers and jacket. She rummaged around the pockets and found them—the ring of keys. Having returned the key to the ring herself, she recognized it immediately. On the way out, she told the nurse to get someone in the room to help Ewan.

The elevator doors opened onto the fourth floor. The hallway was not as black as it had been that other night, but the doors to the patients' rooms blocked much of the dawn light. She repeated her steps down the passageway into the lab once more. Here, the morning light glowed through the window. Carefully examining the counter and shelves, Sophie realized that her first impression had been correct. The lab had not been used in years. Ignoring the ECT room, she walked forward again. It was at the next set of doors that she noticed them. Her friends were waiting for her.

"Hello," she said. "What is it now?"

The spirits circled but not so erratically as before. Perhaps her lack of resistance to their advice had calmed them.

"Is it this next ward?"

They reversed direction.

Sophie opened the doors very slowly and looked in. "Duncan?" she asked. "Are you in here?"

There was indeed a modern-looking lab beyond the doors. Undraped windows, lining the walls of the large open space, drew in the light. The counters sported several microscopes, and large machines skirted the wall. She did not see Duncan but noticed the windowed refrigerator at the end of the counter. Petrie dishes cloaked the shelves. The blood-red agar was dotted with clear spots that cut through the medium to the glass on the bottom. Then Sophie gazed at the items on top of the counter. Beyond the microscopes at the far end, sat a broken beaker. There was no liquid around because it had evaporated, but Sophie wondered what substance might have spilled onto the counter and dripped onto the floor. No one had bothered to pick up the shards.

The entities were back, brushing her cheeks and mussing her hair.

"I get it," Sophie assured them. "This is bad stuff. I won't touch any of it."

They continued to circle her face and then brushed her hair back away from it. Her reaction was immediate. Tears began to fall as she thought of him the first time he made love to her, having placed his hands on the side of her face and brushed the hair back so he could gaze at her. He had such a gentle touch like the spirits that continued to sweep by.

"Ewan," she whispered, watching the entities twist and entwine until they became the shape of a human figure. "I love you, Ewan. Please don't go yet."

Spurred by the urgency to save him, she scanned the counter for the notes and spun around to see a desk. Pulling out all the drawers, she found nothing. She cleared the book shelves before discovering a filing cabinet against the opposite wall. A folder labeled "Beta Streptococcus" sat on top of it. She grabbed it and quickly headed back to the elevator.

At the first nurse's station, Sophie stopped and called Ewan's number. "Dr. Brewer, I have his notes. Ewan was evidently studying the bacteria in a lab here in the hospital. I don't want to give these notes to anyone else. Please come."

Fearing that if she put them down anywhere, they would disappear, and cognizant of Ewan's insistence that the notes go to Dr. Brewer, she walked to the lobby and sat down, the notes on her lap. He was there in ten minutes, and she handed them over.

"Ewan said these are important. Do something to help him," she pleaded, returning to the east wing hallway.

When she got to the ward, she ran into Dr. Charles exiting the room. Noticing the look on his face, she lunged forward, taking the door from him. He stopped her before she entered.

"I'm sorry, Sophie. Cardiac arrest. Nothin' could be done, nor do I think he would have wanted it," he said. "I'll let you stay with him for a while. Tell the nurse when you're ready."

Sobbing, Sophie sat with his body for an hour. Her friend, Dr. Ellis, finally came in and urged her to leave.

"Come on, Sophie," he said. "I think we have work to do."

"What do you mean, Dan?"

"You're doing the service, aren't you? Shouldn't you be thinking about what you're going to say at that? Someone's got to plan a funeral and get him buried."

"What about his relatives?"

"What about them? Who else but you can make sure the proper people are notified?"

The service was beautiful. Sophie officiated over the funeral at St. Luke's Anglican church in St. Mark. She waited for the doctors to release the body and then made sure his mother was able to fly from Scotland. It was a wonderful service for a man who deserved every bit of it. His mother let him be buried in the cemetery just outside of town. At the site itself, a wind came up, and the attendees around the circle had to nestle against each other to stay warm. But Sophie did not feel it. She repeated the prayers as if she were talking to God personally.

Langley Brewer entered the chapel.

At her office desk, Sophie slowly packed her things into a box. "Hello," she said. "Please sit."

"Let's go into the chapel and talk. It's so much more peaceful. Bring the box of tissue. We both might need it."

Sophie smiled and followed him into a pew.

"I just wanted to get back to you, Ms. Hawkins. I think you might wish to know what happened."

Sophie hesitated. "Yes, I guess I do."

"Dr. Charles was fired today and will probably be brought up on charges."

"He knew about the lab?"

"Yes. He hired Dr. Black for that purpose."

"I can't believe he kept quiet and did nothing even when Ewan became so ill," Sophie mused. "Oliver should have gone to the fourth floor himself and looked for the notes, yet he was too worried about his job."

"When it all began to unravel, I think Charles believed he could get away with it. He probably didn't know you had investigated the fourth floor already nor did he think that Ewan would regain conciousness and tell you."

"I actually didn't discover Ewan's lab the first time."

"And Charles was already under investigation."

Sophie grabbed a tissue and dabbed her eye. "Ewan knew it was illegal too, I suppose."

"Yes. Dr. Black came here because he couldn't study the bacteria in Scotland. There are labs where one can do this kind of research, but Dr. Black wanted to be the boss of his own lab and wasn't allowed to do it in Scotland without the proper credentials. He moved to Canada to try to get a lab here. Dr. Charles suggested he use the fourth floor."

"Is that legal?"

"No. But that was something the head of surgery didn't seem to worry about. Putting the lab upstairs was lucrative. Dr. Black, unable to get grants to fund the lab because he wasn't supposed to be doing it, used family money and paid Charles handsomely."

"But the hospital is short of funds. They keep the lights on the third floor dim in order to save money."

"I said Charles was paid. I'm not sure any cash ever made it to the hospital. Anyway, the lab had an accident. Evidently, Dr. Black broke a beaker containing the bacteria."

"First of all, I don't think he'd break it. He was a surgeon and not clumsy at all. Secondly, if he had, he would've protected himself. He wouldn't have put his hand in it. Duncan must have done it."

"Maybe the flask wasn't supposed to contain the bacteria. We'll never know. MacLeish was picked up in Scotland. He claims he didn't spill it. But of course, even if he didn't, he's still up on charges."

"He probably did it."

"Who knows? He evidently left town three weeks earlier. He had sent a letter to the authorities here to inform them about the illegal lab on the fourth floor. It was postmarked three weeks ago in Scotland. The timeline just isn't right. If he had spilled the bacteria before he left, I'm not sure it would have been virulent enough to infect Dr. Black a week and a half ago. I don't know. I have people pouring over the notes to see if he and MacLeish even discovered anything new about the disease."

Sophie thought about the spirits that had protected her. She wondered if they tried to do the same for him. "If he had lived, he would have gone to jail, wouldn't he?"

"Most likely. The crime was serious and whatever his intentions, he knew the dangers. That said, his desire to study the disease process—the same sort of bacteria that poses danger for fishermen here—was a noble one."

Sophie handed a dry tissue back to Dr. Brewer. "I guess we'll never know. But at least the cancer is being excised from the beast."

"You mean the hospital? I hope so. I'd hate to see the authorities have to close her."

"That would be a shame, indeed. Well, if you'll excuse me, I'm going to continue to pack. I turned my resignation in to the bishop and need to get away."

"That sounds like a permanent move."

"I suppose I need to move on, and resigning will give me an opportunity to do so. That fourth floor made me come to terms with some of my demons too. Now I think I'm ready to take the next step.

Chapter 21

The Cavalry

Her bags packed, Sophie sat cross-legged on the bed in her apartment and talked into the receiver. She wiped a tear from her eye. "I have to speak with you, Griffon. I've resigned my job. You must tell me what I should do next."

"I doubt I need to instruct you, Sophie. I've heard you were doing a wonderful job there."

"Everything has turned upside down, and I don't know if I can handle the next few weeks alone."

""I can meet you in Grand Falls. Can you make it that far?"

"Yes. I'll be ready to leave in an hour. I can get a room in Grand Falls and meet you tomorrow morning if you're free."

"I'll get you the room. The rector of St. Paul's will gladly let you stay at the rectory. We can meet in the church in the morning."

Noah continued to work with his warden as if nothing had occurred. The thousand dollars emptied his personal account, but it seemed to appease Lemon. Noah knew he would have to contact Mathias but put off any thought of meeting with him for now.

A few weeks later, he sat down to write a letter to his spiritual director. He deliberated over its contents for two days before finally telling the priest that he sought an appointment for some time in July. There were things he needed to discuss with him about how to proceed with the vestry. Dropping the letter at the post office, Noah felt immediate relief. He had taken the initiative and would be frank with Gabriel. He did not really want to give up on Brandy Point but felt he needed something else in his life before everything had progressed too far to manage. That was it. He had somehow lost control and looked for help getting it back. Gabriel would know what it was like, losing the faith of your parishioners. It was probably more common than he knew.

When he received the letter, Mathias Gabriel tried to call Noah on the phone. He left messages, but the priest did not return his phone calls. Finally, he wrote a letter:

Dear Father Noah,

I will definitely be available to you anytime in July and will make the appointment right away. I do think, however, that June or maybe even this month might be better. It is always preferable to take care of these things as soon as they crop up. If the problems are reparable, we can get started trying to solve the difficulty right away. If, however, there is a personal crisis, you may want to go on a retreat. That would allow you the opportunity to pray and see if you want to make adjustments in your calling. If being a rector does not suit you, I'm sure there are other positions in which you might feel more comfortable.

Sincerely,

The Reverend Mathias Gabriel

Noah threw down the letter. He knew Gabriel would take it wrong. He had inadvertently opened the door. Gabriel would jump on it. Getting rid of Noah would solve all his problems. The bishop would be hoodwinked into removing his star priest because somehow Noah had requested a move. How was he going to deal with Gabriel now? How could he stave off the appointment until July?

The phone suddenly rang, and Noah picked up the receiver.

"Noah? This is Mathias. Did you get my letter?"

"Yes. I was just reading it. I don't think the crisis is such a big deal. It was more a question on how to handle my warden."

"Oh?"

"Yes. He seems to want to get the diocese to pay for everything."

"Like?"

"Like rebuilding the church in Black Inlet."

"I thought you guys would do fundraisers. Isn't that working?"

"Yes and no. Even though we'll get the funds eventually, Lemon still thinks the money should come from the diocese."

"Ah. Does he blame you for the accident?"

"Yes."

"And you can't regain his respect?"

"No."

"That sounds like a problem for Andrew. Why don't you call your boss? I'm sure he'll head out there and talk to your warden for you."

"Uh. Okay, I'll see if I can get to that."

"Do you still want an appointment in July?"

"Uh. Yes I would."

"Noah, you are very skilled at convincing people that they need to act. Why do you think you can't convince Lemon?"

"I don't know, he just wants to control everything."

"I see. Did you say he was the warden? What are the warden's responsibilities, Noah?"

"The business end of the parish," Noah replied, his stomach sinking.

"And what are your responsibilities, Noah?""I know what you're saying and you're right, Mathias. It's just that—"

"It's better if you manage the whole thing? Is that what you wanted to say?"

"I understand you."

"Are you free in June?"

"Toward the end of the month, Mathias. I have some things to take care of first."

"The fifteenth of June then. I'll come there this time, Noah. Until then, try to concentrate on your responsibilities and leave the rest to your warden. That way you won't be stretched too thin. I want you to be comfortable when I talk to you, okay?"

The day was drizzly as spring and winter continued to fight for dominance. Sophie navigated the roads easily and made it to Grand Falls in a little over six hours. Father Clement and his wife had a bed ready, and exhaustion let sleep overcome her as soon as her head hit the pillow. Late the next morning, Father Clement led her to his office in the parish hall and left her alone with Dr. Fairbourne.

Sophie smiled when she saw him. He stood up and she ran to him, letting him hold her. "It's been so long."

"You really didn't need me, did you. Sit down," he said, taking a seat behind Clement's desk. "Actually, I would have been concerned if you hadn't called me."

"So you heard there was a problem?"

"The bishop phoned me yesterday. He didn't even know there was a something afoot until you sent him your resignation letter. I think that hurt his ego more than anything else though," he said, the corners of his mouth turning up at the idea. "Why don't you tell me when you started to have doubts?"

"Such a broad question, Griffon. I'd forgotten how you could make me work," she said sitting back. "Let me see. I became engaged to a young surgeon who was visiting from Scotland. Everything was going fine until he got sick just a few weeks ago. He contracted a Strep infection that moved into his bloodstream, and early the next morning, he died. At that point I discovered that he was involved in a scandal that brought down the administration of the hospital. He and an assistant had a lab on the fourth floor. They were studying bacteria that caused infections in fisherman, and one of them, beta Streptococcus, was being tested in the laboratory. Before my Dr. Black died, he came to the conclusion that his notes could help save his life. He sent me to his lab to find his notes and hand them to a government official, an epidemiologist named Dr. Brewer. Of course, the lab was illegal, and the chief administrator was fired."

"And that's the whole thing?"

"Pretty much," she said, squirming. "Well, it's more complicated than that, I guess."

"So everything went well from the day you got there. I understand that there are medical problems in any hospital that can cause nervous tension. I believe, however, that Sophie Hawkins was prepared for that, and her patients didn't give her too many sleepless nights."

"That's true."

"Tell me about your first impression of the hospital or St. Mark in general."

"My first impressions weren't supported by anything other than neuroses, Griffon."

"That's just up my alley, Sophie. Give me all those quirky things that happened that were caused by fear or other forms of paranoia."

Sophie smiled. She trusted him. There was no doubt about that. "It's a long story," she warned him.

"I'm here and I'm comfortable."

Sophie told him about the voices she heard as she entered the city, about how dark and isolated the third floor of the east wing seemed, and how odd Dr. Charles acted. She also described Dr. Black and how many weeks it took before she became intimate with him. Then she told Dr. Fairbourne about the louder noises and lights in the windows of the fourth floor.

"Dr. Charles told me that it had been a psychiatric ward in the forties and fifties," she said. "The hospital closed the ward but never cleared or renovated the floor because they had all the space they needed."

"You said the lights on the third floor crackled and dimmed while you were there."

"Yes. Once the elevator cage stopped, and the light went out while I was riding in it."

"Did you ever tie that to the activity on the fourth floor?"

"No, not definitively. But when Ewan started doing research in clinics in Labrador and left me to water his plants, I found his ring of keys on the desk. Most employees weren't allowed access to the fourth floor. The fourth floor button on the panel in the elevator needed a key, and the door to the stairs was also locked. The nurses essentially told me to mind my own business. When I saw a key that looked like it fit the lock allowing access to the fourth floor, my curiosity, already piqued from failing to get good answers to my questions about the activity, convinced me to pocket it. Then one night, I took the elevator up."

"Were you frightened?"

"Very. I had a flashlight," she said, pausing. "And I saw the rooms to a psychiatric ward, just as Dr. Charles had described. The voices got louder and the spirits appeared."

"Could they have appeared because of your anxiety?"

"Perhaps. But I was in trouble and didn't know it. In the next ward was an old laboratory and a shock therapy machine that had been left on."

"So you ignored the ghosts. Where were they?"

"They were circling my head like they had before. No. I didn't ignore them. You told me they were there to protect me so I tried to talk to them."

"Did they answer?""No. But when I approached the machine used to shock the patients, they became disturbed."

"What do you mean?"

"I tripped over some wires and knocked something off the table that looked like earphones. When I started to bend down to pick them up, the ghosts went wild, swooshing past my face and through my hair. I stood up and turned the machine off, and that made them calm down again."

"So you controlled the entities yourself. You must have been aware in the back of your mind that you were in danger but didn't completely realize how much until you forced yourself to stop and think."

"Maybe. But I believe it was more than that. I think these were the spirits of the patients who had been locked up there. Is that possible?"

"Anything is possible. What made you think that?"

"Because they were soothed when I told them I acknowledged that they were probably victims of that terrible treatment."

"Okay. So you got out of there. Who had turned on the machine?"

"I don't know but I narrowly escaped. Someone was up there with me. I heard footsteps and ran through the shadows only to discover that I couldn't call the elevator without the key. I escaped into a dark corner and found the door to the stairwell."

"And?"

"And nothing. I never found out who it was. But I now suspect someone."

"And Dr. Black. Why did he have the key? Did you confront him?"

"No. He traveled quite a bit over the winter, and when he was at home, I quickly forgot to ask him."

"Ah, love."

"In the early spring, he asked me to marry him, and I said, 'yes,'" she explained, reaching for the tissue box Fairbourne had carefully placed on her side of the desk. "Shortly after that, I ran into him at the hospital. He had bandages on his hand and told me he had contracted a nasty infection in a cut and had to return to our hospital to get it fixed. Then he took off again. One day, I stumbled upon his car, parked in an odd place. He would have needed his car to take the ferry to Labrador, so I figured he had returned early. I couldn't find him and even asked Dr. Charles who claimed he had no idea where Ewan was. Oliver maintained that he wasn't involved with what Ewan did. I now see how funny that was. Ewan was a fellow surgeon, and the two would have had to coordinate who was performing what surgery. Of course because of that, Oliver would need to know the comings and goings of his closest associate."

"Had Dr. Black returned?"

"Yes," said Sophie

"Do you believe he ever really took any trips?"

"Yes, maybe a few. I knew he wasn't at his cottage a number of times, but after that, I just believed him. Maybe I trusted him too much."

"It sounds like you have strong doubts," Fairbourne said. "Go on."

Sophie explained what occurred that night—how Ewan asked her to go to the fourth floor, and what she found there."

"Did you see your friends again?"

"Yes. They protected me from getting into the bacteria in Ewan's lab. But then something odd happened," she said, dabbing at the tears starting to fill her eyes. "They entwined and became one figure. The fingers of what looked like a hand brushed against my face."

"Who do you think it was?"

"Ewan. He used to love to touch my face. When I got downstairs, he was already dead. I think he was saying good-bye."

The psychiatrist let Sophie regain her composure. "So Dr. Black infected himself by accident," he finally said.

"I guess. No one's sure. All I know is that the lab was illegal. He had an assistant, a Duncan MacLeish, who'd returned to Scotland a few weeks earlier. I think it was Duncan who was on the fourth floor the night I was there and Duncan who'd turned on the ECT machine. It was also Duncan who exposed the lab to the authorities, though I never learned why. The letter to the Canadian oversight agency was postmarked "Scotland" with a date far enough back to make him innocent of being responsible for the accident. I don't believe it, though. I think the beaker wasn't suppose to have bacteria in it. I think Duncan knew that Ewan would use the beaker and set him up for the accident."

"If MacLeish had left three weeks earlier, Dr. Black would have returned to find the lab empty. Could MacLeish have confronted Dr. Black before that and warned him he was going to leave?"

"Ewan talked about my finding MacLeish that night as if he didn't know that Duncan was already gone, but he could've been delirious. If you look at it the way you mention, I suppose you could conjecture that his assistant threatened to report the lab. If a fight ensued, Ewan could've been cut in the fight with Duncan. Then, unpracticed in working with the equipment in the lab because Duncan had always done it—"

"And in a hurry because MacLeish threatened to shut him down—"

"Ewan spilled the liquid and got bacteria too close to his cut."

"And Dr. Black's spirit hasn't appeared to tell you what happened?"

"No. But I'm not sure I want to see him again. He was guilty of running a lab that was dangerous to the patients in the hospital. I can't see him doing it for noble reasons."

"And you haven't forgiven him yet."

"Nor will I anytime soon. He knew I was concerned about what was happening on the fourth floor and never told me he had a key."

"What else, Sophie? What else do you feel?"

Sophie blew her nose. "I feel stupid. Where the hell was my gift?"

"You expected your gift to tell you what?"

"I expected to know that he was a fraud. I fell in love with a fraud!"

"Not that he was going to die?"

Sophie thought about it. "It didn't tell me that either. I felt odd. Everything was surreal, but it had been that way since the day of my arrival."

"So maybe we should write that down. Sophie's gift doesn't work when she's in love. When else? When she's too busy being wrapped up in a mystery concerning tortured souls who were somehow living on the fourth floor because their terrible experiences fifty years ago prevented them from flying up to heaven, Sophie can't predict the future."

"You're laughing at me," she said, staring at her hands. "I did see something once. I helped a little blind boy who had a tumor and warned the doctor to take a second look at the diagnosis. But I didn't see that anybody was about to die."

"Did you see the images of the boy's tumor in your mind?"

"I don't remember. I'm not even sure I was positive about it. I think it just popped into my head."

"Like a voice?"

"Perhaps," she said. "What about you? You once told me you had the gift of prophecy. How did you know your bishop was going to be washed away?"

"I don't know. I'm not sure I have a true gift, though. You see, things like that don't occur every day. I figure I just happen to be open to God's words at the right time. He tells me to do something, and I do it."

"Really? You mean that maybe I don't have a gift?"

"We all have gifts, Sophie. We all try to listen to what God tells us. Those who do see things that are difficult to comprehend pray for God's help so they can interpret them. The Bible tells us that some of us have special gifts, that we are more alert to the responses and are better at praying for someone's health. You probably are more sensitive to God's messages, and when you are receptive, when you aren't bombarded with other emotions, you hear and understand them."

Relieved, Sophie smiled.

"So." he continued. "Let's talk about Bishop Edmonds. He was more than a little upset by your resignation and ripped up the letter before he could contain himself."

"I don't want to go back to the hospital, Griffon."

"What do you want to do? Do you need a retreat? Do you need to pray? What can the Church do for you, Sophie?"

"I need to find something out. I confess that I talked with friends from my past just a few weeks before the problems in the hospital blew up. I believe this is one of those crossroads my professors talked about. There's a part of my life I thought I could do without."

"Love?"

"Companionship," she corrected, embarrassment making her face glow. "But now that I have experienced it, I seem to want to explore it more. I need to find out if I'm destined to have a relationship that will last for a lifetime. I have to make a decision about it before I go back to thinking about my career."

"I'm sure the bishop would certainly not want to interfere with that. But don't close any doors, Sophie. Love and relationships can take many forms. You might find something that allows you the comfort of lifetime love and companionship, but it may not be what you envision," he counseled. "What do you want me to tell Bishop Edmonds?"

"Tell him that I'll contact him in a few weeks. I'm just not sure what the answer will be."

Chapter 22

Home

Once her head hit the pillow, Sophie could not get up again. Nearly thirteen hours later, Noah entered her room with a breakfast tray.

"Okay, futter, I can't take any more of this languor. You should be ready to get out of bed by now. Eat first, and then we talk. I want to hear how just a month after we were all here having fun you ended up in my rectory in such bad shape."

Sophie sat up and gratefully accepted the meal. "This looks great," she said. "I know. I'm messing up your work. It's so late. Maybe you should go back to your office. I can meet you there after I've eaten and showered."

"Nonsense. The fact is you've saved me from it. I'll be downstairs. I have to help Angus collect cuckoos in an hour or so. Jacob can't go because he and his fiancée are in Corner Brook shopping for their wedding."

"Oooh, when's that?"

"By the end of the summer, I think. So far, he and Angus seem to be pretty successful with their enterprising efforts to sell whelk to the fish plant."

"If I'm ready in time, would you two mind if I come along? Even though I grew up on the coast, I've never been out on the water."

"Of course. Dress warmly. I'll meet you downstairs."

Sophie plunked down near the bow, clinging to the sides of Noah's dinghy as the boat skipped over the rolling waves. She felt the spray on her cheeks and inhaled its salty odor. "How far out do we go?" she yelled to the skipper.

"Just to those buoys out there. We have to pull them in and take the pots back to port. Angus is collecting the booty from the villages farther north. At first, he only did it for Sandy Rock, Black Inlet, and Daisy Cove, but some of the villages farther on wanted to try out trapping whelk too. I think there are six involved now. Angus and Jacob are making a bundle."

He slowed the motor as they approached the first buoy. Noah showed Sophie how to steer and adjust the power so he could pull the traps in. When they had collected them all, they headed back to the pier where they would empty them, throwing the catch into buckets. It would take an hour longer for Angus to return, just in time to meet the truck pulling up beside the pier. When the buckets had been delivered to the back of the truck and the small group had accepted more bait, Angus divided it up and took off again. The sun was already low in the cloudless sky, but Angus did not mind. He was used to navigating the coast by moonlight.

Noah and Sophie divvied up their share among the pots, ready for them to be attached to buoys at the trapping site in the morning. When they were finished, Noah let Sophie steer the dinghy back out to his rocks off the beach. She was already a pro.

The next day, Sophie decided to help Noah with parish work and strode down the road to Millie's.

"Come on in, Sophie," Millie said. "I s'pose you knows why I called.

"You need help with your religious ed group?"

"Yes. But I gots other ideas too. Effie and I be plannin' a card game to beat all card games."

"Oh?" Sophie said, taking a seat on an old sofa while Millie went into the kitchen to pour her some tea.

"Angus ain't the only one with ideas, you know," she called out. "The church needs patchin' as soon as the winds die down. The sidin' on the parish hall is startin' to fall off. Effie and I figures we can get more money by playin' cards with others outside the parish. Milk?" she asked, carrying in the tray.

Sophie stood up when she heard the sudden loud thump that made the house shake. "What's that?" she asked, looking in the direction of the noise.

A human form masked the window on the far side of the room. Sophie's heart leapt.

"Don't worry, girl. That just be Patrick. He be fixin' the sidin' where it be comin' loose. Patrick may look like he's gonna fall off that ladder but he never does. Oh yes. Come to think on it, he did once, but bags full of garbage breaked his fall."

Sophie sat back down. "Is he good?"

"At fallin' or fixin'?"

"Is he a good builder?"

"The best, though I don't like to admit it. If I be too nice to him, he'll be in here beggin' me to take him back."

"Now, then," said Sophie, hesitant to continue the conversation in that vain. "Tell me how the religious ed program is going."

Millie sat down beside Sophie and talked about each and every one of the students in the parish, telling her how many teachers she needed and how she thought she would approach it. But the conversation soon turned back to cards.

"Effie's sister, Marley, goes to another church up the road a bit. Her husband, Harold, told her she should go to the same church he does. It be called the Apostolic Beginnin's or something like that. He's a case, let me tell you. Marley has to follow his rules 'bout most everything *but* cards. Anyway, the women at this church claims they makes lots of money playin' other groups cuz they be real good at cards."

"Did Marley approach Effie about playing the women in our parish?"

"Not just women, but the men too cuz Jacob be pretty good himself."

"Are you sure we're up to it?" Sophie asked.

"I figure with you and Jacob, we be real good since I seen both of you plays afore now. I don't know why we didn't think on it afore. Don't worry 'bout nuthin'. Effie and Angus have played with both Harold and Marley. She swears they're lousy."

"And it's not a trick? They could be luring us into playing them by acting like they're no good in front of Effie."

"Nah. Just cuz Harold's not faithful 'nough to be a good Christian, don't mean he be a sleeveen. I don't think he's smart 'nough to sting us."

Sophie stood up to go. Millie walked her toward the door and helped her put her on coat.

"Just one more thing. We was wonderin'—"

"We?"

"Yea, those in the parish was wonderin' if you and Father Noah was thinkin' of runnin' this parish together."

Sophie smiled. "Really?"

"It's not that Father Noah can't do it himself. He done a credible job so far, 'cept for a few yes-ma'ams longs the way," she said, trying to choose her words carefully. "It's just that he gets so low-minded sometimes. We thinks he might gets lonely, fadgin' the whole parish by himself."

Sophie smiled. "Just because he's alone doesn't mean he's lonely, Millie. I'm not sure the bishop would go for this parish getting two priests, even if you guys are bucky and quite good at raising dollars when you need to."

Sophie pulled into the church lot at Sandy Rock in time to make the vestry meeting. Noah sat on the other side of his warden. Sam leaned on the table beside Effie, Jacob, and Mr. Dawe. Sophie nodded at the group.

"Hello, Sophie," Noah said, standing up. "I think you know most of the people here. Have you met Francis Dawe? He and his wife, Bonnie, keep this church up. I know you've met Sam and Effie. Have you been introduced to my senior warden, Hugh Lemon? We were just talking about the Black Inlet church building and could use any ideas you might have."

Sophie sat down next to Hugh. "How much money have you collected so far?" she asked him.

"We have thirteen hundred," Hugh answered readily.

"Is that the normal cost for something this big?"

Hugh seemed happy to explain it all to her. "We need someone to give us an estimate. We don't have anyone that qualified here. I don't trust Minty's figures. He be a twillick when it comes to plannin' a complete job."

"Dey's doin' 'struction up da road a bit," Dawe said. "We could ask dem who'd be willin' to come and eye it fer us."

"That's where Patrick worked, isn't it?" Hugh asked.

"Why can't Patrick do it?" Sophie offered. "Doesn't he have the experience?"

"Patrick be long gone," said Hugh. "He took off when Rose died."

"I just saw him at Millie's. At least Millie told me the man in the window was Patrick. He was fixing her house."

Hugh turned to her with the hint of a smile. "If he be back, maybe we can get an estimate out of him. We'd almost given up hope, Sophie. We're sure glad you decided to join us today."

On the way out, she waited for Noah. "Hugh wasn't so bad."

"He's taken a liking to you. Believe me, he's a scutty man to everyone else. Watch out. He can flice you before you know what's happening."

"You sound like you've experienced his more spity nature a time or two," she teased.

"Listen. Follow me back to Brandy Point. I need some help with the sermon this weekend."

"I'd be happy to help you write it."

"No. I mean you're giving them on Saturday. I'll do it Sunday."

"I don't do sermons."

"No arguing until we get back to the parish house, okay? Just follow me."

It had started to rain soon after Sophie's first service began. The inside of the church in Sandy Rock was dark and drops spattered the windowpanes, but Sophie had little problem. The only member of the audience who made her nervous was Noah who sat in the last pew.

He patted her on the back after she had greeted the last person to exit the church. "That was very good. I didn't hear any snickers or guffaws. You had them listening to your every word."

"I think they were preparing for me to swoon. Francis was sitting in the front row like he was ready to run forward if my knees began to buckle."

"But he didn't have to. It'll get easier."

The rain continued to come down on Sunday morning, but the winds increased as the afternoon wore on. Writing letters, Sophie sat on the sofa in the rectory living room. Noah started a fire and sat down beside her.

"I'm writing Ben and Rachel," she said. "I told them you said, 'Hi.'"

"Do you have enough light?"

Mustering her courage, Sophie looked directly at him. "Rachel told me when we were all here in early April that you told her that you made friends with her to be near me. That doesn't sound like something you would say."

"What did you tell her?"

"I told her that when I was around you'd never been anything but a gentleman. If you did have feelings for me, you never showed them. But I swore to Dr. Fairbourne just a few days ago that I'd find out before deciding if I wanted to stay in the diocese."

Noah took her hand. "I definitely have feelings for you. It's just that—"

"That they're not that kind of feelings. I understand."

"It's just that I'm not sure falling for you would be good for either of us. Mathias pointed out that I was attracted to strong women because I didn't see my mother as strong, but at the same time, I couldn't handle *not* being in charge."

Sophie laughed. "And you see me as taking over? Remember that I didn't want to give the sermons. It was your idea."

"I don't think that's what I meant," he said, his brow furrowed. "I don't know what I mean around you. It's clear you're strong, but I don't know when you're being that way. You just walk in, and there you are—strong and elegant and beautiful."

"I don't feel like that, especially lately. And I never wanted to be strong. I wasn't dominant when I was with Ewan."

"No? Didn't you mention sneaking around a psych ward on your own because you found his key?"

"I would've been able to save him had I insisted he confess that he was going to the hospital instead of to Labrador."

Noah got up to pour them some wine. "Yes," he said, handing her a glass. "Yes, I told Rachel that I wanted to be close to you. I'm sorry I didn't make it clear."

"Why didn't you say anything?" she asked, standing.

"I don't know," he said obviously contemplating his answer. "I guess I was shy. Cheers."

Sophie laughed. "I know that's not true."

"All right. I would've been in your way. You were so good with your classes. You really deserved to make it, and I was afraid I might convince you to quit like Rachel did."

"I didn't quit, did I? I made it."

"Yes," he said, leaning over to kiss her on the lips.

She pulled away. "Do you want dinner?"

"Yes, I guess. I'll help you."

The heavy clouds brought darkness early. Sophie and Noah ate slowly and washed the dishes.

"Why don't we go to bed early?" he suggested. "The power will probably go off soon."

Sophie smiled. "Does it usually go off in storms?"

"Yes. All too often."

"How romantic."

Lightening lit up the bedroom ceiling, and Noah sat up as if waiting for the crash. It flashed again. He must have seen the silhouette of her figure hesitantly standing in the doorway of her room across the hall. He turned back the corner of his blanket, and she scurried across the floor to crawl in. He held her close through the boom of thunder. She looked up at his brown eyes, once confident, but now not so positive. He looked vulnerable, unsure of what to do next. She lifted her chin and kissed him, and he responded, slowly at first. Was he waiting for her reaction? She closed her eyes and pushed against his hard body—felt him breathe, felt his hand stroke her back and hips. She longed to respond and soon could not hold back. What she experienced was indescribable as she let him come in and be one with her. And when it was over, she fell asleep in his arms—content and happier than she had ever been.

Hours must have passed. The storm whipped through every crack in the rectory, producing whistles and whines that might have scared Sophie but for the fact that she was in his arms. The ring from downstairs sounded distant—in another world.

"Is that the phone?" she asked him, rousing.

"Shit!" he said, climbing over her to get out of bed. "I'll be right back." He pulled on some pants and grabbed a robe.

She could hear his voice downstairs, angry and hoarse. Sophie slipped into her robe and came down. Reaching the bottom step, she realized there were others in the kitchen with him. He pushed past her to climb the stairs.

"Sorry for wakin' you, Sophie," Millie said, standing in the kitchen doorway. "This here be Effie's brother, Stone. He be stayin' with the Clarks for a time."

"Can I get you two some tea?" Sophie asked, walking into the kitchen. "I guess I don't understand why you're out on a night like this."

Noah entered, dressed to go outside. He grabbed his jacket by the door. "Sorry, Sophie, Angus and Jacob are missing, and I have to get the boat out to look for them."

Sophie felt the jolt. "What do you mean missing?"

"They goes out in the boat to deliver bait round six," said Millie. "We've not seen 'em since."

"Maybe they took ashore in Black Inlet or Sandy Rock."

"We called round," Stone said. "Nobody seen 'em for at least an hour now."

"Was any bait delivered?"

"Yes, both Sam and Francis hooked the bait in the pots hours ago," Millie explained. "Instead of goin' back out to the buoys, though, they puts the pots in a shed so they don't get blowed away."

"I have to go now, Sophie. I promise I'll be quiet when I come in. Millie, Stone, you go tell Effie I'm going out to look, okay?"

"You aren't going alone, are you?" Sophie asked, her voice sounding high.

"I know what I'm doing, Sophie. I grew up on these waters, remember?" he said, touching her cheek softly.

Noah pushed his boat away from the rocks only to have the wind blow it back over them, scraping the bottom. He took an oar and pushed hard against the boulder, turning the boat around as it headed toward shallow water. Once past the larger rock, he was able to start the motor.

The trip was difficult and treacherous. The bow jumped high over the top of each menacing crest like he was in the wake of a huge ship. Then it dove down the other side, the motor racing when the propeller popped out of the churning water. He passed the first group of pots, and afraid of getting tangled in them, gave them a wide berth. Then he circled the group to make sure that whenever the raging waves dipped to give him a glimpse there was no odd movement around the buoys.

At the end of the headland, he turned north, the waves now pummeling him broadside and filling the dinghy. Noah steered, but at the same time, scooped and poured with the pail he had stowed under the thwart. The motor roared as the boat grew heavy, taking on more water than he could bail out. It was in the bay near Black Inlet that he noticed something. He could hear nothing other than the howl of the wind over breaking waves, like a roll of thunder through a heavy layer of clouds. But beside the row of buoys Hugh had set up, he saw something that did not look right. They seemed to be tied in a line so tight that the water had to wash over the unyielding barrier. But the splash was taller at one end of the line.

"Ho!" yelled Noah as the dinghy crawled toward the buoys.

He turned off the engine to slide in next to what looked like a raft, but the wind and waves stopped him short, and he had to start up the motor again so he could continue edging toward it. "What the hell?" he whispered.

The raft was actually the bottom of a capsized boat. Noah drew the dinghy alongside.

Clinging to the keel, Jacob's head bobbed. "Get Angus," he said, his voice eerily faint.

"Where *is* Angus?"

"On the rope. Hurry!"

Noah pushed Angus's boat to one side. There in water up to his neck was Angus. His hair billowing with the tide, only his face was exposed above the black surface. Noah drew up to him and put out his hand.

"Go away!" he said. "Get Jacob!"

"Give me your hand, Angus. I'll need help pulling Jacob in."

Water washed over Angus's face, and the man sputtered. "I'm stuck. I'm tangled in the stupid 'traption Lemon built to scare poachers 'way from his pots."

"What?"

"Ropes! I be catched in the ropes!"

"Give me your hand, Angus! I'll pull you free."

"That be what Jacob tried. That be what tipped his boat and lets in the water. Save Jacob! He be gettin' married next month."

Noah wanted to run. His stomach churned. "I'll get Jacob, and we'll both pull you free," he finally said.

The priest leaned out over the top of the upturned boat. "Give me your hand, Jacob."

"I c-c-can't," he responded.

Noah pushed his dinghy away and started the motor, edging up its other side. "You've got to move toward me, Jacob. Follow the keel until I can reach you."

A wave suddenly hit the dinghy broadside, sending Noah tumbling over the thwart. The pain in his side was excruciating, but he pulled himself up and grabbed at the keel of Angus's boat once more. Jacob inched toward him, neither hand letting go.

"Try to hurry, Jacob. We have to get Angus."

Jacob whimpered. "My hands," he said. "I can't let go!"

Icy pellets hit the side of Noah's face sending tendrils of cold water down his neck. "Shit! It's hailing," he said, unable to hear himself.

"I c-c-can't do this, Noah. I can't release it! Go back and save Angus!"

"I'll hold the keel steady, Jacob. I won't let go."

Jacob released his grip and slid off the side of the boat, waving helplessly for Noah's hand. Noah let go of the keel and reached for the bubble in the young man's jacket. In seconds, it would be discharged, and Jacob would sink into the black hole that encircled them. Noah fell to his knees and grabbed desperately at the jacket, carrying it up in one motion. When he saw Jacob's head against the outside of the dinghy, he slipped his other hand under the arm and somehow managed to pull Jacob's trunk in beside him. Then he reached over for a thigh, grasping at the cloth of Jacob's trousers, until he finally hauled in his prize. Unsure if Jacob was still breathing, Noah felt for one of the blankets floating in the water that had accumulated in the bottom of the boat and wrapped the heavy sheet around Jacob's shoulders.

Returning to the motor, he repeated his actions to help Angus, but just as he pulled away from the capsized boat, he heard a sucking sound, like the soapy drain in his bathroom sink after he had shaved. Angus's boat disappeared. Behind it was nothing but blackness. He could see no Angus, no ropes, nothing to mark where the man had been.

"Angus!" he wailed. "Oh dear God, help me! He must be here some place!"

He moved forward and then turned around and circled back, but the farther he got from the spot where the boat had been, the more lost he became. Finally gunning the engine, he raced back toward Brandy Point, knowing the clinic would be the only place that could save Jacob. Again the waves poured water into his boat until he felt like it was moving in slow motion. With both hands gripping the pail, he scooped and scooped before reaching back to correct the direction the dinghy traveled. As he rounded the head and entered the bay, he calmed. His hands were numb and stiff, but he could just make out a few lights on shore.

About ten meters out, catastrophe hit. One huge wave, sneaking past the headlands, struck the dinghy just right, upsetting it enough for the water to pour in. Jacob's body, still and silent since they had left Black Inlet, rolled toward the deluge so that Noah could not gain control. Both men tumbled into the icy sea. All Noah could do was grab what he thought was Jacob's jacket and push on, scissor kicking and tugging at the salty water with all his might. They would both go down if he did not get to shore. His strength rapidly waning, he gasped for one last breath. Unwilling to let go of Jacob, and still kicking, he sank into the black water. Miraculously, he soon felt the rocky sand under his knees. Painfully planting his boots and impelling himself forward, he tugged at the lifeless body like he would have beached his dinghy on a sunny day. Minutes later, the span of the waves was behind them. He dropped Jacob, and hoping to find a dry blanket, made for the shed just off the beach. The door was locked. Unable to open it, he pounded in frustration.

"Hell! What fool be out here in a storm like dis one?" Patrick yelled as he unlatched the lock and pulled the door open. "Dat be you, Fader?"

"Jacob," was all Noah could say. He pointed toward the beach and then passed out.

Chapter 23

The Celebration

Noah awakened early. The storm had run its course, and a bright sunrise threw its first rays through a window above his head.

"Father Noah, glad you're back with us," she said, clasping his wrist to check his pulse. "I'm afraid it's a little early. Nursin' Sister Laura told me that I should administer more sedative. I was just gettin' it ready. You've got some nasty bruises on those ribs."

Noah seized her wrist. "Please," he said, his voice hoarse. "Please call someone for me."

"Who?" she asked. She pulled away and held up a syringe, tapping it gently with her finger.

Noah reached for a sheet of paper at his bedside and clutched the pen from the breast pocket of her uniform.

"I'll write it," she said, putting the syringe down.

Noah mumbled the number. "It's Mathias in Corner Brook. Tell him to come at once. I need him."

Then Noah fell back onto the pillow, wanting to tell her to call Sophie too, but unable to say anything more. He did not feel the prick of the needle in his arm, having already slipped back into a hazy sleep.

It must have been late afternoon when Noah roused again. He turned onto his side and came face to face with his friend, Mathias Gabriel.

"Good afternoon, Noah. Nursing Sister Eileen is off duty now but I think you'll like Miriam just as well," he said, his voice smooth and calm.

"Jacob," Noah muttered.

"He's alive. They flew him to St. Mark. He'll need to be watched for a while."

Noah suddenly sat up straight. "Angus! He's by the pots. I left Angus because I couldn't find him!"

"He drowned with his boat, Noah," the priest said, touching the young man's arm. "There was nothing you could do. Jacob was very upset too. He had tied Angus to his boat to keep the fisherman's head up. Jacob was afraid that if he moved, if he somehow let go, the boat would go down and take Angus with it. That's why it was so hard to rescue Jacob. Unfortunately, he blames himself."

"Oh God!" Noah wailed. "I killed him! I can't do anything right!"

"You didn't kill him. You didn't know Angus was tied to the boat. You only thought he was tangled in the ropes. You made the right decision. You saved the one person you could save. God doesn't expect you to work miracles. Only he can do that. God just expects you to perform the miracles that are possible to perform. I think he's smiling right now because you didn't leave them both out there in order to save yourself."

"Effie will never forgive me," he said, covering his eyes. "And Sophie!" he said, sitting up once again. "Poor Sophie is worrying about me."

"Sophie was here and sat with you until I arrived. I hope you don't mind. She was worried about Effie too, and I sent her to stay with Effie. I like Sophie, by the way. I think she's very capable of helping Angus's family through the ordeal."

"I can't face it," Noah whispered, lying back down. "I can't face any of them."

"I think I understand. There's a place near St. John's. It's a monastery of sorts in Mount Pilot. I say that because it's actually a group of men sharing a big old house on the edge of town. They have some property with trees and tall bushes and they have a vegetable garden. I called them and asked if you could do a retreat there. Just for a few weeks or so—however long it takes you to make up your mind what you want to do. If you don't want to be a rector any more, I'm sure there are other positions in the church that might interest you."

The priest's voice had already lulled Noah into a half-sleep.

"They said you might be released tomorrow. You can go back to the rectory, pack a few things, and say good-bye to Sophie. Then we can drive to St. John's."

"I love Sophie," Noah said softly.

"I know," Mathias said. "And making yourself healthy so you can see her again is very important."

The next day, Mathias accompanied Noah to the rectory door but then returned to the car. "Don't pack too much, Noah. I'll wait out here."

When Noah entered the front room, he saw her there, her slim figure silhouetted in the kitchen door.

"Thank God," she said, running forward to greet him. She wrapped her arms around his neck.

"I have to go," he said. "I don't know how to ask you to stay and take care of everyone."

"I'll stay. Jacob's on the mend, and Tulla insists she wants the wedding soon after Angus's funeral. I'm going to be busy."

He wanted to tell her how much he loved her, how much he desired her but did not dare. She might ask him to stay, and then he would not be able to go, could not tear himself away from her embrace. She leaned into him, and he kissed her on the cheek. A lone tear sliding over his lips was the only sign that he wanted to be with her. He waited a moment before walking around her and climbing the stairs.

When he finally carried his bag out the door, he found her on the landing. She gave him her hand, and he held it for a few seconds before dropping it and walking to the car. Mathias took the bag and opened the rear door for him. Noah slid in but did not face the front. Instead, he stared out the rear window. Sophie's figure shrank until the car turned onto the highway, and she disappeared from view.

The morning sun slithered through the bedroom window. Sophie stuffed the letters back into their envelopes and buried them in her suitcase. She descended the stairs to find Ben and Rachel having breakfast.

"Good morning, Sophie," said Rachel, walking over to hug her old friend. "So this is the big day. Sit down at the table so I can serve you breakfast."

"Yes, the big day," Sophie repeated. "Last night, I dreamt that I tripped over my alb and knocked over Andrew's chair! Maybe someone can take a picture so I can hang it up."

"Is he the chief consecrator?" Ben asked, putting down his newspaper.

"Yes. At least he knows I'm not just a lungy girl. I don't want to eat too much. Remember what I did after my first ordination."

"You did better when Andrew went to Brandy Point for your priesting, didn't you?"

"I wasn't in great shape. Noah had just made up his mind that he wasn't coming back, and Andrew thought it was about time I became a real priest and rector."

"You'll do fine. You know all these people, Sophie. Tell yourself that this is just another service. Your hair looks good."

"There isn't much I can do with it. The color looks awful."

"What do you mean? It's almost completely white. I thought you hated the red. Isn't that what you used to say?"

"I probably did. I wouldn't have complained so much if I had known how old I would look with white."

"You look great, like a bishop, and your hair won't clash with any color they vest you in," Rachel said, serving Sophie some eggs and toast. "I hear you were busy yesterday. Ben tells me that his students asked you to give your whole history."

"At least they didn't go to sleep. What about you? Did you enjoy your evening out?"

"I always love to get away."

The two women stopped talking when they heard someone come in the front door.

"Hi, Aunt Sophie. How are you?"

"Jessie!" Sophie said, standing. "I haven't seen you in years! Tell me what you're doing. I hear you're moving out."

"Finally," she said, putting her arms around Sophie's neck.

Sophie pulled her away to look at her. Jessie's short hair, a dark blond, stuck out in all directions, and her brown eyes were serious until she smiled, a wide smile lighting up her whole face. Sophie put her hand over her mouth.

"Mom, I'm getting some stuff and then picking up a friend at the airport. Do you need me for anything?"

"I don't think so," Rachel said to the retreating figure.

"Good luck today, Aunt Sophie," Jessie said as she climbed the stairs.

"I'm so sorry, Sophie," Rachel commented as soon as Jessie disappeared.

"Does she know?"

"Yes," said Ben. "She's actually visited him a few times."

"How long have you known, Ben?"

"Noah and I both knew about it before the wedding," Ben said. "I suppose it would have been better if we had told you too, but until the last few years, she really didn't look so much like him, and I guess we thought it would be nicer for Rachel and me if we were able to keep the whole thing a secret. Believe me, Jessie only found out when she was sixteen or seventeen, and her response was understandably harsh."

"What was Noah's reaction to her discovery?"

"We discussed it with him ahead of time. He had no trouble with it, and they seem to get along."

"Please, Sophie, don't let this spoil your day," Rachel implored. "I have worried so much about how to tell you."

"What about you? Are you two okay?

"We've adjusted, Sophie, but thanks," Ben said. "We'll never forget what you did for Jessie. I'm just happy the doctors discovered the problem in time."

"I was so angry with what you told me at the reunion," Rachel explained. "I thought you were trying to get me back for revealing how Noah felt about you. But I did listen. If I hadn't, the doctors might not have discovered the leukemia in time."

"We anguished over whether or not you should know the truth then," Ben added.

"Since Noah and I never got serious, I guess it's okay. I might have been angry if we had decided to stay together."

"I can't believe it didn't work out," Rachel said. "I remember that there was some sort of accident and that he had to go for a retreat to recover. Then you took over officially as rector of Brandy Point. What happened?"

"I didn't become rector right away. Noah was supposed to regain his health at the monastery and return in a few weeks. Unfortunately, it took months. By the time he was healthy, he had already decided that the life suited him and stayed there. That's all. The parishioners informed Andrew they wanted me to remain there so I was priested and became the rector. It was and still is a wonderful place. I continue to visit my friends there now and then. I stayed on as rector for nearly ten years before a young newly-ordained deacon and his wife arrived to replace me. As you know, I went on to that other parish in the south for a few years before Andrew asked me to help out in Corner Brook. I taught at the college in Corner Brook while I assisted in the bishop's office."

"Didn't you also finish your PhD in Psychology while there?" asked Ben, getting out of his chair. "Well, we had better get going. We wouldn't want to be late for your consecration. I get to be a presenter. Hope I don't look too nervous."

"You'll do fine, Ben. You might have to hold me up, though," Sophie admitted.

It was a sunny day, a bit cold for May, but the blue sky was cloudless, and the sun shone down in an attempt to warm them up. Sophie could hear the glorious music wafting out the open doors as the line of priests slowly filed into the narthex ahead of her. Ben was somewhere behind her, but fearing that she might trip, she did not dare turn around. Soon, she too was crossing through the narthex and entering the nave of the cathedral she had visited so many times before. About twenty heads in front of her, she could make out the altar and pulpit. The place was packed. She did not dare look directly at the congregation, but in the pit of her stomach, she could feel them. The procession made its way to the front faster than Sophie had hoped. Just before the sanctuary, she turned left into a row of chairs set up in front of the first pew and sat down next to her old friend, Griffon Fairbourne. The two of them listened to the final passages of a flute and organ voluntary. Looking up, Sophie noticed a group of visiting bishops, including Andrew Edmonds, seated in front of the chancel. She was grateful when Griffon took her hand. The music ended. Sophie stood while Ben and others presented her to the presiding bishop, and the testimonials were read.

Finally, Andrew stood and began to speak. "Please come closer, Sophie. As the bishop-elect, we expect you to make the following promise," he said, gazing at her over the top of his glasses. "In the Name of the Father, and of the Son, and of the Holy Spirit, I, Sophie Hawkins, solemnly declare that I do believe..."

Sophie repeated the promise after him. Then the people in the pews joined in, testifying that Sophie was indeed the elected bishop of the Eastern Diocese of Newfoundland. For the first time, she turned to gaze at them, recognizing several from the Western Diocese. She let her eyes scan the pews and noticed Cyril and Kieran several rows back. She spotted Rachel, and sitting with his wife, the now longtime rector of Brandy Point. Sophie knew she would be able to talk to them further at a luncheon planned in her honor. She did not, however, see Noah and turned around to face the front, trying hard to hide her disappointment.

After more hymns sung by the choir, they listened to the readings and gospel before sitting down to hear the sermon. Sophie was surprised when Griffon did not stand and walk over to the steps that led to the pulpit. He was supposed to give the sermon. Instead, the priest still held onto her hand! Had he forgotten? She glanced up. Someone else was in the pulpit. Sophie could not believe who stood there. His figure still lean, he stood straight and tall in a simple black robe, gathered with a cincture tied loosely so that it rested on his hips. Noah appeared different. His hair, now gray, was much thinner. But when he looked down at Sophie, his wide smile was the same. Tears filled her eyes, and Griffon slid her a tissue.

Taking his time, Noah leaned forward to grasp the sides of the dais. "Ladies and Gentleman, in today's gospel, the disciples receive a treat. Remember that Jesus has just died on the cross. They have witnessed it and have heard from Mary Magdalene that he has arisen—that he has joined his father. The disciples are meeting in a house to discuss what to do next. They are frightened and lock the doors, having just seen their leader executed for crimes they have espoused. Suddenly, a man appears among them. He may look like Jesus and talk like Jesus, but remember that Mary Magdalene at first mistook him for a gardener because she couldn't believe he was standing in front of her. So it is understandable that they don't recognize him. Jesus shows them his wounds, and seeing the proof, they rejoice, forgetting their fears. And Jesus tells them, 'Peace be with you. As the Father has sent me, so I send you.'

"We must all appreciate this as something enormous in church history. Keep in mind that just weeks before his death, telling Him that he had fulfilled his duty, Jesus had prayed to his Father. He had spread God's word to the people so they would know Him. But Jesus knew he wouldn't be there much longer and asked his Father for a favor. He said, 'Sanctify them in the truth; your word is truth. As you have sent me into the world, so I have sent them into the world. And for their sakes I sanctify myself, so that they also may be sanctified in truth,'" Noah said, pausing. "Think about it. Jesus, the son of God, is handing over his powers to his disciples.

"How many of us sometimes wish that Jesus were still here among us? Would we recognize him? If a man came up to you and asked you to look at his wounds and those wounds were in the exact same places that the Bible has said that Jesus' wounds were when he was taken down from the cross, would you believe him? Would you kneel down in front of him and do what he instructed you? Probably not. We're pretty cynical about that nowadays. But the disciples did finally believe Jesus was among them. They knew him in person. How well do we know him? How hard do we try to know him? Their faith was soon rewarded." Noah paused again, glancing down at his notes.

"But rejoicing in his presence, knowing that his spirit was still alive is probably not really the point John is making here. What is important is that Jesus passes the authority on, the authority that symbolizes God's charge to him, to those who are capable of representing Him. Jesus breathes on them and tells them to be ready to receive the Holy Spirit and says, 'If you forgive the sins of any, they are forgiven them; if you retain the sins of any, they are retained.' Jesus thus hands his power, the power granted to him by God himself, to these men. By bestowing this authority, Jesus' death is no longer the requisite for us to receive God's love and penance. And so through the centuries, the authority to represent God and his son has continued to be passed down. Through those of us in the Church, we too learn what God wants for us and expects from us. We are teachers so that all around us believe in eternal life. We are confessors so that we can all be forgiven. We celebrate the gift that God has given us through his son, Jesus, and share the feast."

Sophie listened intently as did those packed into the pews. Noah's ability to draw attention to his words had not disappeared. His confident voice and natural gestures kept everyone rapt, knowing that he was going to tie the words of John into the events of today.

"At this celebration, the church bestows these same powers on one of our fellow priests, Sophie Hawkins. She, of course, has already been practicing them as a priest. In her new position, as a bishop, she will step into the same role Jesus played in that house two thousand years ago. She will pass the authority to grant forgiveness for man's sins on to her disciples so that God's promise of eternal life will be repeated in future generations.

"I can think of no other person who is more capable of taking on this burden. I have known Sophie Hawkins for over thirty years. Like most of us in Newfoundland, she comes from humble beginnings. She has witnessed horrendous acts by those who profess to speak God's words while taking advantage of those around them, who have judged rather than understood, and who have never asked for forgiveness themselves. Sophie, on the other hand, has an almost unlimited capacity to forgive. At an early age, she realized that no man is purely evil but the product of happenings around him. We shall conquer evil by demonstrating that we are good, illustrating to him that we can forgive, showing him that we aren't afraid because God has granted us eternal life. If we aren't afraid of death, what else is there to fear?"

Noah looked down at Sophie and smiled. "As a bishop, Sophie Hawkins will pass her authority on to priests, and these priests will have the power to forgive us our sins. I once heard that she thought she was born with special gifts—prophecy and healing. I believe she has them because I've seen her use them. Sophie could see the strength of character in those living in villages where I was once rector. When the parishioners needed her, she was there. You see, while I could stand in front of them and tell them so eloquently what they should know about Jesus, Sophie lived among them like Jesus did among us. When there was pain, she soothed them. When there was joy, she shared it with them. When they were scared, she honestly told them that there was nothing to fear. Sophie's real gift is that she can see the good in people and get the best out of them. I believe Sophie will be an inspiring bishop, a leader among her disciples, helping to spread the word of God."

Mathias Gabriel, sitting in the front pew behind Sophie and Griffon, stood up just as Noah stepped down from the pulpit. He walked over to his charge and took Noah's arm, leading him out a door in the north transept. Sophie felt the blow to her chest and wanted so badly to follow him, but Griffon urged her to stand for the examination, which would soon be upon her.

Then she heard Andrew say, "My sister, the people have chosen you and have affirmed their trust in you by acclaiming your election. A bishop in God's holy Church is called to be one with the apostles in proclaiming Christ's resurrection and interpreting the Gospel, and to testify to Christ's sovereignty as Lord of lords and King of kings…"

Sophie listened in disbelief as he called off her duties. And when he asked her if she was convinced that God had called her to the office of bishop, she answered in a clear voice and without hesitation, "I am so persuaded."

After several more declarations, she turned to those in the pews. Everyone stood and watched as she knelt in front of Andrew's knee for her consecration. Listening to his prayer, it finally came upon her what was happening. When she stood up, she was vested with the stole, much like Griffon's, the cope, the mitre and finally a chasuble. Then Andrew turned her to face the filled pews once more and presented their new bishop to the people.

"I cannot say I remember celebrating the Eucharist as the new bishop," Sophie would later tell students in another of Ben's university classes. "In fact, the whole day still seems like it's in a haze. But I can tell you all that becoming bishop wasn't the goal. I never thought about it before I was consecrated, and to tell you the truth, I'm still surprised to hear someone call me that now. The ultimate goal is to make sure I've lived up to the tenets of my job. I'm to ordain priests and deacons and help ordain other bishops. That's fun as well as gratifying, I'll admit to that. But I also have to make sure that everyone retains faith. I have to make sure everyone around me knows that God has appointed disciples who have the power to forgive them their sins and to remind them that the ultimate reward is eternal life with all of those we have loved in our lives here on earth."

Sophie sat back, realizing what she had just said. One day, she might see Lety and Gracie and even Ewan. One day, she might again be with Noah, and hopefully this time he would not need to walk away.

CPSIA information can be obtained at www.ICGtesting.com
Printed in the USA
LVOW07s1454250913

354111LV00002B/330/A

9 780978 731809